THE DUKE OF ICE

❧ The Untouchables ❧

DARCY BURKE

The Duke of Ice
Copyright © 2017 Darcy Burke
All rights reserved.

ISBN: 1944576231
ISBN-13: 9781944576233

Book design: © Darcy Burke.
Book Cover Design © Carrie Divine/Seductive Designs
Photo copyright: © Period Images
Photo copyright: © FairytaleDesign/Depositphotos
Photo copyright: © FairytaleDesign/marcink3333
Editing: Linda Ingmanson.

For my lovely and talented friend, Christy Carlyle

Chapter One

October 1817

RAIN CLOUDS MOVED in from the horizon, promising a drenching in the next thirty minutes or so. Nicholas Bateman, tenth Duke of Kilve, was glad he'd completed his outdoor activities for the day. He stared at the expanse of ocean stretching beyond the cliffs, never failing to appreciate the immensity and treachery of the world around him. Or how small and insignificant it made him feel.

"Your Grace?"

The sound of Markley's gentle query drew Nick to turn from the window. He looked at the butler in silent response.

"His Grace, the Duke of Romsey, has arrived."

A jolt of surprise hummed through Nick's frame. He hadn't expected to see his oldest—his only, really— friend until next month when they would meet at Simon's hunting lodge in the north of England.

Nick leaned back in his chair. "Show him in."

With a nod, Markley pivoted and departed. A few moments later, Simon strode into Nick's office, his dark hair artfully disheveled—as it usually was—and his brown eyes alight with some sort of mischief. When one considered Simon's background, it was no small feat that he was a near-constant source of wit and humor.

Simon deposited himself into a high-backed chair

and stretched his long legs out before him.

"Comfortable?" Nick asked.

"Not yet, but I'll get there. It was a hell of a ride. I was trying to beat the weather."

"Well done of you," Nick said. "To what do I owe this surprise?"

Simon slipped his hand into an inner pocket on the front of his coat and withdrew an envelope. He rose from the chair and tossed the missive on Nick's desk before falling back onto the cushion.

Wordlessly, Nick opened the parchment and read the contents. The ill humor he worked to keep at bay stole over him as surely as the storm clouds moving rapidly toward the shore.

He dropped the letter on his desk and fixed his friend with an icy stare. "So?"

Simon exhaled with great exasperation. "It's an invitation. I realize it's been eons since either of us has received one, but surely you recall what they look like."

"Vaguely." Nick didn't bother trying to remember. What was the point? He didn't want to go to house parties or balls or any of the other nonsense that mattered to the ninnyhammers in Society. Nick wasn't ever supposed to be one of their number, and he would never forget that.

"You're being purposely morose."

"It's my way."

Simon rolled his eyes. "Yes. However, it is not mine. I am thrilled to finally be invited to something, and I'll be damned if you're going to keep me from it."

Nick shrugged before resting his elbows on the arms of his chair. "I wouldn't dream of doing so. You should go."

Simon pulled his legs up and leaned forward. "Didn't

you read it? I am heartily encouraged to attend the party *with* the Duke of Ice."

"It didn't say that."

"No, it said Duke of Kilve, but let's call a spade a spade, shall we?" Simon gave him a bland smile. "Anyway, it's not nearly so derogatory a nickname as mine. Plus, it fits." Simon leaned back in his chair with a resigned sigh. "I suppose mine does too."

Not by half, but that was because Nick knew Simon better than anyone, and his friend didn't deserve to be called the Duke of Ruin. Nick, on the other hand, *was* the bloody Duke of Ice whether he liked it or not. And truth be told, he liked it. Or at least preferred it. When people thought you were incapable of interaction, they generally left you alone. And that made Nick quite content.

"Yes, mine fits. Yours, however, does not, and I'll not argue with you about that."

Simon shook his head. "Heaven forbid anyone debate you."

Nick snorted. "You debate me constantly. Your insisting I go to this house party is ample evidence."

"True," Simon said with a grin. "So you'll go?"

"I'd rather have my entrails removed through my nose."

Simon let out a bark of laughter. "What a disgusting image. But I do believe you would prefer that. Still, because you're my dearest friend, you're going to do it."

Nick glanced down at the letter and recalled the details. It was a house party hosted by Mr. and Mrs. Linford.

"It's not terribly far—just outside Wells," Simon said. "And we'll go to my lodge after that. It's on the way, if you think about it."

"It isn't, but that's a nice attempt," Nick said wryly. "If it's terrible, we'll leave early."

"Agreed. Does that mean you'll go?"

"No. I'm humoring you." Nick gestured toward the invitation on his desk. "It doesn't say you have to go with me."

"I take 'heartily encouraged' as a demand. I don't think it would do me any favors to arrive without you."

Nick made a guttural sound in his throat. "Then perhaps they should have invited me."

Simon arched a brow at him. "Do you know they didn't? I thought Markley burned any invitations upon receipt."

Yes, he did. Nick called for the butler, who returned to the study with alacrity. "Yes, Your Grace? Should I bring tea?"

"I suppose, but that isn't why I called for you. Did I receive an invitation from the Linfords in Somerset?"

"Indeed you did." A bit of color leached from Markley's middle-aged face. "I'm afraid I disposed of it as usual. Was that a mistake?"

"Of course not. I will advise you if I wish the procedure to change. Thank you, that will be all. Except for the tea."

An expression of relief crossed Markley's features before he departed.

"They're still petrified of you," Simon said.

"They're deferential, as they should be."

Simon's response was an inarticulate sound that managed to convey his disagreement.

"Why the hell do you want to go to this party?" Nick asked. "Society has been horrible to you." It was universally accepted that Simon had killed his wife four years ago, though he was never prosecuted for the crime. The fact that Simon had been drunk out of his mind and couldn't remember a thing hadn't helped matters. He'd also done nothing to defend himself, but he hadn't imbibed a drop of spirits since. Indeed, his surrender of drink had only served to make him look guilty in the eyes of many. Such judgment by strangers only reinforced Nick's need for isolation.

Simon's dark brows pitched low over his eyes as he steepled his fingers and stared at the windows beyond Nick. "Unlike you, I get lonely. One can only read so many books or visit so many corners of the kingdom before one begins to go mad."

His eyes met Nick's, and for a fleeting moment, Nick saw the hollow darkness that Simon tried so hard to bury. That was where they differed. Simon tried to keep his past from dragging him into an abyss, whereas Nick refused to forget the tragedies that had led him to his cold solitude.

"What do you hope to gain?" Nick asked softly.

Simon dropped his hands to the arms of the chair and lifted a shoulder. "Diversion? That's all I ever hope for."

"Will we know anyone there? I can't say I'm acquainted with Mr. or Mrs. Linford."

"Linford was at Oxford at the same time as us. He was in New College, if memory serves." Simon shook his head. "Might've been Hertford."

"I wouldn't know," Nick said. "Clearly, we barely knew him. Why would he suddenly attempt to rekindle the acquaintance?"

"I can't say."

Nick narrowed his eyes. "I find it suspicious."

"Just come with me, stay for one bloody night, and

then continue to the lodge."

"Won't you come with me?"

Simon shrugged. "It depends on whether I'm enjoying myself. If I'm uncomfortable, I'll leave with you."

"I'll do my best to ensure you're uncomfortable, then." A rare smile curved Nick's lips provoking a shout of laughter from Simon.

"There's my old friend."

"Since you're here, you should stay the night," Nick said. "Unless you've somewhere else to be?"

Simon's country home was a two-day ride at a swift pace, longer if one wasn't in a hurry. But Nick doubted Simon would go back there. The house party was in a little over a week, and Simon would use that time to explore Cornwall or perhaps even venture into Wales. He had a hard time staying in one place.

"I don't, as well you know. I'd be delighted to stay for a day or two. Perhaps we can go searching for the elusive dragon in the caves."

Nick snorted at his mention of the old legend of Blue Ben. "It's far more likely we'll run into a smuggler."

"Indeed?" Simon's brows rose.

"Perhaps. Although I've done my part in quashing the activity."

"Of course you have. You're nothing if not a staunch patriot." Simon said this with a somber note, silently referencing Nick's service to King and country as well as the great sacrifice his family had made.

Thankfully, Markley entered with the tea, putting an effective end to that line of conversation. While Nick would never forget, he also chose not to discuss those matters. It was enough that they all lived in his mind.

Rain began to batter the windows as the storm moved over the house. Markley served the tea and departed.

Simon sipped his tea, peering over the rim of the cup at Nick.

Nick braced himself for another unwelcome topic. Could it be worse than cajoling him into attending a house party?

"Since we're going to the Linfords' party, should we discuss whether we're on the Marriage Mart?"

Oh yes, it could be much, much worse.

"No." The single word dropped into the room like a shard of ice.

Simon, heedless as ever when it came to Nick's irritation, cocked his head to the side. "No we shouldn't discuss it, or no we aren't on the Marriage Mart?"

"I've no idea where the hell you are, although I might suggest an asylum."

Simon grinned as he grabbed a cake from the tray Markley had perched on Nick's desk. "It probably doesn't matter. I can't imagine anyone would consider us marriage material. Not yet anyway."

Nick detected a note of hope in Simon's voice. "Do you really wish to marry again?" he asked quietly. It seemed almost sacrilegious to even pose the question.

"I think I do," Simon said, his tone equally soft. He shook his head. "I don't know. I *think* I do, but when I consider it—actually think of how that would play out—I think not." He shoved the rest of the cake into his mouth.

"I don't even consider it." How could he without sacrificing the memories of Jacinda and Elias? To look for, let alone accept, someone else would be to lay them to rest forever. He wasn't sure he could do that.

"No, I don't imagine you do."

They drank in silence for a few minutes before Simon said, "Perhaps it's time we consider it. We're dukes. We have a responsibility to our titles."

"I have cousins who can inherit."

"Do you?"

The question made Nick wince. He had a cousin or two but hadn't established a connection with them, for fear of what might happen. Just as he feared what might happen to the woman he was selfish enough to wed.

"My apologies, of course you do," Simon said.

Nick steered the conversation back to Simon since he'd brought up the infernal topic. "That is your goal, then? You're going to this party with the hope of finding a wife?"

Simon shrugged. "I have no expectations. I may very well walk into the Linfords' drawing room and receive the cut direct from everyone in attendance."

"And you'd risk that?" It wouldn't bother Nick, but he wasn't sure about his friend.

"I prefer it to sitting alone and staring at the sea," he answered dryly.

Nick smirked at Simon's jest. "We're an odd pair. I hope the Linfords and their guests are ready for us."

"Indeed." Simon's eyes glowed with mirth. "I'm pleased to hear your enthusiasm."

"Do not take my surrender to your pitiful pleas as enthusiasm. I am going to support you, and I will leave at the earliest opportunity. On that I want to be quite clear."

"Understood." Simon stood and stretched. "I'm going upstairs to change and then I shall beat you at chess."

"You can try."

Nick watched his friend leave, his mind churning over the hell he'd just agreed to. A house party? When he was in London to conduct business and perform his duty in the House of Lords, he kept to himself. He hadn't the first notion who was who, nor did he care. Yes, he'd go to support Simon, and he'd do his damnedest to keep to himself as he always did.

Markley entered to remove the tea tray. As he gathered up the implements, he shot a quick, curious glance at Nick. "May I say how nice it is to see His Grace here? His visits always brighten things."

What he meant was that when Simon was around, Nick was somewhat palatable. "Yes."

Nick knew he was difficult. But he was also patient and generous when it came to his retainers and tenants. So they didn't love him or particularly like him. It was for the best.

To care for Nick was to commit yourself to misery. Nick had tried to warn Simon off, but he only rolled his eyes and told Nick to lighten up.

And now he was going to a house party where he *should* be light of mood. Except that wasn't who he was. He *was* the Duke of Ice.

That was precisely who the Linfords and their guests would   get.

Chapter Two

BY DESIGN, LADY Violet Pendleton was the first to arrive at the Linfords' house party. Hannah Linford was her closest friend, and Violet always supported her social endeavors.

Hannah swept into the drawing room after Violet had already finished a cup of tea. She offered a half smile as she drew Violet into a quick hug. "I'm running late, of course."

"Of course," Violet murmured.

Laughing, Hannah shot her a mock indignant look. "You didn't have to agree!"

"You're always running late. Should we pretend otherwise?"

"No." Hannah's dark brown eyes twinkled with mirth. "You had a pleasant journey?"

Violet lived in Bath, only a few hours away by coach. She'd left early that morning in order to be the first guest to arrive. "Yes, although it does look as though the weather is going to turn. Hopefully it will hold until evening so that your guests may get here safely. Are you expecting everyone today?"

Hannah, always full of nervous energy, paced before the hearth. "Yes, and I'm so anxious. This is either going to be the most successful house party ever or the biggest disaster." She paused to look at Violet. "Either way, it will be the most talked about."

"That is your goal, is it not?" Violet loved her friend dearly but had never understood her need to be recognized among the leaders of Society.

"It's all I have," she said. "I haven't a title like you."

Violet had married a viscount, but she would've gladly traded the *lady* preceding her name for true happiness such as Hannah had with her husband, Irving. They had two small children and were the epitome of what Violet had once wanted. What had once been in her grasp.

"I'd give it to you, if I could," Violet said.

Hannah exhaled, her lips curving into a warm smile. "I know you would, dear."

Violet smoothed her hands over her skirt. "Now, what do you need me to do? Will Lady Dunn be here?"

Sometimes Hannah asked her to pay particular attention to certain guests, to ensure they were content and to let Hannah know if anything was amiss. Lady Dunn was one such guest. She was a charming old biddy, given to gossip, but thankfully none of the more salacious kind.

"She will not," Hannah said. "Which is unfortunate because I anticipate that rumors will run amok, and she is quite good at keeping things from escalating."

"That is true." For all that she liked to gossip, the elderly viscountess was adept at putting things in perspective. "Is there anyone else I should pay attention to?"

Hannah floated to the settee and sat down beside Violet, like a hummingbird taking a brief but necessary respite. Her eyes fairly glowed with anticipation. "I'm particularly anxious about this party because two Untouchables will be here."

Untouchables…noblemen who were seen as particularly difficult to snare on the Marriage Mart, or so Violet thought based on what she'd heard. Details like this always failed to sufficiently root in her memory. "That's well done of you."

"Oh, these are not the ordinary Untouchables. These are dukes that literally no one dares touch—at least not socially."

Violet had no idea who they could be. She was the opposite of Lady Dunn—she detested gossip and typically put it from her mind the moment she heard it. This was why she wasn't entirely certain about what an Untouchable might be, particularly ones that weren't *ordinary*. "If no one dares to include them socially, why ever are you?"

"Because it will be *the* on-dit of the season! The Duke of Ice never attends social gatherings, though he is occasionally invited." Hannah tipped her head to the side. "I suppose it's unfair to say that no one dares to touch him. They simply aren't successful. And he's apparently quite haughty. He has no time for parties such as this, or so the rumors go."

"And yet he's coming here?"

Hannah lifted her hand to her mouth as a giggle escaped. "I'm afraid I manipulated his attendance by inviting the Duke of Ruin. Now *he* isn't invited *anywhere*, but he and Ice are friends. Furthermore, unlike Ice, Ruin actually accepts the paltry few invitations he receives. I invited him on the condition that he bring Ice along."

"You didn't." Violet pursed her lips. She loved her friend very much, but such machinations flirted with boorishness.

"I'm afraid I did." A look of contrition flashed in Hannah's eyes. She quickly rose and started pacing once more, the lull over. "It will all work out marvelously. You'll see."

"What is it you wish me to do?" For the first time, Violet considered refusing her friend's request. She wanted no part in any scheme that might bring unwanted notoriety to these…Untouchables.

"Nothing much, really. Just watch for people's reactions and keep your ears open. To have the Duke of Ice here will surely recommend me. And if he is charming and enjoys himself? Well, that could send me into the upper echelon." Hannah's eyes gleamed with excitement.

Violet knew how much it meant to her friend to find a place among Society's elite, even if it didn't matter at all to her. "Of course. You know I shall always have your best interests at heart—even when you sometimes don't." Hannah could get carried away, and in those instances she never failed to thank Violet for being a voice of reason. "So I'm to watch over the Untouchables and report any gossip to you?"

"Yes." Hannah paused long enough to bestow a look of love on her friend. "Thank you."

The butler came in to announce that guests were beginning to arrive. Color warmed Hannah's face, and she clasped her hands together. "I'll fetch Irving. Here we go!" She grinned at Violet before turning and fluttering from the drawing room.

A maid came and cleared away the tea tray. Violet stood and shook the wrinkles from her gown. She went to the windows and looked out at the gray sky. There would be rain; it was simply a question of when the heavens decided to unleash the torrent.

Over the next few hours, Violet greeted guests, many of whom she'd met on prior occasions. She braced herself when Lady Nixon and Mrs. Law arrived together. They were two of the most formidable women in Society. Hannah invited them for precisely that reason, of course. It was a risk, but if they stamped their approval on this house party, Hannah would likely be invited everywhere.

For that reason alone, Violet affixed a warm smile on her face and heartily welcomed the two women.

Mrs. Law was a few years older than Lady Nixon, with dark hair liberally streaked with gray and sharp, piercing brown eyes. "Lady Pendleton, how lovely to see you here, but then you always attend Mrs. Linford's parties, do you not?"

"Indeed I do. We've been friends for some time." They'd met as newlyweds in London for the Season nearly seven and a half years ago. It had been the first time in London for both of them, and they'd banded together.

Lady Nixon was tall with tawny hair and pale blue eyes. When she looked at you, one had the sense she could see every secret you possessed. She couldn't of course, but Violet knew she'd try to learn them. She never failed to put Violet on her guard. "Mrs. Linford says the Duke of Ice will be here. I will believe that when he presents himself." She exchanged a look of doubt with Mrs. Law.

Oh dear. Violet hoped for Hannah's sake that this duke showed up. If he didn't, Violet might have to hunt him down and cause him bodily harm.

Violet forced herself to continue smiling at the women. "Would you care for refreshment?" She gestured toward a sideboard where food and drink had been laid out for the guests as they arrived.

"Oh, maybe just a cake. Or two." Mrs. Law laughed softly as she made her way toward the refreshments. Once there, she took *three* cakes.

Violet greeted more guests, and while a few went upstairs to rest, most remained in the drawing room, and by late afternoon, there was an air of expectation. Of *anticipation*.

Violet caught Hannah's distressed eye and excused herself from Lady Colton and her daughter. Hannah met her near the doorway.

"Irving says the men want to leave," Hannah whispered urgently.

"I know. I can sense their impatience. Why delay?"

"Because the dukes aren't here yet!" Hannah kept her voice low, but her features reflected her anxiety.

Violet lightly touched her friend's arm and guided her to pivot so that she was no longer facing her guests. "Remain calm. All will be well. Perhaps they were simply delayed."

Hannah shook her head. "I was a fool to pin my hopes on their attendance, wasn't I?"

Perhaps, but Violet wouldn't say so. "It doesn't matter if they come or not. Your party will be a smashing success. And they will be the poorer for not being present."

Hannah's mouth curved into a wobbly smile. "You are the dearest of friends."

The sound of the butler speaking to someone in the hall made Hannah freeze. A moment later, he appeared, leading a gentleman. He was tall, broad-shouldered with brown hair and thick brows cloaking warm brown eyes. This couldn't be the Duke of Ice. He looked far too pleasant.

Furthermore, Hannah didn't relax, which meant he wasn't the duke she was hoping for. This must be the other one, the one she'd had to invite to ensnare the true prize.

Violet suppressed a shudder. Her friend's scheming made her ill at ease. She offered the new arrival a welcoming smile.

Hannah and Violet stepped just inside the drawing room as the butler paused at the doorway. "The Duke of Romsey," he intoned.

Every head in the room turned, and conversation ground to a halt. There was a beat of silence before voices quietly started up again.

Hannah offered a curtsey. "Welcome, Your Grace."

Violet did the same but was prevented from speaking by the hasty arrival of Irving. He welcomed the duke with a bow.

"We deeply appreciate your coming, Your Grace."

The Duke darted a glance toward Violet but focused on his hosts as he answered. "It is my pleasure. Thank you for the kind invitation."

Hannah looked past him, clearly in search of his missing friend. "Did His Grace not accompany you?" she asked, her voice tight with stress.

"Not entirely, no. He should be along shortly."

The manner in which he said the word *should* gave Violet pause. The duke was uncertain of his friend. Violet prayed Hannah hadn't caught that slight intonation.

Violet edged away, giving Hannah and Irving a moment to speak with the duke. As she strolled toward the hearth, she overheard Lady Nixon, who was seated beside Mrs. Law on one of the settees.

"The Duke of Ruin, can you imagine?" If a question could sneer, this one would have. Lady Nixon's face, however, was quite serene. One would never guess at the venom dripping from her tone.

"She said it would be Ice, but we get Ruin instead."

Mrs. Law clucked her tongue. "A veritable disaster. I wonder if anyone will leave now that he's arrived." She blinked at her friend. "I wonder if *we* should leave."

Violet wanted to snap at them that they *should* go and that their destination ought to be where the devil resided. Instead, she moved to the opposite side of the room, where she sent discreet glowers in their direction.

She also looked toward her friend, who seemed thankfully ignorant of the obnoxious conversation taking place on the settee. Hannah did, however, look pale. This was not what she'd planned for—nor what she'd hoped.

Surveying the room, Violet tried to determine what others thought of the duke's arrival. Would anyone leave? Goodness, she hoped not.

At that moment, a flash of light blazed over the lawn, followed a moment later by a loud crash. Then the rain started. Violet smiled in gratitude. Now they had to stay.

"The Duke of Kilve."

The butler's announcement took everyone by surprise, or so it seemed to Violet. They'd all been turned toward the window and the spectacular start of the storm.

Conversation stopped once more, but this was much more pronounced. The length of silence stretched until it was palpable. It might have continued for some time if not for another flare of light and subsequent boom.

Violet turned her body toward the doorway and immediately saw the look of triumph radiating from Hannah's face. *This* must be the Duke of Ice. She glanced toward the biddies on the settee and nearly laughed at the twin looks of shock on their faces.

Hannah had done it.

Giddy with joy for her friend's success, Violet turned her head to investigate this enigmatic duke.

The moment she did so, she understood his nickname, for every part of her went utterly cold.

She knew him.

From the top of his dark head to the small cleft in his chin to the long, athletic length of his legs to the tips of his boots, she knew him. Oh, he looked different—there was a small bump at the bridge of his nose as if it had been broken, and his shoulders were wider, his chest more broad. And his face…his beloved face… It was scarcely the man she'd known and yet it was. His brow was coarser, as if he'd endured more than he'd thought possible. There was a hollowness to his cheeks and a tension in his jaw that made him look uncomfortable. She had the distinct impression he didn't want to be here.

Good heavens, what *was* he doing here?

He's the Duke of Ice, she reminded herself.

A duke! How on earth had Nicholas Bateman become a duke? And how had he earned the name the Duke of Ice?

Violet's body thrummed. She took a step toward the door. His gaze, sweeping the room, stopped when it fell on her. There was a flash of recognition, and then he moved on. He'd seen her, recognized her, then decided she wasn't worth his time.

The pain of eight years ago swept through her frame and nearly sent her to her knees. No, she wouldn't be worth his time. Not after what she'd done. And certainly not that he was now a duke.

He stood in the doorway, his attention pinned to Hannah and Irving as well as the Duke of Romsey. He didn't say much nor did his discomfort seem to wane. His stance was rigid, his jaw stiff. No, he didn't look much like the Nicholas Bateman she had known.

For a moment, she allowed her mind to retreat to that idyllic fortnight in Bath. She'd just come out, and they'd met by chance at the Sydney Hotel. He'd taken her for a stroll through the gardens. He'd been handsome and charming, and his intelligence and wit had completely won her heart. They'd arranged to meet the following day in the Pump Rooms and then danced the next night at the fancy ball at the Upper Assembly Rooms. The day after that, they'd returned to Sydney Gardens, where he'd kissed her in the shadow of a tree, and she'd been lost. Love had claimed her heart and owned it ever since.

Chapter Three

THE SIGHT OF her across the drawing room made Nick's blood run cold. His vision tunneled until he feared it would fade altogether. He'd immediately turned his attention to the Linfords and Simon and kept it there. Nevertheless, he was acutely aware of her presence.

Violet Caulfield was as achingly beautiful now as she'd been eight years ago. But no, she wasn't Violet Caulfield. She was Lady Pendleton. He wondered where her husband was.

The ice he was known for slid through his veins. He never should have come here and would leave immediately.

Light spilled into the drawing room as the storm raged again. Thunder clapped nearby as rain sluiced down the windows, and he realized he wasn't going anywhere.

"Hopefully, this storm won't last," Mrs. Linford was saying. "But if it does, we'll have plenty of inside activities tomorrow. Would either of you care for refreshment?" She gestured toward a table that was thankfully nowhere near Violet.

Violet.

He couldn't call her that, nor should he think of her in such familiar terms. Yes, they'd known each other as intimately as two people could, but that had been a long time ago. A lifetime ago.

Elias's lifetime.

"That sounds excellent, thank you," Simon said. He nudged Nick's arm and darted his eyes toward the refreshment table.

Nick didn't want any bloody refreshments. Actually, he did. Whiskey, preferably. Instead, he moved toward the table with Simon without saying a word to his hosts.

"Could you manage a smile?" Simon asked. "Or at least a less murderous glower."

"I'm not glowering," Nick muttered. He was intensely aware of the eyes turned toward him, of the air of expectation. "I never should have let you talk me into this."

"Perhaps," Simon murmured. "However, we are here. It's too late to run."

"No, it isn't. I'll be doing just that at the earliest opportunity." He looked toward the windows as he reached the table. "I'd leave now if not for the storm."

"Storm or not, you promised me you'd stay one night."

Nick eyed the cakes and biscuits but didn't pick any of them up.

Simon's brow darkened. "Hell, someone's coming this way. Could you at least endeavor to look bored? Or maybe ill?"

That wouldn't be too difficult, Nick thought. Being the center of attention, even for such a relatively small gathering of what, thirty or forty people, made him feel unsettled. He hadn't been raised to be a duke, and though he'd carried the title for five years now, it still felt odd, particularly around others.

The man who'd approached cleared his throat. "Don't know if you remember me, Duke, but we met several years ago in London." He spoke directly to

Nick, clearly indicating which "Duke" he meant. "I'm Lord Colton." He gestured to the woman at his side. "This is my wife, and allow me to present my daughter, Miss Colton." He made the introduction with clear intent: Miss Colton was on the Marriage Mart.

Nick offered a bow to the young lady. "A pleasure to meet you, Miss Colton." He noticed the viscount didn't introduce his daughter to Simon, which only soured Nick's already dismal mood. "This is my dear friend, the Duke of Romsey."

Simon bowed, and Miss Colton offered a curtsey. Lady Colton's face pinched and Lord Colton's cheeks lost a bit of their robust color. Nick wanted to turn and stalk away, effectively giving them the cut direct. How dare they insult Simon?

As if reading Nick's mind—and maybe, *probably*, his outrage was evident on his face—Simon briefly clasped Nick's elbow. "Shall we move on?" he murmured.

"Please excuse us." Simon gave them an undeserved smile and guided Nick away. When they were out of earshot, he said, "You're going to have to do better than that."

"Why? I don't want to be here, particularly if people are going to be rude to you."

"They weren't rude. They were reticent. I *do* want to be here, and you promised me one goddamn night." Simon took a deep breath. "Compose yourself and let us continue."

"For how long? I need a drink." He cast Simon an apologetic glance.

Simon shook his head imperceptibly—their friendship was long enough and close enough that Nick didn't need to censor himself. Still sometimes, particularly in moments of stress like this one, he tried to be more mindful. "You *do* need a drink," Simon said. "But first, we circuit the room. I promise it won't take long." He looked ahead. "We'll start with that woman. She looks quite harmless."

Nick stopped moving and dug his feet into the carpet. "No."

Simon halted alongside him. Nick angled his body so he couldn't see Violet. They stood near the windows, and another flash of light brightened the sky. "Why not?" Simon asked.

"I don't want to speak with her. You may take me anywhere else. *Anywhere.*"

Simon dashed a glance toward her, his brows gathering together in consternation. "You know her? I don't think I've ever seen her before. How do you know someone I don't?"

"Leave it," Nick growled low in his throat. The urge to stalk from the room was nearly overwhelming.

"Calm yourself," Simon said soothingly. "We'll discuss it later." He gave Nick a look that clearly communicated he wasn't going to forget the topic.

They spent a half hour—or maybe it was a lifetime—meeting everyone else in the room. There were several unwed ladies, all of them interested in meeting Nick and nervous about having to meet Simon too. By the time they'd finished, Nick was ready to walk directly into the storm and hopefully be struck by lightning.

"You've one more person to meet," Mrs. Linford said brightly as Nick and Simon made their way toward the door. "Come." She lightly touched Nick's arm, and Simon inclined his head to go along.

A moment later, Nick stood three feet from the woman who'd broken his heart.

"Violet, may I present Their Graces, the Duke of

Kilve and the Duke of Romsey."

Violet offered a rather deep curtsey. "It's a pleasure to make your acquaintance." She inclined her head to both of them, and Nick acknowledged that she was the first and only person in the room who'd given Simon the same deference and courtesy she'd given him. Perversely, that didn't improve his disposition.

"Violet is Lady Pendleton," Mrs. Linford said.

Simon took her hand and bowed. "The pleasure is mine, my lady."

Nick forced himself to make a curt bow. He said nothing and avoided looking at her. Except he couldn't. She was even lovelier now than in her youth. Her eyes were still full of warmth and intelligence—moss-green irises that melted to rich brown at the edges. She had more curves now and a set to her chin that suggested experience and confidence. Her dark pink lips were as full and lush as he remembered. That mouth had drawn him in from the start, especially when she'd laughed. He'd compared it to music.

He'd been a foolish boy.

Mr. Linford cleared his throat loudly, drawing everyone to turn toward the doorway. "Gentlemen, if you'd care to repair to the billiards room with me, you are most welcome."

Hell yes. "If you'll excuse us," Nick said, turning. He didn't wait for a response before stalking toward his host.

A few minutes later, he entered the billiards room on Linford's heels. A footman stood at a sideboard and offered spirits. Nick accepted a glass of whiskey and took a welcome drink as he made his way to a corner.

Simon joined him there, his eyes dark and his lips pressed together. "You were incredibly rude."

"Not *incredibly*." He took another sip of whiskey. "It's not as though I gave her the cut direct."

Simon exhaled sharply. "I know you've a name to live up to, but must you be a beast?"

"You insisted on dragging me here. You may not complain about how I comport myself."

A groan of frustration vibrated low in Simon's throat. "Who is she?"

"I met her several years ago. Before my uncle bought my commission." He and Simon hadn't been as close during that period after Oxford. While Nick, a mere mister at the time, had gone home to Bath, Simon had been a marquess with a penchant for gaming and drink. And women. He'd done his best to become the most notorious rake in London.

"You never told me about her."

"There's nothing to tell." That was an egregious lie, but the story was ancient history. Surely it didn't matter now.

Except she was here. And the past was playing merry hell with his well-ordered life. No, *Simon* had played merry hell with his well-ordered life. "I never should've allowed you to persuade me to come here," Nick said before taking another drink.

"Perhaps not," Simon said with resignation. "But you *are* here. Can we not try to make the best of it? If the weather clears, there will be fishing tomorrow. Linford's lake is excellent, I hear."

Nick did love to fish. And there wouldn't be any women there. Perhaps if he kept to this room as well as his own chamber, he could suffer through this infernal party. "How long are we supposed to be here?"

"A week," Simon said. "Dare I hope you are reconsidering your desire to flee?"

"As you said, we are here, and there is fishing."

Simon grinned. "There are also several marriageable females. You can also reconsider your decision to avoid matrimony."

Nick grunted before sipping his whiskey.

"I think there are several candidates. And you've an excellent chance with any of them."

"I'll leave the courtship to you," Nick said.

"Oh no, everyone is interested in you," Simon said cheerfully. "*You* didn't kill your wife."

Nick looked at his friend sharply. He joked about the rumor sometimes, and it was the nearest they came to discussing it. There were just some things you didn't share with anyone, not even those closest to you.

Such as the fact that Nick *had* killed his wife. If not for him, she would still be alive. Nick was cursed. Indeed, perhaps if he removed himself from Simon, his friend might begin to emerge from the cloud of fear and distrust that surrounded him wherever he went.

Nick swirled the whiskey in his glass before downing the rest of the amber liquid. "You should find a better friend."

Simon snorted. "No one will have me. So I'm afraid you're stuck."

"Perhaps your luck would improve without me."

"Is that what you think?" Simon let out a huff of laughter. "Right now, you're the only luck I have. Without you, I wouldn't even be here. So you're not getting rid of me. Let us try to enjoy ourselves this week, and if the future presents itself, you ought to embrace it."

Nick felt suddenly contrite. If Simon could be optimistic, Nick owed it to him to try. Still, there were limits to what he could do. What he was capable of.

"I'm not going to fall in love."

"You sound quite adamant."

"If there was a marriage—and I'm not saying there will be—she would have to agree to an arrangement in which love played no part." That was essential. For her own well-being.

"How cold, but then you are—"

Nick glared at him. "Don't say it."

Simon raised his hand in self-defense. "I won't." He eyed Nick intently. "Could you do that? Take a wife without emotion."

"I do everything without emotion."

"Mostly, yes." Simon let out a breath and turned to look at the windows. The lightning had died down, but a sudden sharp bolt rent the sky. "Sometimes, however, there's a glimmer of hope." He slid a look at Nick and the corner of his mouth ticked up. "I'll cling to that. And so should you."

No. Nick had long given up on that particular emotion. Hope was for people who believed in happy endings.

Nick most certainly did not.

LATER THAT EVENING, Violet entered the drawing room after dinner. Most of the ladies sat down to play cards, but she'd never particularly cared for cards. Instead, she made her way to a seating area in the corner where she could have a good vantage point of the activities. She'd also be able to see when Nick came into the room.

She mustn't think of him so familiarly. He was the Duke of Kilve now. The Duke of Ice.

How he embodied that nickname. The frigidity in his gaze had been matched only by the frostiness of his tone and the chill of his overall demeanor. At dinner, he'd sat at Irving Linford's right with Mrs. Linford, Irving's mother, on his other side. Violet had watched him covertly throughout the meal, but he hadn't once looked in her direction. He'd seemed to engage in conversation with Irving and his mother, but they'd done the majority of the talking as far as Violet could tell. Nick had sat stiff and tall, like an icicle frozen in place and absolutely impervious to warmth.

That wasn't the Nick she'd known eight years ago. What had happened to him? Curiosity ate through her, but she wasn't going to ask about him. Although she was certain Lady Nixon and Mrs. Law would tell her everything she wanted to know. If she strained to listen, she'd be able to hear them from across the room. They'd talked incessantly since entering the drawing room and were the primary reason Violet had chosen to remove herself from the card playing.

The younger set of women, a trio of bright-faced young ladies, made their way to Violet's seating area. "Do you mind if we join you?" one of them asked. She was a petite, almost fairylike creature with large blue eyes, glowing ivory skin, and dark, nearly black hair. Her name was Miss Diana Kingman. Her father was a baronet and, from what Violet could tell, a bit of a braggart. He believed his daughter to be the most beautiful and the most charming young woman on the Marriage Mart, and he made sure everyone knew it.

"Not at all," Violet said warmly. "Please sit."

Miss Kingman took the chair near Violet, while the other two—Lady Lavinia Gillingham and Miss Sarah Colton—lowered themselves to the small settee.

"We hope you don't mind, but we thought we might ask your advice," Miss Colton said tentatively.

Violet wasn't sure she was in a position to advise these young women. "If I can help, I certainly will. What do you wish to know?"

Lady Lavinia smoothed the back of her dark red-brown hair and glanced between the other two, as if seeking courage. "It's our first house party." She squinted at Violet, making her wonder if the girl needed spectacles. "What do we *need* to know?"

Violet thought back to her first house party. She'd been wed to Clifford for nearly a year, and, newly with child, she'd been rather ill. He'd taken that opportunity to do what many gentlemen did at such events— philander. But she wouldn't discuss *that* with these young ladies.

"I daresay there isn't anything you *need* to know. Mrs. Linford has planned a great many diversions for everyone, so there is bound to be plenty for you to keep busy."

"I'm eager for the excursion to see St. Andrew's Cathedral in Wells," Lady Lavinia said.

"I've seen it and it's stunning." Miss Colton's blue eyes sparkled with anticipation. "I'm looking forward to shopping."

When Miss Kingman didn't contribute her opinion regarding the scheduled activities, Violet turned to her and asked, "And you, Miss Kingman?"

"The cathedral will be excellent, I think. But I'll only be allowed to go if certain other guests go too." However she felt about this was carefully guarded by her placid demeanor.

The other two women gazed sympathetically at Miss Kingman, and Lady Lavinia leaned toward Violet. "Her father is keen to marry her off." She kept her voice low.

Violet studied Miss Kingman to see her reaction, but her features were remarkably impassive. The young woman was a study in reservation. Violet completely understood. She'd quickly learned to repress most of her emotions after marrying Pendleton, and though he'd been dead nearly three years, she still kept things close. Or perhaps that was maturity, as her mother often noted.

"I should like to be married," Miss Kingman said evenly. She glanced around at the other two young ladies. "Wouldn't you?"

Miss Colton's shoulder twitched. "I suppose. My parents certainly want that."

"I *do* want to marry," Lady Lavinia said. "But perhaps not immediately." She winked at Miss Kingman before turning her gaze to Violet. "How old were you when you wed, Lady Pendleton?"

"Not quite twenty." She hadn't even had a season. That had been the intent, but after Nick, her parents had married her off at the earliest possible opportunity.

Lady Lavinia wrinkled her nose. "I'm two years past that, and I'm not certain I'm ready to be leg shackled."

Violet hadn't been ready either, but that was due to the choice of groom. If she'd been allowed to follow her heart… Well, that hardly mattered now.

Tracing a small flower embroidered on her skirt, Lady Lavinia exhaled. "Still, there are several eligible bachelors here this week, and my father will undoubtedly assess their worth." She shot Miss Kingman a look of commiseration. "I daresay our fathers will put us in direct competition for the Duke of Ice." She laughed, but it was edged with uncertainty.

Or perhaps nervousness.

Miss Colton smiled happily. "I doubt my father will bother trying to match me to an Untouchable, thank goodness. For me, they are truly untouchable."

"Are you sure?" Lady Lavinia asked. "No one would dare touch the Duke of Ruin, and for that reason, he may be quite available. If someone wished to take the risk."

The smile crashed off Miss Colton's face, and her eyes widened with horror. "You would wish that on me?"

"Of course not!" Lady Lavinia's cheeks turned a bright shade of pink. "It was a poor jest."

"What is wrong with the Duke of Ru—the Duke of Romsey?" Violet didn't want to use their nicknames.

All three young ladies swung their heads to stare at Violet.

"How can you not know?" Miss Kingman asked.

"I'm afraid I don't pay much attention to gossip." How many times had she stopped Hannah from sharing the latest on-dit? Too many to count.

"It's quite a lurid tale." Lady Lavinia lowered her voice and glanced about before fixing her stare on Violet. "It is said he killed his wife—pushed her down the stairs."

Violet was instantly outraged for the man. "What a horrid rumor."

"It's not a rumor," Miss Colton said softly. "He has said himself that he doesn't remember what happened."

"Are you saying he doesn't dispute it?" Violet asked.

"That is the rumor," Lady Lavinia said.

This was a prime example of why Violet despised rumors. "Was he formally accused of this crime? Or tried for it in the court?"

"Charges were never brought," Lady Lavinia said, her eyes narrowing slightly. "But everyone knows what truly happened. Such a tragedy. She was apparently expecting their first child to boot."

Violet's gut clenched. She'd lost several children—three—but not because she'd fallen down the stairs. No, her body was simply not able to carry a child, a defect her husband pointed out at every opportunity. "How awful."

"I have to admit that he doesn't look like a murderer." Miss Colton shrugged. "I thought he was rather handsome, to be honest." Color flooded her cheeks, and she looked down at her lap.

Lady Lavinia giggled softly, then reached over and patted Miss Colton's hand. "I did too."

Miss Colton looked up at her and joined in with soft laughter.

"It's his eyes," Miss Kingman said, her lips quirking into a half smile. "Such a rich brown, like velvet. And little gold flecks that make them glimmer."

Lady Lavinia looked at her sharply. "Do you have your sights on him?"

Miss Kingman's gaze cooled. "Of course not. Finding someone attractive doesn't mean they would be a good match."

It was precisely the same sentiment Violet's mother had repeated eight years ago. Violet's "love" for Nick hadn't been real. Finding someone handsome and being drawn to them physically were not nearly as important to a marriage as placement in Society. She'd convinced the young Violet of that truth, that what her heart wanted didn't matter. It seemed Miss Kingman had been schooled in the same manner.

"My mother tells me that all the time," Miss Colton said with a sigh. "I argue with her—love *is* important."

"Companionship at least," Lady Lavinia put in. "I can't imagine marrying a man I didn't even *like*." She gave a delicate shudder.

Miss Kingman showed no outward reaction to the other girls' commiseration. "We must trust that things will work out."

Violet couldn't tell if the young woman believed that or was merely reciting what had been drilled into her head. In her own experience, things hadn't worked out—at least not with regard to her marriage. But now she was a widow and blissfully independent.

Violet coughed delicately. "So the Duke of Romsey isn't someone any of you wish to pursue." All three women shook their heads in the negative. "Well, there are several other eligible bachelors here. Mr. Adair's father is a baron. And I believe Mr. Woodward is heir to a viscountcy."

"Mr. Seaver is quite charming," Miss Colton said.

Violet didn't know him. "Excellent. I think you'll all be quite entertained."

"I hope the weather clears so that we may fish tomorrow."

Violet turned to look at Miss Kingman, who'd spoken the surprising statement. "You fish?"

She nodded. "Though I won't be allowed tomorrow, I suppose. I shall have to suffer with only watching."

"How unfortunate," Violet said, her mind working. "I can speak to Mrs. Linford. I'm sure she can arrange something."

Miss Kingman went a bit pale. "No, thank you. I wouldn't want to cause a fuss. Truly. I am quite content to watch the men fish." She gave them a serene smile, but Violet wasn't entirely sure she meant it.

"I heard we will be allowed to take the boats out," Lady Lavinia said to Miss Kingman. "Surely that will be diverting."

Miss Kingman's eyes lit with true anticipation. "Indeed it will."

For some reason, it made Violet happy to see Miss Kingman's enthusiasm. Perhaps the young woman reminded her of a past she'd tried to forget, of being a young woman with no choices. Violet would keep an eye on Miss Kingman for the duration of the party.

The gentlemen joined them then, filtering into the drawing room. The air in the space changed, becoming thicker and more charged as the volume climbed. Violet hadn't meant to look for him, but there he was, one of the last to enter. He lingered by the door.

Nick didn't look her way as he stood with the Duke of Romsey for a few minutes. Romsey left his side and made his way to another pair of gentlemen. Nick gravitated to the corner, where he gazed out over the drawing room with heavy-lidded eyes and his mouth pressed into a thin line of dispassion. There was only one word for what he was doing: *brooding*.

When—and more importantly *why*—had he learned to brood?

The young women had continued their chatter while Violet had taken on the role of observer.

"You should go talk to him," Miss Colton urged.

"Who should?" Violet asked.

"Either of them," Miss Colton said with a wave of her hand. "Lavinia probably. She's the most vivacious, I think." She darted a look toward Miss Kingman, who kept casting surreptitious looks in Nick's direction. "But Diana seems as though she wants to…" Miss

Colton's voice trailed off.

"I'm going." Lady Lavinia stood up, her mouth set with determination and her spine straight. She was a bit taller than average, and her pale yellow dress draped her slender frame to perfection. She smoothed the silk, perhaps nervously, before embarking to the opposite side of the room.

"We mustn't stare," Violet said, despite following the young woman's progress. Violet's breath caught as Lady Lavinia stopped in front of Nick. His pale gaze swept over her, but his features registered nothing resembling interest. In fact, they didn't register anything at all.

Miss Colton swung her head back around toward Violet. "I can't watch."

Violet tore her gaze away. "Perhaps you should go speak with Mr. Seaver," she said encouragingly to Miss Colton. Since everyone had been dutifully introduced after arriving earlier, it was perfectly appropriate for her to do so.

The young lady's attention pivoted to the man in question. He stood near the windows in conversation with Mr. Stinnet, an older fellow with an entirely bald pate. "I don't think I'm brave enough to interrupt them."

"I could go with you," Violet offered. She could see herself guiding these young women over the next week and decided that might be rather nice.

"Lavinia is coming back," Miss Kingman said.

Violet and Miss Colton snapped their heads in that direction. Lady Lavinia was indeed returning, her face flushed and her eyes a bit wide. When she sat down in her vacated seat, it was clear she was flustered.

"What happened?" Miss Colton asked in alarm.

"He was rather...abrupt." Lady Lavinia seemed to take great pains not to look in his direction.

"What did he say?" Violet asked, curiosity burning inside her. The Nick she'd met eight years ago in Bath had been charming and witty. Absolutely irresistible.

"Barely anything. I asked if he liked to fish."

Violet recalled that he did. Very much, in fact.

"He said the only fishing he cared to do was in the lake tomorrow." Lady Lavinia blinked at them. "I said, 'Of course. What other fishing would there be?' He snorted then, and asked if I wasn't fishing right then. He told me to swim back to the shallow end."

Violet snapped her head toward Nick. He was staring at her, his pale eyes familiar and yet unrecognizable. He shifted his gaze away. Slowly, as if he didn't care that she'd caught him staring. She looked back to Lady Lavinia. "Are you all right?"

She nodded and pressed a hand to her cheek. It was still a bit pink and likely warm. "Yes. I daresay I won't be doing *that* again." She laughed nervously. "When he said I was fishing, what did he mean?" she asked Violet.

Violet suppressed a frown. "I'm not certain, but I believe he was referring to husband hunting."

Miss Colton's shoulders twitched. "I'm ever so glad I didn't go with you!"

Miss Kingman cast him a look tinged with curiosity. "He *is* the Duke of Ice. What did you expect?"

Violet was more eager than ever to know how he'd attained that nickname. Whatever the reason, it didn't give him permission to behave in such a boorish manner. Without thinking, she stood and stalked toward his corner.

His gaze strayed to hers as she approached, and she

wondered if he'd gained the sobriquet purely by the way his eyes made one feel. She shivered as she came to stand before him. "Duke."

"Lady Pendleton." Or perhaps it was his tone. It fairly dripped with ice.

Words stalled on her tongue. What could she say to this man after eight long, lonely years?

He arched a dark brow at her. It was the prodding she needed.

"Why were you rude to Lady Lavinia?"

"I wasn't rude. I was plainspoken."

"It sounded rude to me."

"And Lady Lavinia would be the first young woman to speak the absolute truth? I find that impossible to believe."

He was referring to her and the promise she'd made to him. The promise she'd broken.

"She said you told her to swim back to the shallow end. That's hardly polite."

"It's honest." He glowered past Violet. "She's in over her head with me."

Words failed Violet again for a moment as she struggled to reconcile the cold man in front of her with the Nick she remembered. "What happened to you?"

His frigid eyes bored into hers. "Haven't you heard? I'm the Duke of Ice now."

"Just today in fact." She searched his face, looking for a trace of the young man she'd fallen in love with. "I'd no idea you were a duke or that you were even in line for a title."

His lips spread into a humorless smile. "Of course you didn't. You wouldn't have thrown me over. A duke surely trumps a viscount."

Of course he was angry with her—he'd every right to

be. What had she expected? Eight years hadn't washed away her emotion for him. She had to assume it was the same for him.

"I am still so very sorry about what happened, as I explained then."

His brow shot up briefly. "Explained? I had no explanation from you."

"I wrote you a letter." Panic bubbled in her chest as she realized he'd never received it. She'd asked her maid to post it—had her parents somehow intervened?

His face settled back into its stoic mask. "Would it have changed anything?"

Defeat, as heavy as it had been then, weighed on her. She would still have married Pendleton. She'd had no choice. "No."

Horror dawned, and her lips parted as she looked up at him. "Is this… Are you like this because of me?"

He let out a sharp snicker. "Don't flatter yourself, Lady Pendleton. You were one disappointment among many, and I daresay you weren't the worst. Not by a great deal." His gaze hardened. "Do not presume to know me. Our brief and ancient association is long dead. I prefer it to remain that way."

He turned and strode from the room, moving much faster than a glacier, but with precisely the same temperature.

As Violet pivoted to return to the trio she'd left, she realized the volume of conversation had dipped. Heads were turned in her direction. Her gaze found Hannah's a few feet away. It looked as though she'd been on her way to Violet—perhaps to intervene in her conversation with Nick. A conversation it seemed, judging by the attention currently directed toward her, everyone had been aware of.

Color leapt up her neck and spread through her face. She spun on her heel and fled the room.

Chapter Four

NICK HANDED HIS fifth salmon of the morning to the footman and set about casting his line again. The sun was just becoming visible over the tree line, which meant his solitude would soon be interrupted.

"You've quite a hand at this, Your Grace," the footman said as he placed the fish in a basket.

Nick said nothing as he sank his line into the pond once more. Fishing allowed him to sit quietly without anyone bothering him or expecting anything from him. Whether he was on a boat in the ocean or beside a lake or stream as he was today, he enjoyed the silence, broken only by the sounds of the water and the creatures in and around it. The trill of a jay reached his ears, and he closed his eyes briefly, grateful for the calm.

"How long have you been out here?" Simon's voice interrupted his peace.

Nick opened his eyes. "Since just before the sun came up."

"Too early for me."

"I didn't expect you to join me."

"Nor would you have wanted me to." Simon clapped his hand on Nick's shoulder briefly before dropping down next to him. The footman handed him a pole.

"You're actually going to fish?" Nick asked, eyeing the equipment in Simon's grip.

Simon grimaced as he cast his line. "I thought I'd *try*."

"Admirable of you."

"Yes, well, I think it behooves me to participate in the party's activities, even if I'm the resident pariah. Though I wonder if I may be in danger of losing that title to you."

Nick glanced at his friend, his mouth pursing. "I'd be happy to take it from you."

"No, you wouldn't. Trust me."

"You forget that I like to be left alone."

"And yet every time I come to visit, you seem to enjoy my presence," Simon said bemusedly. "You're fooling yourself, and someday you'll come to realize that. I just hope it isn't too late."

Nick suffered his friend's concern. "When would that be?"

"When you're old and decrepit and everyone you know is gone." Simon shot him an earnest stare. "I mean *everyone*."

So many people *were* gone already. "That argument will gain you no ground."

Simon exhaled. "I know. But I still have to make it every now and again. Just as I have to point out your atrocious behavior last night."

Nick turned his head. "Atrocious?"

"Don't pretend a stupidity you don't possess. First you stood in the corner sulking like a boy denied his favorite sweet. Then you conversed rather brusquely with not one, but two women. The first went hurrying back across the room, tail between her legs, and I can tell you her father, Lord Balcombe, was *not* pleased. And the second…"

Nick looked back out at the lake, willing a fish to take his bait so that this infernal topic could be interrupted and hopefully avoided.

"It was clear to everyone that your conversation was heated—such a strange word to be associated with the Duke of Ice, or so I heard said—and that Lady Pendleton was flustered. She practically ran from the room."

Nick watched a heron swoop down and take up a position on the opposite side of the lake in the shallows. The graceful bird glanced toward Nick and Simon but paid them no further mind as it stood stock-still in search of prey.

"Have you nothing to say?" Simon demanded.

Nick turned his head once more. "Did you ask me a question?"

Simon snorted. "You're a beast. You should apologize to both women. You're never going to find a wife if you behave in that fashion."

"May I remind you that finding a wife is your endeavor? Furthermore, we're dukes. We can behave in whatever fashion we please and still find wives."

"There you are wrong, my friend," Simon said good-naturedly. "As it happens, if you are rumored to have killed your wife, your marital opportunities are rather limited. If not nonexistent."

"You didn't kill her," Nick muttered, knowing this was a futile argument, much as Simon's regarding his chosen solitude.

"If only I could be as certain as you."

They sat in silence for a few minutes before Simon spoke again. "Who is Lady Pendleton? It seemed as though you knew her when we were introduced yesterday."

Nick didn't want to talk about her. Or think about her. Or remember anything to do with her. But he'd dreamed of her last night for the first time in ages.

Only she hadn't been the young, dewy-eyed girl he'd met eight years ago. She'd looked as he'd seen her last night—her high cheekbones more pronounced, her lips a deeper pink. And her eyes, so clear and honest in their youth, had been perceptive, more experienced, like stones polished after years and years in the bed of a stream.

"She's no one important."

"But you know her?" Simon persisted.

Nick ground his teeth. "Yes."

"And she clearly strikes a nerve."

She did indeed. Last night he *had* been sulking. Or perhaps brooding was a better word. Then that chit had come over to speak with him, and he'd done his best to scare her off. Not because he was a beast, but because it was better for everyone, especially the young woman.

Then Violet had approached him, and every inch of his body had reacted in a combination of hurt, regret, anger, and something wholly surprising: yearning. For a fleeting moment, he'd recalled what it had felt like to want her. He'd embraced the other emotions instead.

Even so, he couldn't forget the glimmer he'd seen, the reminder of a time long past. A time before he'd gone to war, before he'd lost the rest of his family, before Jacinda and Elias.

"I knew her a long time ago," Nick said softly, his gaze trained on the heron.

"Before we met at Oxford?"

Nick shook his head. "After."

"You never told me about…" Simon sucked in a breath. "She was the woman. Christ, I'd forgotten all about her."

Nick had told him he'd met a woman, but that she'd

married someone else. By then, Nick had progressed from grief to anger. "You were busy at the time."

"Raising hell," Simon said with more than a touch of regret. He'd been doing what heirs to dukedoms did in London—gambling, chasing women, and drinking.

Nick was sure there were many things Simon didn't remember, and he didn't hold it against his friend. Simon had been through his own trials and managed to come through them with a far better disposition than Nick.

"I'm sure you don't wish to speak of it, but remind me what happened beyond the fact that she broke your heart?"

"I don't think there's much else to tell, is there?" What good would it do to relive that fortnight?

Her parents hadn't been in Bath when they'd met, and so he hadn't been able to ask to court her. They'd met in secret, and Nick had anticipated asking for permission from her father to wed as soon as he came to Bath. However, when Nick went to Violet's aunt's town house to make his case for her hand, he'd learned that she'd left town the day before just as soon as her parents had arrived. His mind shuttered against what he'd discovered that day. He gripped the fishing pole tightly, the muscles of his hand clenching. "In hindsight, I don't think my feelings were really that strong."

"How can you know?" Simon asked. "Your relationship ended before it had really begun. It's hard to say what would have bloomed if the seeds had been allowed to grow."

"Stop trying to be a bloody poet."

Simon flashed a broad smile. "Don't pretend I don't amuse you."

A loud cacophony of chatter amidst the rustling of bushes heralded the arrival of the male members of the house party.

"Ho there! I heard you'd come down early, Your Grace," Linford said with a hearty grin. He turned his smile on Simon as well. "And here you are, Your Grace. I am beginning to think that where I may find one of you, I shall find the other. How easy it will be for the young ladies to spot you." He chortled and looked about to see if anyone else was joining him in his mirth. Seeing that they were not, his laughter turned to coughing and then he cleared his throat. "Shall we fish?"

Footmen had toted the fishing equipment, which the men were now clamoring to claim. Nick resisted the urge to pull up his line and return to the house. He doubted there would be much more to catch with all this commotion, but told himself to stay for Simon's sake.

It was true that most of the attendees treated Simon with an odd deference that smelled a bit of fear. Some of these imbeciles clearly believed that he *had* killed his wife. If nothing else, Nick should do his best to disabuse them of that notion and encourage them to get to know Simon instead of listening to vicious rumors.

How in the hell was he—a man who sought and coveted his solitude—supposed to do that? He'd long forgotten how to be affable or charming.

Blood of the devil. His mood, already soured by the disruption of his peace and quiet, threatened to turn even darker.

He glanced over at Simon, noting that no one had sat on his other side. Reeling in his line, he stood. "This is an excellent spot. I've already caught several salmon."

Lord Colton stepped toward him. "Indeed?"

"Go ahead, take it."

"Are you certain?" the viscount asked.

"I insist." Nick offered a bland smile before taking himself away from the crowd. He found an outcropping of rock, an ideal spot above the deepest water of the lake. He'd considered camping there earlier, but it had been rather slick at that dark hour. Now, it was mostly dried out thanks to the sun.

Nick sat down on the rock and wished he'd grabbed one of the blankets the footmen had brought. The stone was rather hard and cold. Ah well, at least he was relatively alone. He cast his line and tried to relax. Just as he was beginning to feel comfortable, he saw a flash of color across the lake. *Blast.* The women of the house party had come to the lake.

A handful of boats bobbed around a small dock. Evidently, they'd come to row. There'd be absolutely no fishing now. At least not with any success. Who the hell had planned this activity?

Several of the gentlemen called out across the water. The women waved in response. Though he tried not to, Nick picked out Violet among the group. She was taller than most, her blond locks covered with a tall, dark green hat that made her even easier to spot. She wore a costume that was a bit reminiscent of a riding habit, with a buttoned coat and sleek velvet trim. She was stunning.

He turned his head to find the heron and was disappointed to see it had gone. *Lucky bird,* he mused.

He tried to ignore the women clambering into the boats, but it was rather distracting given the noise they were making. He watched as Violet got into a skiff with one of the young unmarried women he was trying to avoid. Hell, wasn't he trying to avoid everyone?

Scowling to himself, he averted his gaze from the boats. The lake wasn't terribly large, so it was only a matter of minutes before one of them rowed into his line of sight. He hoped they knew enough to stay well away from the fishing lines.

To hell with it. He wasn't going to catch anything else today. He stood and reeled in his line. Then he heard the loud clack of two boats colliding. He looked up from his pole just as one boat capsized. His eye caught a tall, dark green hat just before the boat went over.

Tossing his pole aside, he didn't think. He dove into the lake and swam like hell.

◆ɞ•Ʒ◆

THE SKIFF COMPLETELY flipped over, not only plunging Violet into the lake but into darkness as the boat landed on top of her. It didn't strike her, instead creating a void above the water. She heard a shriek— from a distance—and surmised that she was alone beneath the boat.

The water was cold and thick, sucking at her skirts. She worried she would be pulled under from the weight of her wet clothing. She knew how to swim, due to Uncle Bertrand's lessons, much to her aunt's horror.

Violet pushed at the boat but wasn't able to flip it back. She'd have to duck under it. Sucking in a deep breath, she braced herself to submerge. Before she could go completely under, she realized her hat would pose a problem. Bobbing back up, she pulled the accessory from her head and tossed it aside. Taking another breath, she tried again, this time dropping beneath the surface.

As soon as she was underwater, she felt a moment's panic. The weight around her legs seemed heavier. She pumped her arms, trying to propel herself clear of the boat.

Suddenly, someone clasped her bicep and pulled her to the surface. She inhaled sharply and opened her eyes, blinking rapidly against the moisture clinging to her lashes.

Her vision filled with a familiar visage: Nick.

His gray eyes had taken on the color of storm clouds, and his lips were pressed into a nearly nonexistent line. "Are you all right?"

"I think so." She tried to regain her equilibrium, and her gaze caught a dark head bobbing beneath the water several feet away. "*Miss Kingman.* You must help her." She looked pleadingly at Nick.

"I'm not letting you go." He used his free arm to pull the boat—which had somehow been flipped back over, perhaps by him. "Can you hold on to this?"

Violet nodded. "Yes." She reached for the edge and clasped it with both hands.

"Don't pull on it," he warned brusquely. "It will flip again. Just hold on enough to keep your head up. Can you do that?"

She nodded again as her teeth began to chatter with cold.

He left her then and struck out, swimming beautifully, his arms slicing through the water, toward Miss Kingman. He pulled her above the surface and began to drag her toward the dock. She worked to keep her head up as he swam.

When they were almost to the dock and Violet felt as if her entire body was encased in ice, a boat came toward her. "Nearly there, Lady Pendleton!"

The Duke of Romsey rowed toward her. He came alongside the boat she clung to, trapping her between the boats. He came off the seat and sat down in the middle of the boat. "We must be careful not to capsize. I'm going to lift you. But I need you to turn and let go of the boat."

Violet knew she would drop like a stone as soon as she let go. "I'll sink."

"You won't." He grabbed the back of the neck of her gown, startling her. "I've got you. Ready?" At her nod, he said, "Let go!"

She did as he instructed and relinquished her grip. She tried to turn, but she could barely move her legs in the weight of her skirts. And she was so cold.

Nevertheless, she left the water as he pulled her up over the side of the boat. He dragged her inside, and she collapsed on top of him, her back to his front.

"Don't move," he said, breathing heavily. After a moment, he wriggled from beneath her. "We need to even our weight across the skiff. Can you move to that end?" He gestured to the front, where she was facing.

"Yes." Feeling as though she was draped in armor, she slowly worked her way forward to the front of the boat.

"That's it. Wonderful." With his encouragement, she made it all the way, then turned her head. He was at the back and had already picked up the oars. "And away we go," he said cheerfully, as if she hadn't just fallen from a boat and wasn't shivering so badly, she feared her teeth might fall out.

The duke rowed them to the dock, where a footman grasped the side of the boat and another one helped Violet step out. She was quickly bundled into a blanket, and Hannah rushed toward her. Her friend's face was stricken. "Are you all right?"

"I-I-I'll be f-f-fine," Violet managed. As she stepped from the dock onto the path, she saw Miss Kingman wrapped in a blanket between her parents, who were ushering her toward the house.

"What a disaster," Hannah cried softly. "I do hope you and Miss Kingman don't catch cold." She glanced up at the bright sky. "I'm grateful yesterday's storm has given way to fairer weather today. Even so, we need to get you to the house."

Violet wondered what had become of Nick. She turned her head and saw him standing about twenty feet away, his gaze locked on her. His features were impassive, but in the lake, she'd seen the concern in his eyes. Was there any chance he might still feel something for her? Something other than animosity? He'd been so cold last night, but today, he'd come to her rescue. Hope fluttered in her chest, and she smiled.

He turned abruptly and started toward the house, his long legs devouring the uneven earth as he skirted the path. Another chill swept over Violet, and she shuddered.

"Come, let's get you to the house," Hannah said.

"You sh-should stay with your g-guests," Violet said with a weak smile. "I'll find my way."

"I should be happy to accompany you," the Duke of Romsey offered. "I'd give you my arm, but I daresay you should keep yourself as covered with that blanket as possible."

"Yes, probably." Violet took in her friend's expression of distress. She truly looked as though she might cry. "Everything will be fine, Hannah. This will be an amusing story, you'll see."

Hannah nodded but didn't appear entirely convinced.

Violet started up the path alongside the duke. "Thank you for r-r-rescuing me."

"It was my pleasure. Indeed, perhaps this will improve my reputation at last."

She looked at him askance and saw that he was grinning. Plus, she'd heard the self-deprecation in his voice that said he was no stranger to being maligned. "I hope so. I'm afraid I can't believe the rumors about you. You seem far too kind."

"Rumors, I've found, are usually based on at least a kernel of truth."

It was an enigmatic statement, but she wasn't sure she had the courage to ask what he meant. Was he trying to say he had somehow been involved in his wife's death? Violet was saved from a response of any kind when he continued.

"Take Nick—Kilve, I mean. He's the Duke of Ice, and it's not a wrong description. He is as cold and unemotional as they come."

Now. Violet barely recognized this Nick.

"He wasn't always like this—I've known him since we were at Oxford together. Longer than you, I think."

She snapped her head to look at him. "He told you about me?"

"A bit."

Those two strained words hinted at things she didn't want to revisit—not just now. "No, he wasn't always like this. Nor was he a duke. How did that happen?"

"A series of misfortunes befell his family. He inherited from his uncle."

"I take it his brother died?" Though their affair had lasted only a fortnight, Violet had learned many things about him. Still, there was so much she didn't know.

And likely never would.

"At Badajoz, fighting alongside Nick, actually."

She looked over at the duke. "Nick served in the army?" She hadn't known what happened to him after she'd left. Her parents had removed her from Bath as quickly as possible and nearly as quickly had married her off to Pendleton. She hadn't looked back, despite wondering what had happened to Nick. She'd decided it was too painful to hold on to something—someone—she couldn't have.

"His uncle bought him a commission."

She imagined him going off to war. Would he have done that if she hadn't left? She recalled that his older brother had been a soldier. "Did he go because of his brother?"

"I think so. And he…needed a change. Or so he said. I admit we weren't terribly close at that time. I was too busy drinking my way through London."

"I see," she murmured, not knowing quite what to say to that. "But you're close now?"

"As close as he allows. He was different after Badajoz and…other things that aren't my place to discuss."

Curiosity fairly burned inside her, but she wouldn't ask him to disclose Nick's secrets. "I cared for him a great deal. It pains me to see him so removed. So cold."

"It does me as well, I must admit." The duke's gait slowed as they neared the house. "Is there a chance you still care for him?"

Though she was still quite cold, Violet paused and turned toward him. "I will always care for him."

It was more than that, but she wouldn't say so. She loved him still, and seeing him again had only reminded her of that fact. She'd thought she could keep him in the back of her mind, a distant memory that, if handled with care, could bring her joy.

"That's good to hear. Nick needs people who care for him. He works damn hard to make sure they don't."

"Why would he do that?"

"I'm not sure I know the answer to that. It's complicated. *He's* complicated. He's been through a great many trying circumstances, and I think he's perhaps forgotten how to live. If there's any chance at all you could remind him, I would encourage you to do so."

"What exactly are you saying, Duke?"

"I think you should call me Simon. I saved you, after all." He grinned at her, and she decided she liked him no matter what. "I'm saying that Nick needs *something*. Or someone. I was able to get him to this party—which was no small feat—but I fear that he'll return home and go right back to his solitude."

"I don't know if I can prevent that." Aside from rushing to her aid in the lake, Nick had given her no inkling that he was interested in having a conversation with her, let alone any kind of relationship.

"I don't know if you can either. But if you wanted to try, I'd be grateful."

The breeze stirred, and she shivered again.

Simon rolled his eyes. "I am the worst rescuer, keeping you out here in the cool autumn air. Come, let's get you inside." He ushered her into the house, where a maid informed her that a hot bath was being prepared in her chamber.

As Violet climbed the stairs, she looked forward to being warm. More than that, she looked forward to seeing if she could thaw Nick and bring him warmth too.

Chapter Five

NICK FROWNED AT his reflection in the mirror. Not because his appearance was lacking, but because he really *was* cursed. He'd barely spent one day with people and catastrophe had already struck. He only hoped Miss Kingman and Violet were all right.

They'd both been pale and sodden, their eyes wide with fright. Actually, the latter had just been Miss Kingman. Violet's gaze had reflected more surprise than anything else. Surprise at finding herself plunged in the lake or because he'd come to her rescue?

He was surprised.

He told himself he'd gone to her first because she'd been a bit closer than Miss Kingman. However, he knew that Violet could swim. That was one of the *many* things he knew about her. Along with her love of ices, her penchant for reading poetry, and the way her toes curled when she was kissed.

Swearing under his breath, he turned from the glass.

"Something amiss, Your Grace?" his valet, Rand, asked.

Nick glanced over at the young man and shook his head. "No."

"Is there anything else you require?"

"My coach so we may depart?"

Rand blinked at him. "Would you like me to pack?"

Nick exhaled. "No," he lied. He *did* want to leave. He'd promised Simon one night, and he'd fulfilled that bargain. And yet here he was dressed for dinner.

Because he wanted to ensure that both women were well after their unplanned swim. If either of them took ill…

It didn't bear thinking about.

A knock on the door drew him from taking that dark path. Rand answered the summons but didn't need to announce the arrival as Nick heard Simon's voice. "Evening, Rand. I'm here to fetch the Duke."

Rand stepped aside and held the door wide for Simon to enter. He stopped short and surveyed Nick from head to toe. "Christ, you look as if you've eaten bad soup. Have you? I didn't see you for luncheon."

"I didn't eat soup." He'd barely eaten anything, save a few cakes from the tea tray that had been sent up that afternoon.

Simon flicked a glance at Rand. "What's wrong with him?"

Rand appeared mildly alarmed, his jaw tightening and his eyes widening slightly. "Nothing." He looked at Nick in question—and apology.

Nick glowered at Simon. "Don't scare my valet."

"I doubt that's possible. He's in service to *you*," Simon quipped. "Are you ready for dinner or are you indeed ill?"

No, and he hoped Miss Kingman and Violet weren't either. The only way to verify that was to go to dinner. "I'm ready, and I'm not ill." He turned and checked his reflection in the glass. He looked fine. Or at least not peaked. "Do you know if Lady Pendleton or Miss Kingman have recovered from this morning?" He avoided looking at Simon as he asked the question.

After a moment, Simon answered slowly. "No. But I begin to see why you look as you do."

Nick brushed at a nonexistent speck on his coat and

pivoted from the mirror. "I don't 'look' like anything."

"You're concerned about them—I can hear it in your tone. I've no idea how they fared. Neither came to luncheon."

Nick wasn't able to suppress a flinch.

"You *are* concerned."

"You don't find it odd that as soon as I venture back out into Society, two women are endangered?" As soon as he uttered the question, he wanted to take it back.

Simon stared at him a moment, then did the unthinkable. He laughed.

Nick scowled.

"That's a question *I* should ask. *I'm* the one who's a menace." Simon's laughter faded. "Or something."

"And *I* am cursed. Need I point out to you that everyone I've cared about has died?"

Simon laid his hand over his chest. "I'm wounded. Here I thought you cared about me."

"I should clarify—everyone in my family. You are not a member of my family."

A loud sniff punctuated the air as Simon wrinkled his nose. "I see." He shook out his shoulders and looked Nick squarely in the eye. "That's all nonsense."

It wasn't, but Nick wouldn't debate him. "I'm planning on leaving in the morning."

"You *can't*." Simon narrowed his eyes. "You made me a promise."

"Which I've more than kept. Tonight will be two nights, and I only pledged one."

"You can't go, not when I'm on the verge of a true breakthrough. After my rescue of Lady Pendleton this morning, I am enjoying a bit of positive notoriety for once."

Hell. How could he abandon his friend now? "I am,

of course, thrilled for you. However, you don't need me to remain."

"Perhaps not, but I'd like you to. One more day." Simon cocked his head to the side. "So long as you're already here. Lord knows when you'll venture to such a thing again."

He had a point. "One more day. Can we please go downstairs now so I can stop listening to you whine?"

Simon grinned as he clapped him on the shoulder. "Anything you say."

They left Nick's chamber and went down to the drawing room where everyone was told to gather before dinner.

As soon as they appeared in the doorway, Linford clapped his hands. "It's our resident heroes!"

Everyone joined in with applause, their heads swiveling to the doorway. Nick wanted to melt into the floor. He looked askance at Simon and saw a faint blush at the top of his friend's neck. Yes, he was enjoying this, and well he should.

Simon flicked his wrist with a flourish and bowed deeply. Nick belatedly copied him, albeit with just a stiff bow.

As he straightened, he scanned the room. Miss Kingman was perched between her two young friends on a settee. Some of the tension left his frame. However, it returned as soon as he realized Violet wasn't present. Was she ill?

A few of the ladies intercepted them, smiling and preening. They didn't ignore Simon, but their attention was first directed at Nick.

Lady Balcombe looked up at Nick, her lashes fluttering. "However did you learn to swim like that, Duke?"

"In the ocean," Nick answered, looking about the room once more as if he could will Violet to appear.

"My goodness," Lady Adair said. "That must have been terribly difficult. How strong you must've been, even as a child. Assuming you learned as a child. I never did. Learn, that is."

Nick focused on her for a brief, irritating moment. "I live on the coast. Learning to swim in the ocean is rather necessary. If you'll excuse me." He stalked to the opposite corner, where he could take up a vantage point from which he could see the doorway. That way, he wouldn't miss Violet's entry.

He caught the perturbed stare Simon quickly directed his way and lifted a shoulder in response. He knew he'd been short, but he didn't want to make inane chitchat, especially about himself.

The expression he'd donned was clearly enough to deter anyone from approaching him. It looked a few times as though someone wanted to come speak with him, but then thought better of it. Mrs. Linford smiled at him and took a few steps in his direction, but stopped abruptly and made her way to another group of guests. And Lord Adair had inclined his head, then angled his body as if he might come Nick's way. His wife had intercepted him and cast a wary glance at Nick.

Good, he preferred they all stay away.

With each minute of Violet's absence, his gut churned. Ice spread across his shoulder blades and down his spine. When he was on the brink of quitting the room, she appeared in the doorway. Her honey-colored hair was piled atop her head with a jeweled comb while curls kissed her cheekbones. Her ruby-red gown hugged her frame, accentuating the swell of her breasts and the creaminess of her skin. Her gaze swept the room as his had done, but instead of finding it wanting, she settled on him. A shock went through him as their eyes met.

He'd felt something similar in the lake when he'd pulled her from the water, desperate to make sure she wasn't going down beneath the boat. Leaving her to save Miss Kingman had been difficult—painful almost—but he'd done what he must. He'd seen Violet safe and gone to help the flailing young woman. But with every stroke, he thought of Violet's hazel eyes—a beguiling mixture of strength, determination, and vulnerability.

That last one scared him to death.

He didn't like vulnerability. He'd had far too much of it.

Her lips curved up, and she started toward him. He didn't want to speak with her. Turning abruptly, he nearly crashed straight into Mrs. Padmore, a matron with sharp eyes and an even sharper tongue. She faltered but steadied herself. "My goodness." She gave him a thorough but critical assessment. "Are you in a hurry?"

She wasn't alone. Mrs. Stinnet, another matron but with far kinder eyes and a more retiring demeanor, stood at her side. "Of course he's not," she said to the other woman. "He just didn't see us."

"No, I did not." But he *had* been in a hurry—to escape Violet. "I beg your pardon." He offered them an awkward bow and attempted to move past them, but Mrs. Padmore moved into his path so that he'd have to barrel into her again if he wanted to leave.

"That was a brave thing you did this morning, jumping into the lake," she said. "I didn't see it, but I hear it was magnificent."

"Yes, quite dashing," Mrs. Stinnet said with a wide smile. "I'm sorry to have missed it."

He didn't like this attention. Or the accolades. "It wasn't meant to be a show."

The women stared at him, nonplussed. *Good.*

Before they could pester him with more nonsense, the butler announced dinner. Relief poured through Nick, and he turned away from the women with alacrity.

He went directly to Linford's mother, whom he'd escorted to dinner last night at Linford's behest. Nick had also sat next to her at the table. She was rather reserved and provided an excellent buffer between him and the rest of the guests. Hopefully, he'd be seated next to her again.

Striding to her side, he offered her his arm and looked forward to leaving tomorrow.

"HE'S RUINING MY house party!" Hannah cried as she and Violet huddled together in the corner of the drawing room. "He was supposed to complement the party. *Elevate* it."

Violet patted her friend's forearm briefly. "You mustn't fuss. Or draw attention," she murmured.

As soon as dinner had finished, Hannah had steered Violet into the corner where they could talk somewhat privately. Still, Hannah's stress was evident, and Lady Nixon and Mrs. Law were casting suspicious glances in their direction.

Hannah straightened. "You're right, of course. I refuse to let him ruin things." Her eyes hardened, and her jaw stiffened with determination.

"That's the spirit. Who needs him anyway when the Duke of Romsey is turning out to be so charming?"

"Is he?" Hannah sounded uncertain. "I suppose his involvement in this morning's boating debacle has improved people's opinion." She groaned softly. "Between that disaster and the Duke of Ice's behavior, I may never be able to host another house party again."

Violet felt for her friend. She was, invariably, a people pleaser, going out of her way to ensure that those around her were happy and satisfied. That, in turn, made *her* happy and satisfied. "I don't think anyone is having a bad time."

With the exception of Nick. He'd been obnoxious before dinner—tales of his boorishness had traveled around the opposite end of the table from where he sat, again between Irving and Mrs. Linford. Simon's counsel from earlier floated through her mind. Perhaps she should try to speak with Nick.

"I'll talk to the Duke," Violet offered.

"Kilve?" Hannah asked. At Violet's nod, her shoulders drooped with relief. "I should be ever so grateful. Now, I must go speak with Lady Nixon and Mrs. Law and make sure they are indeed enjoying themselves."

"Are you joking? Of course they are. What you see as a disaster is their premium gossip. I'm sure they're thrilled." Violet didn't bother keeping the edge of derision from her tone.

Hannah smiled, and Violet was glad to see it. "You're right, of course. Still, I'd prefer *nicer* gossip. And I know you would too." She gave Violet's hand a pat. "Thank you. I don't know what I would do without you."

Violet watched Hannah rise and go to where the

scandalmongers were sitting. Violet's gaze drifted to the trio of young women who sat in the same area they had last night when they'd joined Violet. She stood to go see how Miss Kingman was faring.

The three women smiled up at her, welcoming her approach. Lady Lavinia patted the empty chair beside her. "Come sit with us, Lady Pendleton."

"Good evening, ladies," Violet said before turning her attention to Miss Kingman. "I trust you are recovered after this morning's swim?"

The young lady gave a delicate shudder. "I admit it was petrifying. I wish I knew how to swim. I asked to learn when I was younger, but my father was unhappy enough that my grandfather taught me to fish."

"Your grandfather sounds wonderful," Violet said, thinking of her Uncle Bertrand, who'd encouraged her in ways her own parents hadn't. "I highly recommend swimming. My uncle introduced me to the water when I was ten."

"Is that why you seemed so calm this morning?" Miss Colton asked. "You didn't look frightened at all after you came up out of the lake."

"I admit I was—just a bit," Violet confided. "Mostly because when I did learn to swim, I wasn't bogged down with such heavy skirts."

All three young women were riveted on Violet. "Whatever did you wear?" Lady Lavinia asked, sounding somewhat scandalized.

Violet looked around before lowering her voice. "A boy's shirt and pair of breeches."

Three pairs of eyes rounded, then Miss Colton giggled. The others joined in.

"How scandalous!" Miss Colton said from behind her hand as she tried to keep her mirth in check.

"Perhaps, but it was just me and my uncle and my older brother." Uncle Bertrand had promised to teach Henry, and when Violet had asked to be included, he couldn't think of a reason she shouldn't. How she missed her uncle.

Now composed, Miss Kingman said, "His Grace is certainly an excellent swimmer. He carried me all the way to the dock and hardly seemed fatigued."

"Too bad he's a clod," Lady Lavinia said, wrinkling her nose.

Miss Kingman narrowed her eyes slightly. "He's not a clod. He's simply unused to events like this."

Violet eyed Miss Kingman, curious as to her defense of Nick.

Lady Lavinia rolled her eyes at her friend. "I suppose you must defend him. If your father has his way, you'll be the next Duchess of Ice."

Miss Kingman looked away as a bit of color stole up her neck.

"It's a shame you can't talk your father into the Duke of Romsey instead. He seems far more affable." Miss Colton turned eagerly to Violet. "He rescued you from the water and escorted you to the house. Perhaps the Duke already has his sights set on someone." She gave Violet a coy smile.

"I am not in the market for a husband," Violet assured her. "I will say that he was quite charming, and whomever he does set his sights on will be very lucky."

"You'll have a hard time convincing them." Lady Lavinia inclined her head toward the opposite side of the room, where Lady Nixon and Mrs. Law were holding court. "My mother hangs on their every word, and they said they are not persuaded by the Duke of Ruin's performance this morning."

Performance? "I hardly think it was an act." Violet looked down to keep her acidic glare from shooting across the room.

Lady Lavinia rose from her chair. "I'm afraid I need to visit the retiring room, and I want to hurry before the gentlemen return."

Miss Colton jumped up. "I'll join you."

They excused themselves and departed, leaving Violet alone with Miss Kingman.

"I'm glad you are all right," Violet said. "That water was rather cold."

Miss Kingman shivered. "Just thinking of it makes my skin prickle. I am incredibly grateful to the Duke for saving me. And so are my parents."

"Is it true that your father hopes for a match with him?" Violet was surprised the question came out sounding even. Her heart was beating, and her throat was dry. Thinking of him marrying someone else made her want to toss up her accounts. And yet she'd done precisely that to him—married someone else. Had he felt the same sense of sickness? Her heart twisted.

Miss Kingman nodded. "Yes. He says I'm more than worthy of a duke. Whatever that means."

Violet wondered at the young woman's true feelings on the matter. "And what is it you want?"

The young woman blinked at Violet, her ink-black lashes falling briefly over her vivid blue eyes. "I want whatever is best. My parents say he is best."

She sounded so much like Violet had eight years ago. It was amazing the lies one could tell oneself even while one's heart was breaking. *Especially* when one's heart was breaking. "Make sure it's what will really make you happy. Marriage will change your life."

Forever. *Unless your despicable husband has the grace to die.*

Though Violet was far happier now, she took no joy in Clifford's death.

She'd long wondered how different things would have been if she'd been allowed to marry Nick. Or if she'd done as they'd discussed and eloped in the event that her parents refused him.

The gentlemen took that moment to enter the drawing room. Violet half expected Nick to be absent. He *had* behaved rather obnoxiously before dinner. Perhaps he would beg off the rest of the evening, especially since Hannah had planned dancing.

But no, he filed into the room alongside Simon, although he quickly veered to the right and took up his usual brooding stance in the corner. Before she could think better of it, Violet stood. "Please excuse me, Miss Kingman."

The young woman grabbed Violet's hand briefly, drawing Violet to look down at her in concern.

"You're not going to speak to him about me, are you?"

"I was not. Do you want me to?" Violet couldn't believe she'd asked the question. She didn't want to play matchmaker, not when she wanted him for herself.

Goodness, that sounded so selfish. Yet honest. She'd made a mistake eight years ago, and it seemed Fate was giving her a second chance. She'd be a fool to let it pass her by again.

"Only if you want to." Her tone was less than enthusiastic, and again Violet had to wonder if she was truly interested in marrying Nick. Or if she was interested in marrying at all.

Violet gave her a meaningful look that she hoped the young woman would understand. "If you need someone to confide in—about anything—I hope you know that I'll listen. And whatever you say will be kept in confidence." She gave her a warm smile before turning to face the dragon.

Now he was a dragon?

Standing in the corner as he was, his arms crossed, his mouth drawn into a near frown, he looked every bit an imposing figure. Violet refused to be intimidated.

As she neared him, he dropped his hands to his sides and looked her over—rather thoroughly. His regard heated her, reminding her of the way he used to look at her. His eyes would light up, and his lips would curve into the most devastating smile. What she wouldn't give to see that expression on his face again.

"I wanted to thank you for rescuing me from beneath the boat this morning."

"You look well, Lady Pendleton. I am glad to see it." He *could* be polite.

She was encouraged. "Miss Kingman is also grateful for your assistance."

"I understand she is also in fine health."

"She is," Violet said, feeling suddenly nervous. She tried to recall what Simon had told her, that Nick needed something. Or someone. "You seem a bit more at ease. Has it been an adjustment being here? I take it you don't spend much time socializing."

He stared at her a moment, long enough that discomfort snaked beneath her skin. "No, I do not. I find it tedious."

There was the Duke of Ice—how she hated that name!—who'd disappointed Hannah. "Then why did you come?"

"As a favor to Simon—Romsey."

"So you don't wish to be here?"

"Not at all. In fact, I plan to leave tomorrow."

Hannah would be crushed. As horribly as he was behaving, she would take his departure as a mark of failure. "I wish you wouldn't. My friend Mrs. Linford has planned a marvelous party. Perhaps if you let down your guard, or whatever it is you've erected over the past eight years, you might enjoy yourself."

They stood perhaps a foot apart, but he leaned slightly closer. She caught his scent of leather and clove. "Don't speak to me as if we are friends. Don't even speak to me as if we are acquainted."

Her heart beat faster in response to his ire. "But we are."

"The man you knew doesn't exist anymore."

Anger and sadness coiled inside her and fought for release. "I'm beginning to see that. When I saw that *you* were the Duke of Ice, I was astonished. But now I see how cold you are." She edged closer, her yearning for him overtaking the other emotions he'd wrought. "What happened to you, Nick?"

He flinched when she said his name. His jaw clenched, but he said nothing.

It was agony to see him like this, but maybe he was right. Maybe the man she loved *was* gone, and she'd have to accept that. Except Simon had said he needed people who cared about him and that he'd maybe forgotten how to live. Perhaps coming here had been the first step in living again—whether he knew that or not.

Violet withdrew slightly and stiffened her spine. She looked him square in the eye. "You've come here for a reason. Whether it's to support your friend or something else, it doesn't matter. You're here, and you made a commitment to attend the party. If you leave, you'll devastate my dear friend Mrs. Linford. She doesn't deserve that. I don't want you leaving on my account. I'll stay away from you if you promise to stay." It was the opposite of what Simon had asked her to do, but Nick had just told her they couldn't be friends.

His gaze flickered with something, but she couldn't say what it was. She *could* say what it *wasn't*. Since his arrival yesterday, he'd had a dark, frigid, rather practiced stare. This was something else.

"I'll think about it," he said at last. Then he pivoted and stalked from the room.

Violet realized she'd been holding her breath and let it out in a rush. A moment later, Simon joined her.

"That looked rather tense," he said quietly. "Are you all right?"

She appreciated his concern and again wondered how anyone could think he'd purposely killed his wife. "I'm fine. Your friend, on the other hand, is awful. How do you continue to stand by him?"

Simon shrugged. "Because he needs me. And I need him. In some ways, we're all each other has."

"Well, you have me now—as a friend."

A smile settled over his face, lighting his entire expression. "I am fortunate indeed. Thank you."

Irritated over her encounter with Nick, Violet was pleased to talk of something else. She glanced out toward the various groupings about the room. "I daresay your fortunes have changed, and I'm delighted to see it. Hannah has planned dancing for this evening. Will you stay?"

"Certainly, though I wonder if I ought to persuade Nick to return. He's leaving tomorrow, so he should come dance before he retreats into self-banishment once more."

"He may not be leaving," Violet said. "I am

optimistic I convinced him to stay. After I promised I'd leave him alone." She turned her gaze sharply to Simon. "What do you mean, 'self-banishment'?"

Simon barely winced, but Violet caught it. "He just prefers his solitude, that's all." He cocked his head to the side and regarded her intently for a moment. "I'm pleased to see that you convinced him to stay. I know you said you'd leave him alone, but again I would encourage you not to do so. The fact that you changed his mind is a massive shift."

"He was quite clear in his animosity. He said we weren't friends. Or acquaintances even."

Simon waved his hand. "He's just being beastly."

"I don't know him as well as you." That admission pained her, but it was true. She ought to know him better than anyone, but she'd relinquished that opportunity long ago. "He does seem to enjoy his solitude and frigidity. We can't help him if he doesn't want to be helped."

"And that's what I'm saying. I think he *does* want to be helped, even if he doesn't know it yet. I've been trying to persuade him to reengage in Society with me for years. He's always refused me." Simon's eyes gleamed with purpose. "Until now."

Violet looked at him intently, hoping they could help Nick. "What do you think changed?"

"I've no idea, nor do I care. He's here and he's staying. Somewhere inside him is the Nick we both used to know. We just have to find him and draw him out."

Chapter Six

❖⟨❖⟩❖

BY THE TIME Nick rode back to Linford's stables, he was windblown, damp, and cold enough to make his nickname accurate. It felt good. It felt like home, because he spent many a day riding along the windswept coast regardless of the weather. Being outside allowed him to feel untethered; his thoughts as careless as the breeze.

Except today, he'd been thinking. Last night, he'd tossed and turned, hardly able to sleep after his confrontation with Violet. He'd recalled their time together, their happiness and anticipation, when they'd forecast a life and marriage before them. Since then, everything had gone to hell, and he realized now that a part of him blamed her. As if *she'd* caused all his misfortune.

But he knew that wasn't true. The curse was his. She seemed content and had maintained her charm, even if she was more subdued than she'd been eight years ago. He remembered a young woman who was quick to laugh, her eyes alight with a constant gleam of excitement and joy—as if every day were a new adventure. And he supposed it had been. For that blissfully short time.

Had that been the happiest period of his life? He wasn't sure. He wanted to say it was his marriage to Jacinda, but he'd wed her out of duty. Yes, he'd grown to care for her, but he'd never experienced what he'd felt for Violet. And therein lay a part of his guilt.

He shook his head as he dismounted in the yard and handed the reins to a groom. He hadn't thought of such things in a very long time, if he'd ever considered them so deeply. Normally, he did his best to thrust such thoughts away. It seemed, however, that in the presence of Violet, he wasn't able to do that.

And if she could somehow resurrect him from the prison he'd created—and yes, it *was* a prison—shouldn't he let her?

He stopped short as he approached the house, the wind nearly whipping his hat from his head. What was he saying? Was he thinking of rekindling their affair?

Would that be so terrible? A tiny voice whispered in the back of his mind.

He hadn't had a lover in ages, and house parties seemed rife with opportunity for just such an endeavor. She was, he now knew, a widow, which was also beneficial. He allowed his curiosity about her to rise. How had she become widowed? Did she have children? Had she been happy?

It felt wrong to care about those things—about her—given what he'd endured, but perhaps it was past time he released his emotions. At least a little.

As Simon and Violet had pointed out, he was here at this party. Perhaps he could try to make the best of it, for Simon if not for himself. He was glad for Simon—he was ready to move forward even if Nick wasn't. And if Nick could help him do that, he should.

Nick started toward the house once more, a buoyancy to his step that had been absent for far too long.

It was past luncheon—he'd purposely gone for his ride during that time to avoid the gathering, just as he'd broken his fast in his chamber instead of downstairs.

The house seemed quiet, and he wondered if people had retired for a respite or had perhaps left on an excursion. If it was the latter, they would've done so on foot because the stables hadn't reflected any sort of activity that supported transporting guests. He supposed he ought to pay attention to what the devil was going on at this party if he intended to stay. And since he hadn't left yet, he had to accept that he'd made his decision.

He ducked into Linford's library, which wasn't terribly impressive, to select a book for the afternoon. He stiffened, his feet planting into the carpet, upon seeing Violet perched on a cushioned seat set into the bowed window.

She looked up, and color instantly flooded her cheeks when she saw him.

He wanted to turn and leave, but he didn't. He could do this. Taking a deep inhalation through his nose, he strolled forward until he was a few feet from her.

She closed the book, keeping her place with her forefinger. "Good afternoon. We missed you at luncheon."

"I was riding."

"And you came back." A smile teased her mouth, but only for a moment.

He was sorry not to see it bloom. "Evidently," he said wryly. "I've decided to stay. It looks as if it will rain."

She glanced out the window at the darkening sky. "Yes, I'm afraid so. Hannah had planned a walk earlier, but we feared becoming drenched, so they played cards instead."

"*They* played cards," he said knowingly. "While you came here to find poetry." He glanced at the book in her hand.

"You remembered." Blushing slightly, she tipped her head back toward the window. "We'll take the walk tomorrow—if the weather allows."

A large, fat drop hit the window and slid down the glass. "There it is."

With her free hand, she traced the water's descent. Nick had a flash of her forefinger moving down his chest. The memory jolted him.

She turned her head and looked up at him. "I'm glad you're staying. After last night, I wasn't sure. I will stay out of your way."

That would probably be best. She was rousing all sorts of memories and emotions that he didn't entirely want to face. That voice at the back of his head piped up again. *She's not your enemy.*

No, but he'd cast her as a villain for so long, he wasn't sure he could think of her any other way. Did she really deserve that?

"You…agitate me." He surprised himself by admitting it.

She stood from the window seat, which brought them closer together. She was so familiar to him and yet a stranger. It was an odd sensation. "I can see that. Am I the reason you're the Duke of Ice?"

"Partly." He had the urge to touch her, just a brief stroke of his finger along her jaw, to see if the connection between them was still there.

But he didn't. This was enough. For now.

"Did you really not know I was a duke?" he asked. "Mrs. Linford is your friend. You could have asked her to invite me. Now that I *am* a duke, I imagine I'm worthy of your attention."

Her color turned a bit gray, and he regretted

provoking her. "I deserved that," she said softly, looking him in the eye. "You were always worthy of my attention." She dropped her gaze to the floor. "It's me who isn't worthy. Truly, I didn't know you were a duke. I purposely ignored anything to do with you—Nicholas Bateman, that is. And I pay little to no attention to the goings-on in Society."

"That's something we have in common, then." Something inside him loosened, like a caged butterfly set free.

She looked back up at him, her eyes the color of grass and earth, basic and elemental. "I was glad to see you. I'd always wondered how you were. Simon—the Duke of Romsey—said you were in the army. I was sorry to hear about your brother."

With that sentiment, he snapped back into his usual self. The ice crept back over him. He grasped for a safer subject. "You're first-naming Simon?"

"He asked me to. He seems a good man."

"He is. And since I'm at this infernal party, I've decided I should make the most of it—for his sake. He persuaded me to come here so that he could attend. He would like to move on with his life, find another wife. If that's even possible."

"I should think so." The muscles around her eyes twitched, and she glanced away. "Actually, I'm not certain. He's been treated with reticence since his arrival, though things have improved since yesterday's events."

"He said as much."

"It's the younger women mostly. Convincing their parents that he's a good match may be difficult." She paused a beat to consider him. "You, on the other hand, are highly sought after."

He grunted, his lips twisting with disgust.

"You aren't interested in marrying?" she asked.

"I've *been* married," he said. "I don't particularly wish to do it again." He quickly looked away, directing his gaze at the rain streaming down the windows. "But Simon does, so I'll help him in any way that I can."

She took a moment to respond, and he was certain she wanted to ask about his wife. When she didn't, he breathed softly with relief. He never should've brought it up. Images of Jacinda and of his son, Elias, flashed in his mind. He briefly closed his eyes to banish them for now.

"I'd like to help," she said. "If I may."

He looked down at her, surprised to find himself forging an alliance with her. "I was hoping you'd say that. What can we do?"

"It might be best if you made it clear you are not wife hunting. Then the parents who wish to make a match will look elsewhere."

"I despise making my business public."

A smile teased her lips. "Something else we have in common. Well, I have good news. If you continue behaving like a boor, I doubt anyone would have you." Her breath caught. "Except... I do believe Sir Barnard has his eye on you for his daughter, Miss Kingman, regardless of your temperament."

"I believe you're correct. He's cornered me in conversation after dinner the past two nights and extolled his daughter's attributes at length."

"I've become friendly with Miss Kingman. I can relate to her that you aren't interested and that perhaps she should shift her interest to Simon."

He considered her suggestion but decided he didn't want to wish the baronet on his friend. "I'm not sure

Simon should have to tolerate Kingman as a father-in-law. What are his other options here?"

"Few, I'm afraid. Lady Lavinia and Miss Colton aren't terribly enthusiastic about marriage. Yet. That doesn't mean they couldn't be. Both seem to want to fall in love." Her cheeks pinked, and she busied herself transferring her book from one hand to the other, careful to keep her place.

Oh, to be young and full of dreams again. Nick pitied them, for it was likely those dreams would be dashed. "Even if he doesn't find a wife here, making sure everyone in attendance leaves here with an improved opinion of him should be our goal."

She nodded and looked back up at him, her chin determined and her eyes carrying some of the sparkle he recognized from so long ago. "Agreed."

"I'm afraid you'll have to tell me what to do. My social ineptitude is epic in nature."

The music of her laughter soothed his spirit, and he nearly smiled. "You take care of the gentlemen—do what you can to show them that Simon is a good sort. Leave the women to me." She wrinkled her nose. "I suppose I'll have to talk with Lady Nixon and Mrs. Law. If I can gain their support of him, he'll practically have carte blanche in Society."

"If you could do that, he—I—would be eternally grateful."

She stared up at him, her lips slightly parted. He felt a pull toward her, like a bee drawn to a bright, beautiful flower.

"It's the least I can do," she murmured. Her fingertips grazed his chest, and he had his answer—the connection was still there. "I'd do anything to help you. Or your friend. I'll see you at dinner."

She turned from him and left the room.

He watched her go, his body thrumming with long-suppressed arousal. Well, that had been unexpected. As was the sensation currently tripping through him—an interest in tomorrow.

❦

HE'D BEEN MARRIED.

The information had shocked and saddened Violet—because he'd married someone other than her, but mostly because, like her, he'd lost his spouse. Had his union been happier than hers? She hoped so.

Such thoughts had taken over her brain since she'd seen him that afternoon. All through dinner, she'd stolen looks at him down the table where he'd sat beside Simon. Violet had asked Hannah to seat them together in the hope that Nick would be able to support their effort to elevate Simon's reputation. It had seemed to work since that area of the table had been a source of laughter and general good cheer.

Violet slowly made her way to the drawing room. For her part on Simon's behalf, she should talk with Lady Nixon and Mrs. Law. She wasn't looking forward to it.

Hannah caught up to her just before they reached the doorway to the drawing room. Her smile was wide, and her eyes sparkled with joy. "Thank you ever so much, Violet. I don't know what you did to improve His Grace's disposition, but I daresay he was a different person at dinner."

Violet had told her friend that she'd spoken briefly to Nick. She hadn't elaborated about their past relationship. The habit of keeping that part of her history buried was long and difficult to break apparently. "I think he was just trying to gain his bearing. It's been a long time since he attended a house party."

"That makes perfect sense," Hannah said. "Now, if the weather will just hold tomorrow so that we may have our archery contest."

"I thought tomorrow was bowls."

"In the afternoon. Again, if the weather cooperates." She sighed. "This is what comes from hosting a house party in October."

"October is a perfectly lovely month, and you aren't competing with other parties."

Hannah winked at her. "That was my primary objective, as you know. It does seem as though things are going well. Ice is warming up." She laughed at her not-so-subtle pun. "And Ruin seems to be far more charming than his dark reputation would have us believe."

"I agree. I couldn't be more delighted to see his character redeemed."

Hannah's mother approached them. "If you're speaking of the Duke of Romsey, do not get too optimistic. Lady Nixon and Mrs. Law are not convinced."

Blast. Violet turned toward the drawing room and suppressed a grimace. "I will go and speak with them."

"I doubt you'll gain much ground," Mrs. Parker said, shaking her head. She looked at Hannah in resignation. "Daughter, I know why you invited them, but I hope after this, you'll decide it isn't worth the aggravation."

Hannah twisted her mouth and gave a small nod. "Yes, Mother."

If Violet knew Hannah, her friend had no intention of leaving the likes of Lady Nixon and Mrs. Law out of future invitations, not if they gave her their stamp of approval. Accordingly, Violet ought to make sure that happened. "Please excuse me," she said before taking herself into the drawing room.

A brief survey of the room showed that the ladies were holding a small court in their usual spot. They monopolized the largest seating area, each of them occupying two tall-backed, stuffed chairs. They were surrounded by most of the other ladies of the party, save the younger trio who were in their usual spot. Lady Lavinia looked at Violet in open invitation, and Miss Colton went so far as to beckon Violet with her hand. She smiled at them but shook her head very slightly. Gathering her courage—and patience—she strolled into the lionesses' den.

"Lady Pendleton, how unexpected of you to join us this evening," Mrs. Law said. "We'd thought you'd taken on the duty of chaperoning the young ladies."

Anything to avoid sitting with you lot. Violet smiled blandly, then looked pointedly at Ladies Colton, Balcombe, and Kingman. "They're lovely girls."

"We do appreciate your solicitude," Lady Balcombe said. "One can never have too many examples of grace and propriety."

Propriety. Violet thought back to her own youth, specifically eight years ago. If they knew how she'd behaved with Nick, it would be an extraordinary scandal.

"Indeed," agreed Lady Nixon with a sniff. Her pale blue eyes swiveled to Mrs. Law. "Especially when there are questionable individuals about."

"You're referring to the Duke of Romsey?" Violet asked rather innocently, hoping she successfully kept the edge from her tone.

"Ruin, yes, of course," Mrs. Law said, pursing her lips. "I do understand why Mrs. Linford invited him, and since he did coax Ice out of hiding, we must be grateful, I suppose."

"Yes, but was it really worth it?" Lady Nixon asked. She leaned forward slightly. "I daresay Ice has forgotten how to behave."

"He was quite charming at dinner tonight," Lady Kingman rushed to say. "I even saw him smile."

Lady Nixon arched a pale brow. "Indeed? I must have missed that, surprisingly." The implication—that she'd been surveying him closely—was clear. But then one had only to watch Lady Nixon to know that her powers of observation were sharp and obtrusive.

Violet had missed his smile too, and she was incredibly disappointed. "I've found him to be quite pleasant," she said serenely.

Mrs. Law narrowed her eyes at Violet. "I find that difficult to believe given the interaction you shared with him the other night. It looked rather…tense."

"It was not," Violet lied. "That's the problem with making an assumption about something when you weren't actually there." She gave a placid smile but laced it with some of Nick's ice. "The same can be said of the Duke of *Romsey*." She put special emphasis on his name on purpose.

"There you are wrong," Lady Nixon declared darkly. "There was an eyewitness to the Duke's crime. He pushed his pregnant wife down the stairs."

A few of the women gasped.

"I hadn't heard that," Lady Colton said, her brow creasing with distress. "He truly seems like such an affable gentleman."

"He is." Violet still didn't believe he was capable of

such an act. There had to be an explanation. She blinked at Lady Nixon. "It seems this is news to many people. Who is this eyewitness?"

Lady Nixon's gaze frosted. "One of his retainers. All of them left his employ afterward. What more do you need to hear to know that he's guilty?"

"If he's so guilty, why wasn't he prosecuted?" Violet asked. She looked around at all the women, most of whom lowered their gazes to their laps.

Mrs. Law lifted her chin and shifted her gaze from one side of the group to the other, settling on Violet. "Because that retainer disappeared and was never heard from again. Unfortunately, there wasn't sufficient evidence."

Violet straightened in her chair. "Well, I, for one, refuse to find him guilty of a crime for which he hasn't even been accused or tried. I think he's charming and kind, and I am quite grateful for his assistance in the lake yesterday."

"Oh yes, that was excellent of him to help the Duke of Kilve with his rescue," Lady Kingman said.

Violet noted that she made it seem as if it had been Nick's rescue, and while Nick had been the only gentleman to dive into the lake, Violet gave Simon full credit for his fast thinking. He'd had to dash around the lake—faster than anyone else—and quickly put out a boat to get to her. "He was most solicitous as he walked me to the house," Violet added.

"You were nervous to be escorted by him?" The query came from Mrs. Stinnet, whose arsenal possessed less vitriol than that of Lady Nixon or Mrs. Law.

"Goodness no. I would do so again, in fact." Violet seized the opportunity to be plain in her advocacy. "And if I had a daughter, I wouldn't find fault with him courting her."

"You're still young, Lady Pendleton," Lady Nixon said slyly. "Perhaps he'll court *you*."

Violet couldn't agree without making it seem like she was interested in him—and she wasn't. Instead, she orchestrated a neat maneuver. "I am past courtship, but if I were younger and on the Marriage Mart, I would be flattered by his attentions."

"You must admit he's handsome." This came as a whisper from Lady Balcombe to her neighbor, Lady Colton. When she realized others had heard her, her cheeks blushed the color of Violet's favorite dark pink peony.

"Well, I wouldn't want him courting my daughters," Mrs. Law said haughtily. "If they weren't already well married, that is." She exchanged a superior look with Lady Nixon, and Violet couldn't control her irritation another moment.

"That's ridiculous. *You're* ridiculous." She stood abruptly just as a handful of the men strode into the drawing room.

Spinning about, she nearly collided with Nick. He caught her arm before she barreled into him. His touch streaked through her like the lightning in the sky on the first day of the party—hot and electric.

"In a hurry?" he murmured. "Walk with me." He offered her his arm and escorted her from the room. "They're setting up card tables next door."

"I don't want to play cards."

"I know. But given the malevolent stares cast in your direction by Lady Nixon and Mrs. Law, I thought it best to remove you from the drawing room." He guided her past the sitting room where the card tables were being set.

She tipped her head to look at him and drank in his handsome profile. His ivory cravat stood in sharp contrast to the darker cast of his skin. "Malevolent?"

"Perhaps that's a bit hyperbolic, but not by much. They're dangerous—from what I hear. What did you say to set them off?"

"I called them ridiculous." She winced. "It wasn't well done of me. But they were being incredibly insulting toward Simon." She glanced about. "Where is he?"

He inclined his head to the side and back—toward the room they'd passed. "In the card room helping to set up, which was most fortuitous, I think."

"Yes, his arrival in the drawing room might have caused a scene." Her shoulders sagged. "I was trying to help him. I'm afraid I made things worse."

When they reached the entry hall, he pivoted and led her back the way they'd come. "I doubt that's possible. What's worse than them thinking he's a murderer? They already think that."

"Lady Nixon said there was an eyewitness to the crime. I can't believe it. He would've been prosecuted."

Nick drew her to a stop and turned slightly toward her, keeping her hand over his arm. "There was, in fact, a witness, but she disappeared."

Apprehension seized Violet's chest. "They said as much. I still can't believe it."

"Nor can I, but he doesn't remember what happened. He blames himself, whether he pushed her or not."

"But he shouldn't. Not if it was an accident."

"That wouldn't matter." He turned and started walking once more, his gaze focused straight ahead. "Trust me."

Something in his tone told her there was a wealth of rationale—and emotion—behind that entreaty. She looked up at him and said simply, "I do."

He cast a glance at her, and she caught maybe a hint of surprise in his eyes. She didn't expect him to return the sentiment—his trust was something she'd have to regain. If she even could.

"I do think Simon is making progress," she said as they neared the card room. "Lady Balcombe said he was handsome. And Lady Kingman said his rescue of me was excellent. I still sense some hesitancy, but they aren't maligning his character like Lady Nixon and Mrs. Law."

He stopped again before they got to the card room. "Hmm. We'll need a plan to win them over."

She reluctantly took her hand from his arm. It felt so good to touch him. Familiar and exciting too. Her body wanted to lean into his, but she masked her reaction. "What sort of plan?"

"I'm not sure yet. For now, I suppose I'll have to try to charm them." His face took on a decidedly sour expression, reminiscent of how he looked when he brooded in the corner.

She laughed softly. "Careful. That's the haughty Duke of Ice. I think you need to dig out the charming Nicholas Bateman I met."

His eyes narrowed slightly, and she feared she'd overstepped. They'd reached such a nice truce. She hated to go back to him hating her. Or maybe he did still hate her, and he was simply putting that emotion aside so they could help his friend.

"They won't care."

"How can you be so sure?"

He arched a brow at her. "I'm a duke—made of ice

or not."

His tone was so droll, his expression so wry, she couldn't help but laugh. She also couldn't help thinking *this* was the Nick she'd met. The Nick she'd dreamed of. Her heart leapt and threatened to take flight from her chest.

"Dukes are magic?"

"To people like Lady Nixon and Mrs. Law, yes." He pivoted toward the card room. "I'm going to play. Will you watch?"

She couldn't tell if his question was polite or if he wanted her to join him. She hoped it was the latter and decided she didn't care. She would enjoy this conviviality with him for as long as she could.

Chapter Seven

THE MORNING DAWNED cloudy but dry, and the archery contest was due to take place as planned. As luck would have it—or not, depending on how one felt—Nick left the house just as Lady Nixon and Mrs. Law were making their way to the archery field. Though he needed to speak with them, he decided he was unlucky, for now he'd have to escort them the entire way instead of being able to remove himself if the conversation become intolerable.

He wished it had been Violet leaving the house instead. He'd enjoyed their time together last night, even if it was brief. She'd followed him into the card room for a bit, but then departed and he hadn't seen her again. He'd particularly enjoyed rescuing her again—this time from a potential scene in the drawing room. He'd loved the looks of shock on Lady Nixon's and Mrs. Law's pinched faces when Violet had called them ridiculous. Even if it was ill-advised.

"If it isn't the Duke of Ice," Lady Nixon called as they walked onto the path that led to the archery field, about a hundred yards distant.

Mrs. Law pursed her lips at her friend. "You shouldn't call him that to his face." Since she was saying that loud enough for him to hear, he knew she didn't really find fault with it.

Lady Nixon gave him a mischievous smile. "He is well aware of what everyone calls him. And I think he *likes* it. Indeed, I think he's cultivated that image. It takes effort to cast that much of a chill." She slid a knowing glance toward Mrs. Law. "We should know, dear."

Well, at least they were being honest about their behavior, even if they were talking about him as if he weren't there. "You do realize I can hear you," he said.

Mrs. Law smiled broadly. "Of course, Your Grace. Now, are you going to offer us your escort to the field?"

"It would be my pleasure." He offered each of them an arm and tried not to cringe when they touched him. Just allowing them close made him feel a bit sullied. He might be cold, but he didn't set out to insult anyone. He just preferred they stay away from him. On the contrary, these vulgar beldams liked to be the center of attention.

"We must be honest with you, Duke," Lady Nixon said briskly. "We couldn't help but notice you paid attention to Lady Pendleton last night. We can't presume to know your plans; however, if you were to solicit our advice—and we would endorse such an endeavor—we would encourage you in another direction."

Nick wanted to tell them off in much the same fashion Violet had the night before, but that wouldn't suit his purpose. "I thought it best that I escort Lady Pendleton from the situation last evening. She seemed upset."

"Oh, well done of you," Mrs. Law said, squeezing his arm. "She is fortunate you were so quick thinking."

Lady Nixon craned her neck to look up at him. "It seems you can't help yourself from playing the hero this week. How utterly charming."

"I'm sure you'll agree that my good friend the Duke

of Romsey has done the same. I'm confident he would've acted in the same manner last night if he'd been in the drawing room."

Mrs. Law wrinkled her nose. "Your friendship with him is a bit odd, isn't it?"

These women really had no shame. Or sense of propriety when it came to conversing. Did they think they were immune to Society's rules? "We've been friends since Oxford. I find nothing odd about it. He has been a loyal support, and I treasure his friendship."

"I think I understand what you're attempting to do," Lady Nixon said. "You must understand that our reticence regarding the Duke is not ill-founded."

"No one knows what happened that tragic night, and *no one* is more devastated by that than Romsey." He slowed to a halt and carefully gave each of them his iciest stare. "I would advise you to leave the matter where it belongs—in the past."

Lady Nixon scoffed. "Even before that…*incident*, he was a terrible rake."

Nick detested gossip, but he remembered a few key things, and in this instance, the recollection was going to be quite useful. He lowered his lids and gave her an assessing look. "If memory serves, you would be one to know." At her shocked expression, he stifled a satisfied smile and started walking once more. Luckily, they were almost to the field. "I think I should remind you that he *is* a duke. And not the Duke of Ruin, as you are so fond of calling him. He deserves your deference, if not respect."

Both women were apparently tongue-tied. *Good.*

"Oh, here's Miss Kingman," Mrs. Law said as they reached the field, breaking the blissful silence far too soon. She withdrew her hand from Nick's arm. "Come and join us, dear. Will you be shooting?"

Lady Nixon removed her hand also and took two steps away from Nick.

Miss Kingman, a petite, dark-haired young woman with enigmatic eyes, glided toward them, her light wool skirts skimming the grass. "Yes, I'm looking forward to it."

Mrs. Law turned a smile toward Nick as if he hadn't just taken her to task. "Perhaps His Grace will assist you."

Hell and the devil. He'd neglected to inform them he wasn't on the Marriage Mart.

"Oh yes, that's a capital idea," Lady Nixon agreed. Her gaze narrowed slightly as she regarded him. "You simply must help her."

Every part of him cried out to make his excuses and walk away. And yesterday, he would have done so. But today, he was on a quest to help his friend. "It would be my pleasure to help you practice, Miss Kingman. Shall we?" He gestured toward the footmen who were preparing the bows for shooting.

They strolled toward the shooting area, where a line of targets were set up at varying distances. A few were quite close—maybe fifteen feet. A few more were farther out, at least twenty-five feet. Two were set at a great distance of about seventy yards. "Which target will you be aiming for?" he asked.

Miss Kingman was very young. He'd guess her to be about twenty. "I've only shot a few times, so I'll start with the closest one." She accepted a weapon from one of the footmen.

"You've shot before?" Nick asked while glancing around. Other people were already here taking aim, but not Violet. Simon wasn't here either.

"Yes, but not for a few years." She took a position before one of the nearest targets and lifted the bow. Taking a deep breath, she pulled back the string and let the arrow fly. It fell to the earth about two feet before the target. She laughed nervously. "Well, that was terrible."

"It wasn't, actually. Do you want some advice?"

She turned toward him. "Yes, please."

"Don't hold it so tightly. Relax your hand on the bow before you release. You might also consider widening your stance a bit."

The footman handed her another arrow, and she took her time before pulling the string. She did as he instructed and loosened her grip just before she let the arrow fly. The arrow hit the target but didn't stick.

She turned to him, her eyes bright and her lips parted. "It almost landed."

"You did very well."

She blushed slightly. "You're very kind to help me."

"As I said before, it's my pleasure." Just then, he caught sight of Simon arriving—with Violet on his arm. A bead of irritation worked up his spine.

"Shall I try one more time?" she asked.

Nick tore his gaze from his best friend and his former lover. "Certainly." He resisted the urge to turn his head and focused on assisting Miss Kingman.

She did much better this time, and her arrow hit the target, albeit on the outer edge. "I did it!" she exclaimed.

"After a few more shots, you may be ready for the next distance."

Her expression dimmed, and he noted her gaze was directed past him. He turned to look and saw her father watching them. The baronet smiled and waved.

Miss Kingman touched Nick's sleeve, drawing his attention. "Thank you again." Her gaze was soft and earnest. "I appreciate you spending time with me. But don't feel as if you have to stay."

Was she trying to hint that he should leave? Something about her demeanor reflected discomfort, despite the fact that she'd touched him. He might've thought it was a flirtatious gesture, but he wasn't sure that was her intent.

Regardless, he did want to go. This was the most time he'd spent talking to people he barely knew—first to Lady Nixon and Mrs. Law, and then to Miss Kingman. "I'll leave you to it, then," he said. "I'll keep an eye out in case you require my assistance." He apparently hadn't forgotten how to be polite. This was a surprising relief.

"Thank you." She turned to the footman to get another arrow, and Nick took his leave.

He looked toward Simon but didn't see Violet with him any longer. A quick scan of the field revealed her standing with their hostess, their heads bent in conversation.

Nick strolled toward Simon, who met him more than halfway and set the tone by giving him a sly grin. "Heaven forfend, is the Duke of Ice *thawing*?"

Scowling, Nick offered a grunt in response.

"There's the surly friend I know." Simon's smile didn't falter. "You looked friendly with Miss Kingman. Is there a chance you've changed your mind about seeking a wife?"

"I was helping her shoot. Or maybe I was determining her interest in you. You're the one who wants to remarry."

Simon's eyes rounded briefly. "Egads, no. She's far

too young. I'd prefer a lady of experience. Maybe a widow."

Nick's gaze strayed to Violet. She was a widow. No way in hell was he going to steer Simon in *that* direction. "You shouldn't discount a woman because she's young. You may be surprised. I believe the other single ladies in attendance are a bit older."

"Perhaps slightly." Simon stared at Nick. "Good God, you're trying to play matchmaker."

"Don't look so bloody surprised. You did say you wanted to remarry."

"Yes, but I don't have to find her here." His eyes narrowed slightly, and he turned his head. Toward Violet. "Lady Pendleton is older. And a widow. And rather attractive." He looked back to Nick, his expression unabashed. "Would that be distressing to you given your shared past?"

Hell yes, it would be distressing. Nick had suffered imagining her with her bloody viscount husband. But a friend?

She is your past, not your future.

As usual, he kept his emotions as hidden as possible. "I don't know. It might be…odd." What a goddamned understatement. Seeing her here at this party had shaken him. For the first time in years, he was interacting with people and he was *feeling*. The sooner he could get away from her, the better. If she married Simon—God, the thought of that seared his insides as if with a hot poker—she'd be a part of his life forever. He didn't think he could endure that.

"Well, odd isn't too terrible," Simon said affably.

Was he trying to be provoking? Nick buried another scowl and schooled his features into a hard mask. "Are you going to shoot in the contest?"

"Yes, you can outfish me, but I daresay I will beat you at archery."

Nick's gaze strayed to Violet once more. This time, she was looking straight at him. She smiled, and he turned his head from her quickly. Viciously. Agitation streamed through him as he regarded Simon. "You won't," Nick said softly in response to his challenge. "Prepare to fall."

THE ARCHERY CONTEST began with the women, and the distances to the targets were slightly shorter than the men's. Violet was shooting against Miss Kingman, Lady Lavinia, Hannah, and Lady Adair, the sole woman over the age of thirty who was participating.

They drew straws for places, and Violet, drawing the shortest, was last. In the first round, they all took aim at the nearest targets. Everyone but Hannah hit the target and progressed to the next round. She laughed and leaned close to Violet. "You're going to win anyway."

Violet wasn't sure—Miss Kingman demonstrated some skill, despite being a beginner. And Lady Adair had come rather close to the center of the target. It remained to be seen if this was luck or if she was an accomplished archer.

Lady Adair shot first in the second round as they moved to the next, farther target. Her arrow landed farther out on the target this time. Next up was Lady Lavinia, whose arrow stuck feebly into the bottom of the target for a brief moment before falling to the ground. There was an audible murmur reflecting the spectators' disappointment. Lady Lavinia grinned and gave a shrug as she handed her bow to the footman.

Miss Kingman took her place at the line, which was marked with a wide red ribbon held in place with a pair of rocks on either end, and lifted her bow. Breathing deeply, she focused with intense concentration, the space between her brows puckering. Violet wanted to tell her to hold the string farther back along her fingers. The young woman let her arrow fly, and it landed well within the target, in a better position than Lady Adair's. Her effort was roundly cheered.

A footman handed Violet a bow and arrow. She passed Miss Kingman with a smile. "Well done."

"Good luck," Miss Kingman said.

Taking up her position, Violet scrutinized the target for a moment. She tried not to overthink, but to just feel. This was the way Uncle Bertrand had taught her. She lifted the bow and pulled back the string, exhaling as she let the arrow go. It landed right next to Miss Kingman's.

Violet felt a rush of satisfaction at the applause and cheers that greeted her when she turned from the target. She searched for Nick and saw him standing on the periphery. He clapped, but only briefly. His features were as stoic as they'd been before the contest had started. He seemed to be the Nick of two days ago instead of the man she'd spent time with last night. That short walk had filled her with happiness—and hope.

"Final target," Irving announced loudly. "Whoever comes closest to the center will win!"

Lady Adair curtsied to the guests before taking her bow and moving to the shooting line. She raised her weapon and considered the target for a long minute. Then she pulled the bow and released the arrow. It failed to reach the fifty-yards-distant target.

She turned with a weak smile and gave another curtsey before returning the bow to the footman.

Miss Kingman went next. As she walked past, Violet leaned toward her and whispered, "Try holding the string farther back—behind your knuckles instead of closer to your fingertips. It's much more comfortable and will help your aim."

With a look of surprise, Miss Kingman nodded. "Thank you." She curtsied to the guests, then took her bow and went to the line, where she took even longer than Lady Adair to prepare. She lifted her bow once only to lower it and change her stance. The second time, she hesitated, but, after narrowing her eyes, released her shot, taking Violet's advice. It landed perilously close to the center of the target.

Miss Kingman turned her head toward Violet, her eyes wide with shock and her lips curving into a smile. "Thank you," she mouthed.

Violet flexed her hands as apprehension spiraled through her. Perhaps she ought not to have helped Miss Kingman. As she and Miss Kingman passed each other, Violet said, "*Very* well done."

The young woman blinked, her dark lashes fluttering. "I'm quite shocked. It won't be fair if I win. You helped me."

"I gave you advice. The shot was entirely yours." Violet gave her a look of encouragement as Miss Kingman took a position several feet to Violet's right.

Violet offered a curtsey to the spectators before taking the bow and arrow and turning to the line. She stared at the target, thinking she'd shot farther than this. But it had been a while.

Lifting the bow, she took a deep breath and imagined the arrow striking the dead center of the target. A breeze ruffled the ties beneath her hat, and she belatedly wished she'd taken the thing off. With a firm but relaxed grip, she pulled back the string and let her arrow fly.

It landed in the absolute center. She'd won.

Everyone cheered as Violet turned. She offered a deeper curtsey, her mouth splitting into a wide, uncontrollable grin. She couldn't help but look at Nick; however, the crowd had shifted, and she couldn't see him very well.

"Lady Pendleton has won a boon that she may claim during the remainder of the party," Irving said loudly. "Well done, Lady Pendleton!"

Everyone applauded again, and Violet made another curtsey. Hannah rushed over and gave her a quick hug. "I'm so proud of you! I must oversee the gentlemen's turn." And off she went again.

The targets were adjusted, and the competing men gathered near the line. It would be a wide field that included Simon and Nick, as well as every other bachelor in attendance plus Sir Barnard, Lord Adair, Lord Colton, and, of course, Irving Linford. Apparently, Lord Balcombe had trouble with his shoulder and wasn't able to participate.

After drawing straws, Mr. Seaver went first. Everyone made it through the first round, having hit the target. Simon's arrow was the closest to the center, and Violet was pleased to see him celebrated for it. She hoped he would win, thinking it would only help their cause to rehabilitate his reputation.

But misfortune struck in the second round when his arrow landed in the outer circle of the target. The three men whose arrows were farthest out were eliminated.

He shook his head and came to stand next to Violet.

"I blame the wind. It picked up since you shot."

He was right, as the ribbons of her hat were now blowing quite freely. She glanced up at the sky and saw that darker clouds had moved in. "I believe our afternoon plan for bowls may be ruined."

He looked up as well. "Unfortunately, yes. We'll have to find entertainment indoors."

In fact, Violet's mind was already working on that. She had a boon to claim, and she knew precisely what she wanted. She just needed to corral the younger set this afternoon.

Nick was waiting for his turn, which was second to last. He stared straight ahead, his features impassive.

"Nick seems back to his old self today," Violet said quietly. "Did something happen, or am I mistaken?"

"I'm not certain," Simon said with a slight frown. "He walked to the field with Lady Nixon and Mrs. Law, then spent time assisting Miss Kingman with her shooting." He fell quiet while Lord Adair shot. Then he angled toward Violet. "It may just be exhausting for him. He hasn't had to be social in ages."

Yes, that could be it. Particularly since he'd shared the company of Lady Nixon and Mrs. Law. They were the very definition of taxing. "Why is he such a recluse?"

"He was in deep mourning, and I think he forgot to come out."

Mourning. Her mind instantly went to his brother, but then she remembered that he was also a widower. "Because of his wife?"

Simon nodded grimly. "And son."

Oh God, he'd had a son? "I didn't know."

"Not surprising," Simon said. "It isn't my tale to tell, but to lose Jacinda in childbirth and then Elias such a short time later was devastating." His voice had grown tight, his face pale.

"It pains you too," she said softly, wanting to comfort him. "You are truly a good friend."

"We all have pain, do we not?"

Yes, but for some people, there was unbelievable tragedy, and she began to see how Nick had become the Duke of Ice. She realized Simon had endured a similar calamity. No wonder he spoke of Nick with such compassion. It was perhaps why they were such close friends. She was glad they had each other.

"We do," she said.

"What's yours?" he asked.

Startled by the question, she focused on the contest for a moment. Lord Colton shot, and she clapped along with the others. Nick was up next. She didn't answer while she watched him take his position.

His stance was excellent, his long legs parted, the muscles evident beneath the fit of his breeches. He lifted the bow, and his coat pulled across his shoulders, demonstrating that he was finely formed from head to toe. But then she knew that. She recalled the feel of him beneath her hands, so smooth and warm and hard.

Head straight, grip loose, he pulled back the arrow, and it sailed straight into the heart of the target. Just like Cupid who'd set his sights on her eight years ago. His arrow had struck true, and she'd fallen completely.

"It's him," Simon said softly. "Your pain."

She turned her head slightly but couldn't look at him when she answered. "Yes." Like Nick, she'd shut down after marrying Clifford. It had been a kind of mourning, she supposed, as she'd had to kill the only love she'd ever known.

The three gentlemen whose arrows had hit closest

moved to the last target. Aside from Nick, this included Mr. Seaver and Sir Barnard. She watched in silence next to Simon as first Mr. Seaver shot—his arrow landed fairly close to the middle—and then Sir Barnard hit the center. The crowd cheered and held their collective breath as Nick took his place at the line.

"How can he possibly win?" Violet asked, her breath caught tight in her lungs.

"Watch." Simon's voice held the warmth of a smile.

She did just that and was shocked and amazed when Nick's arrow split Sir Barnard's in two. She gasped.

"I do believe we have a tie," Irving declared.

Lord Colton shook his head. "The Duke should be crowned the victor. Surely his exceptional skill in splitting the arrow would break the tie."

As the spectators exchanged words with their neighbors, Simon nodded. "I would agree with that assessment."

Violet would too.

And it appeared the majority concurred as well, because several people vocalized their support.

Irving glanced toward Sir Barnard, who grimaced but gave a subtle nod that apparently indicated his surrender of a joint victory. Scanning the crowd with a broad grin until his gaze landed on Nick, Irving cried, "It appears the Duke of Kilve is victorious!"

There were shouts and applause. Mr. Seaver shook Nick's hand, grinning widely. Sir Barnard also shook his hand, but looked far less enthusiastic.

"Can't blame Sir Barnard for being disappointed. That was a rare shot."

"Which Nick has done before, apparently." She turned to Simon. "You were expecting it."

Simon nodded. "Nick's wicked with a bow. We're off

to my hunting box after the party. You haven't seen skill until you've seen him take down a stag with a single arrow between the eyes. Quick and painless. Let's go congratulate him, shall we?"

Before she could protest—she found herself feeling uneasy about his demeanor today—Simon had pulled her along. It took a moment for the crowd around him to dissipate enough for them to move forward.

"Well done," Simon said, clapping him on the shoulder.

"Thank you." Nick didn't look like someone who'd just won a hard-fought archery contest with a spectacular shot.

She looked at him tentatively, wary of the ice glazing his expression. "That was amazing."

"Congratulations on your victory," he said without much feeling. It was something one said out of courtesy, not because they were genuinely happy for you.

Violet's insides twisted into knots. She'd been a fool to think they could go back to the way they'd been. But weren't they aligned when it came to Simon? She had a plan for later and hoped Nick would join her in its execution. With Simon beside her, she couldn't bring it up now, nor did she want to. Not when Nick looked as though he was made of frost.

Irving walked to them then and gripped Nick's bicep. "Time for our victory luncheon!" He turned with Nick, saying, "That was a brilliant shot. However do you do that?"

Nick was swept away, and Simon made to follow. He offered Violet his arm. "You coming?"

She saw Hannah standing a few yards away, speaking to the footmen. "I'll be along shortly. I'm going to help

Hannah." She turned and went to her friend, needing a few moments to think.

Hannah's gaze flickered with surprise when she saw Violet. "Aren't you going to the house?"

"With you. Can I help with anything?"

"No, I'm just directing the cleanup. They'll take it from here." She smiled at the footmen and took Violet's arm. "Let's go."

They took up the rear as everyone moved toward the house.

"What an exciting event!" Hannah said, clearly elated. "Lady Nixon said it was the most thrilling archery contest she'd ever seen. Everyone is agog over His Grace's last shot."

Violet wished that had been Simon. Not only would it have helped him, but she was sure Simon would've been happier about it. Nick had seemed as distant as ever. But now she knew why—or at least partially. He'd lost his brother, his wife, his child. That would leave anyone feeling like a hollow shell, where perhaps not even winning an archery contest in spectacular fashion was sufficient to lift one's mood. What would?

"He didn't seem particularly pleased," Violet said.

Hannah waved her hand. "Oh, that's just his disposition, I've come to realize. It does make one wonder what's happened in his past to cause that."

"Me."

Hannah nearly tripped, but caught herself. Her head swung toward Violet. "Pardon?"

"Not *just* me, but I didn't help. He's suffered a great deal of tragedy." She wouldn't say more, at least not about things that weren't her place to say.

"Whatever do you mean? Are you saying you know him?"

Violet nodded. "We met the September before you and I became acquainted."

"You never told me you'd met a duke! We were so nervous during our first Season, even though you were a viscountess."

"He wasn't a duke then."

Hannah watched her as they walked, her arm curled comfortingly through Violet's. "You think you're the reason he's the way he is? How well were you acquainted?"

Violet walked more slowly until there was a good distance between them and the next people in front of them. "As you know, my parents sent me to Bath to prepare for my first Season. I stayed with my aunt and uncle." She'd spent summers with them throughout her childhood. With no children of their own, they'd doted on Violet and her brother. "I met Nick at the Sydney Hotel. He was Mr. Nicholas Bateman then. He was so handsome and so witty. I was smitten immediately."

And he'd been too. "Over the course of a fortnight, we arranged to see each other as much as possible."

"You were in love," Hannah said softly, her voice tinged with awe.

"Helplessly. He asked me to marry him."

Hannah gasped. "What happened?"

"My parents arrived, and when I told them I'd fallen in love with Nick, they took me away immediately. A mister wasn't good enough, not when I was pretty and dowried enough to snag a title. In fact, they already had an interested party."

"Clifford?"

Violet nodded. "Rather than wait until the next spring, my father arranged the union, and we were wed a month later."

"You never saw Nick again?"

"No." Her stomach clenched, and she felt sick, as she had so many times in the intervening years. "We'd planned to meet that evening. There was a revel at the park. We'd discussed the imminent arrival of my parents, and I'd warned him that they might not be in favor of our marriage. He assured me he would win them over. I didn't doubt it—he was so charming." For a moment, she recalled him as he'd been—joyful and teeming with hope for the future. The duke she'd met this week was a stranger, a shadow of that young man. How she wished she could go back and do what he'd suggested. "He'd joked that if he failed, we could always elope. We should have."

"Oh, Violet." Hannah clasped her free hand with Violet's, giving her a squeeze. "I know your marriage wasn't happy—how could it have been when you were married to such a philanderer—but having loved and lost... I wish I'd known." She shook her head and withdrew her hand from Violet's to swipe a finger beneath her eye.

"I promised my parents I would never speak of it."

Plus, Clifford had forbidden her from talking about it. After their wedding night, when he'd learned she wasn't a virgin, he'd been apoplectic. That was the only time he'd touched her in anger, shoving her so hard, she'd fallen into the armoire. She'd earned a massive bump and a subsequent day of dizziness and a crushing headache. It had set a precedent for the darkness of their marriage. He hadn't touched her again until he was certain she wasn't carrying Nick's bastard. Then he'd used her as a broodmare without care or consideration. When she'd failed to carry a child, he'd declared her utterly without value. But that meant, thankfully, that he'd left her alone the last year before he'd taken ill and died.

"It was also easier to banish the past," she continued, hating how the vile memory of Clifford made her want to crawl out of her skin. "For a long time, I pretended Nick was just a dream. I think I'd convinced myself of that until I saw him here."

"I had no idea. I never would've invited him if I'd known it would cause you distress."

"It doesn't." On the contrary, she welcomed the ability to remember that he was real. She was fairly certain he felt the opposite, however. "I'm not sure he would've come if he'd known I was here. He hated me—and rightfully so—for abandoning him without a word." She didn't mention writing a letter. Since he hadn't received her explanation, it was as good as if she'd never written it.

"You still love him."

"Always."

"Have you told him?"

They were almost to the house. Violet stopped and turned toward Hannah. "No, and you mustn't either. No one can know. It's the distant past."

"It isn't. Not when you love him now, and he's here."

He also didn't want anything to do with her—save helping Simon. That was assuming he still wanted to do that. After his behavior today, she wasn't sure. "Promise me you'll leave it alone. I'm fine. I've made my peace with loving him."

Hannah frowned. "I think it's a mistake. Fate brought you together."

Violet laughed, but it sounded a bit hollow. "*You* brought us together."

"I'm happy to help destiny," Hannah said with a smile. "I just want you to be happy, Violet. You deserve it more than anyone I know."

"I am happy," Violet assured her. She turned toward the house, ready to put this conversation and all the uncomfortable memories it had aroused behind her. "What I'd like to do is make sure Nick is happy too, and I'm fairly certain that doesn't involve me."

Chapter Eight

NICK SUFFERED THROUGH the victory luncheon, and every time his attention drifted toward Violet, he steeled himself and took a drink of wine. As a result, he was feeling far more relaxed—and pleasant—than he had been at the archery field.

Which wasn't to say he'd forgotten why his mood had soured. He blamed the time he'd spent with the toxic Lady Nixon and Mrs. Law. But he couldn't ignore Violet's role. Rather, his reaction to Violet.

Simon was seated next to her, which hadn't helped his disposition. His friend couldn't be romantically interested in her, could he? If so, Nick might have to say something. He couldn't bear seeing them together.

But what if it made them happy? Would he want to stop that?

He reached for another drink of wine and was disappointed to find that his glass was empty. Thankfully, the luncheon was nearly finished.

Afterward, the guests would disperse, and Nick would retreat to his room. Mayhap he'd stay there through dinner too.

As they stood, his hostess, who'd been seated to his left, leaned close. "The younger set is meeting in the ballroom for some games this afternoon. You simply *must* attend." Mrs. Linford gazed up at him imploringly.

He wanted to tell her that he *mustn't* do anything he didn't feel like, but she looked so eager, so expectant, that the words died on his tongue. Since when had he started caring about offending other people?

Instead, he challenged her. "Why?"

Surprised by his question, she jerked back slightly, blinking. "Because... It will be incredibly diverting. And you won a boon at the contest. This will be your chance to claim it." She smiled broadly. "See? You *must*."

All the other guests had filed from the dining room, leaving him alone with Mrs. Linford. Perhaps seeing that he was still undecided, she cast her head to the side. "I am a dear friend of Violet's, as you may know. She also won a boon this morning, and it was her idea to have the games since we can't go outside for bowls." The rain had started just after the archery contest and hadn't relented. "It would mean so much to me if you could support her endeavor. She's had such misfortune, you see." She brought her hand to her mouth as her eyes widened slightly. "Forgive me. I shouldn't have said that."

Curiosity seized hold of his judgment. He ought to go up to his room as he'd planned, but he suddenly couldn't move. "What sort of misfortune?"

"I shouldn't say." She waved her hand but lowered her voice conspiratorially. "You'll keep this between us?" At his nod, she continued. "She had a rather unhappy marriage—several children she couldn't carry—and parties like this bring some joy into her lonely, solitary life."

She was lonely?

What an asinine question. She was alone. Except that didn't mean she was lonely. *He* wasn't lonely.

Her loneliness was only a part of it. More concerning was what she'd endured. When she'd left Bath without a word, he'd gone to her aunt and uncle, who'd informed him she was gone. He'd asked for her direction, but Violet's aunt had told him to forget about her. Her uncle had been far kinder. He'd seemed genuinely sorry when he'd informed Nick that she was to wed Viscount Pendleton. He'd spent a great deal of energy wishing her unhappiness and misfortune. It seemed his wishes had come to fruition. Yes, he was fucking cursed.

"I'm sorry to hear what she suffered. I'd hoped her marriage was happy." That was a lie, but in retrospect, given his own travails, he would've preferred she found contentment.

"As I said, I shouldn't have revealed her secrets. You won't say anything, will you?" Mrs. Linford wrung her hands.

"I will not."

She exhaled with relief, her features softening. "And you'll come to the ballroom?"

It seemed he must. "Yes."

She smiled warmly, and they left together. "The ballroom is this way. It's not really a ballroom but a very large reception room. We've used it for a ball or two."

When they arrived, the room was already inhabited by, as Mrs. Linford had termed them, the younger set.

"Well, I'll see you for dinner, then." She turned to go.

"You aren't staying?"

"I wish I could, but I need to see to the other guests. A hostess's duties are never finished, I'm afraid." With a slight wave of her hand, she departed in a swirl of bottle-green skirts.

Nick stepped into the room, and the conversation came to a halt.

"It's about time," Simon said with mock impatience. At least, Nick thought he was pretending. "Tell us, Lady Pendleton, what do you have planned?"

Violet looked around at everyone gathered, her gaze passing quickly over Nick. "I thought we might play some games. We can start with Kiss the Nun."

One of the young women gasped and brought her hand to her mouth to cover a giggle.

"Since it's my boon, I will choose the nun and the grate." She peered at the others, her brow furrowed. "I choose Lady Lavinia as the grate and Miss Kingman as the nun." Now she stared directly at Nick.

Hell and the devil, she wasn't going to choose him as the penitent, was she? He hadn't played this game in ages, but he vaguely remembered it. The penitent tried to kiss the nun's cheek through the grate, which would be Lady Lavinia's hand.

"Duke," Violet said, "since you won the other boon, would you like to choose the penitent?" Her gaze was expectant, and she seemed to be trying to communicate something.

He floundered for a minute, his mind searching until he stupidly realized what she was trying to accomplish. "I choose Romsey." He turned toward his friend with a bland smile.

"Of course you do," Simon muttered. He pivoted toward the ladies and offered a courtly bow. "My pleasure."

Violet dragged a chair to the center of the room, and one of the other gentlemen, Mr. Seaver, placed another beside it. Miss Kingman took one seat, and Lady Lavinia took the other.

Simon moved to stand close to them. "Shall we begin?"

Lady Lavinia splayed her hand against Miss Kingman's cheek.

"Alas these bars, these cruel, cruel bars!" Simon wailed, putting a great depth of emotion into the recitation.

Laughter filled the room, and Simon grinned.

Oh, this was truly brilliant of Violet. Nick was glad he'd allowed Mrs. Linford to talk him into coming.

Miss Kingman fluttered her lashes up at Simon. "They're not so narrow, but you may bestow on me a kiss—one parting kiss!"

As soon as she uttered the word kiss, Simon leaned down and tried to kiss her cheek. Lady Lavinia closed her fingers, and he kissed them instead.

"Take this for your bad management!" she cried, grabbing his ear and giving it a tug.

"Ow!" Simon said, rubbing his ear.

Lady Lavinia blanched. "I'm sorry!"

Simon pressed a kiss to Miss Kingman's cheek. "Ha! I win!"

Miss Kingman frowned at him. "You don't. You're supposed to wait until I say, 'One parting kiss' again."

Simon looked around at everyone else. "Is that right?"

"I'm afraid so," Mr. Adair, a lanky young fellow with light brown hair, said with a laugh. "Guess you'll have to try again."

Simon sighed with resignation. "Again, then."

"I really am sorry about your ear," Lady Lavinia said.

"I may have exaggerated my hurt in order to win."

"Bravo!" the third gentleman, Mr. Woodward, called out.

Lady Lavinia narrowed her eyes. "You cheated."

His eyes sparked with mischief. "I pressed my

advantage."

Nick couldn't help but laugh. Everyone turned to look at him in surprise, reminding him that he rarely laughed. But it was Violet's attention that seared through him. There was a glint of appreciation in her gaze, and a smile teased her mouth. He was captivated.

"Anyway, it did hurt a *little*," Simon said, straightening.

Miss Kingman shook her head at him, but her half smile said she found the situation as amusing as everyone else. "One parting kiss!"

Simon leapt into action and tried to land a kiss against her cheek. Unfortunately, he was foiled again by Lady Lavinia. She repeated the phrase, "Take this for your bad management!" but this time barely touched his ear.

Even so, Simon fell to the ground and pretended agony, grabbing his head and moaning aloud. This was met with sharp laughter and applause.

Lady Lavinia finished her script this time, glaring down at him. "How dare you waste your kisses on cold iron?"

"Are they wasted if you enjoy them?" he asked archly as he rolled to his side, then clambered to his feet. The other gentlemen snickered, and Nick nearly snorted.

Lady Lavinia blushed, and Simon surveyed the scene with his hands on his hips.

"I think I must try a different strategy." He knelt beside Miss Kingman. "Is there a rule against this as well?"

She turned her head and started, perhaps realizing how close he was. Too close for propriety's sake, but these sorts of games pushed the boundaries of acceptability. Which was why they were so entertaining.

"No," Miss Kingman said. She straightened her spine against the back of the chair and looked forward. "One parting kiss!"

Though he was closer, Simon failed again to put his lips to her cheek, kissing Lady Lavinia's knuckles instead. Miss Kingman recited the words once more, "One parting kiss!"

He groaned in frustration. "How much longer must I keep this up?"

Miss Kingman turned a haughty gaze toward him, playing her role to perfection. "Until you kiss me."

"Oh, I'll kiss you all right." He looked at her with determination before kneeling beside her once more. "Again."

She stared at him a moment before turning her head forward. "One parting kiss!"

Simon moved quickly, his body arcing in front of hers. He leaned forward and pressed his mouth to hers. Miss Kingman's eyes rounded, but it was over almost immediately. Simon jumped to his feet with a cry of victory. "That was fair, was it not?"

Lady Lavinia shook her head but was laughing in spite of herself. "You're supposed to kiss her cheek."

"It was never going to work that way." Simon gave Lady Lavinia a stern look, but the tremor of his lips revealed his amusement. "You're a menace, grate."

Lady Lavinia curtsied. "I think that means I win. Do I get to be the nun now?" She looked to Violet.

"I've no objection. Miss Colton, will you be her grate?"

Simon cleared his throat. "And I choose Mr. Seaver to be the penitent." Simon pivoted to Violet. "It's my choice, isn't it?"

"I see no reason why not."

Mr. Seaver went to even greater lengths to try to kiss Lady Lavinia's cheek. After six attempts, he told Miss Colton there was a spider on her head. She shrieked and jumped up, leaving him a clear path to kiss Lady Lavinia.

Everyone was still consumed with laughter when Miss Kingman suggested they play Kiss if You Can next.

"I'm not sure I remember that one," Simon said, wiping his eyes.

Nick was glad he'd asked, because he didn't remember it either.

"A gentleman and a lady will kneel with their backs to each other," Miss Kingman explained. "When the crier says 'make ready,' the lady looks over her left shoulder and the gentleman over his right. At the word *present*, he will lean forward to kiss her cheek, and at the direction *fire*, he will try to kiss her, but she may evade his endeavor."

"How will we decide the pairs?" Mr. Adair asked.

Violet went to a table. "I brought cards. High cards drawn by each sex will face off against each other?"

"Or not, as the game goes," Simon joked.

"An excellent plan," Nick said, joining her at the table where she'd picked up the deck of cards. "Do you want me to shuffle?"

She handed him the cards, and her fingers brushed against his palm. Her touch danced through him, awakening parts of him that had lain dormant for far too long.

He shuffled the deck in his hand several times while Simon and Mr. Adair moved the chairs out of the way. When he was finished, Nick set the cards on the table.

Violet gestured to the table. "If everyone would care

to take a card…"

The ladies drew first. Violet went last, her gaze meeting Nick's as she pulled her card. Her features didn't betray her fortune. It was really too bad that she didn't like to play cards—she'd be a formidable adversary.

The gentlemen went next, and Nick, like Violet, drew last. A king, which meant he'd likely be first up. He tensed waiting for everyone to reveal their card.

"Won't be me going first," Seaver said. "I've the two of clubs."

He tossed his card on the table. Everyone else revealed theirs, and Nick's eye immediately went to Violet's—the queen. He nearly laughed, but checked to see if any of the other women had queens. They didn't, and no kings either.

"Looks like it's you and Lady Pendleton," Simon said. His voice carried a hint of something.

Nick snapped his head toward his friend and detected the glimmer of a smile in his gaze. He was enjoying this. *He* was playing matchmaker. And he had his sights set on Nick and Violet. *Bloody hell.*

Nick wanted to be angry, but his pull toward Violet was too strong. He'd felt it last night and again today when Simon had asked if it would be distressing for him to pursue her. Nick had suppressed his reaction— he'd been jealous. Shockingly, blood-boilingly, desperately jealous.

The realization shook him to the core.

"Who's to be the crier?" Simon asked.

"Why not Mr. Seaver since he won Kiss the Nun?" Adair suggested.

With everyone in agreement, Violet and Nick moved to the center of the room.

"Is this awkward?" she whispered.

"No." His pulse quickened. Should he kiss her or should he fail?

His mind screamed the latter. And really, that was for the best. Jealousy aside, he and Violet had no future, not when their past was so painful.

And yet when they knelt with their backs to each other, he caught her scent of rose and an earthy spice. It was wholly feminine yet slightly wild. He hadn't smelled a rose in the past eight years without thinking of her. His body reacted, heating at her proximity.

"Make ready," Seaver said.

Nick looked over his right shoulder and felt the air move as she looked over her left.

"Present."

Nick leaned close to her cheek. He could feel her warmth, and his skin tingled.

"*Fire.*"

He moved closer, but she sprang up. Instinctively, he reached for her, his arm curling about her waist. He pulled her back down. To stop her from hitting the floor, he spun to his back and sprawled, bringing her down on top of him. He cupped the side of her face and kissed her, his lips sliding over hers for a brief but delicious moment.

"The cheek," she murmured, her gaze locked with his.

He leaned up and brushed his mouth against the soft flesh of her cheek. His lips lingered perhaps a second too long, but he didn't care. Desire coursed through him, and for the first time in years, he felt *alive*.

"Well done!" Simon called, applauding. The others joined in. "Shall we draw again?"

Nick rolled Violet to her side, his arm cradling her

from fully touching the floor. Her eyes never left his, the intensity in their brown-green depths stoking his hunger.

He took her hands and reluctantly stood, drawing her up with him. She took her hands from his, but didn't look away.

"You don't need to draw for this round." Simon came toward them. "But you do need to move," he whispered near Nick's ear.

Shaken from his rapturous stupor, Nick moved to the side of the room. Violet followed him but didn't stand too close as the next players—Miss Colton and Mr. Woodward—took their places.

Nick stole a glance at her profile and wondered if the kiss had affected her as much as it had him. Then he asked himself why it would matter. As he'd determined earlier, they had no future because of their past.

What about the present?

Nick wanted to ignore the voice even as his body screamed for release—for her.

But he was cursed. For that reason, he would leave her alone.

◆≡•℈•≡◆

FOLLOWING DINNER THAT night, Violet made her way to the drawing room with Hannah. Dinner had been the typical affair, with most of the conversation driven by Lady Nixon and Mrs. Law. Violet had spent far too much time watching Nick and thinking of his kiss. Over and over and over again. Though brief, it had far surpassed her eight-year-old memories.

"Just two more full days," Hannah said as they neared the drawing room doorway. "It's evenings like this that I am glad the party is only a week and not a fortnight. I'm exhausted."

"And your mother went home this afternoon?" Violet asked. Hannah's mother, Mrs. Parker, liked to come for a portion of the party, but since Hannah's children were staying at her house near Bath, she was eager to return to them.

"Yes, but I have you here for support." Her eyes lit, and she tugged Violet's arm, leading her to the side of the doorway. "Before we go in, tell me how this afternoon went. I've only heard murmurs, but it seems like it was great fun."

It was certainly memorable. After Kiss if You Can, they'd played a few more games. Nothing had eclipsed her kiss with Nick, however. In fact, she could scarcely recall anything else that had happened.

"It was quite diverting," she said.

Hannah made a face at her. "What a mundane description. Is there nothing exciting to share? At least tell me what you played."

"Just silly games."

Hannah regarded her skeptically. "This is suspicious. It seems as though you're hiding something. Don't make me ask Lady Nixon and Mrs. Law to ferret out the details."

Violet rolled her eyes. "You wouldn't."

"No, but you're being so odd!" She sidled closer and lowered her voice. "Did something scandalous happen?"

"Of course not. As I said, they were silly games." Violet didn't know why she was being so secretive—Nick had kissed her in full view of everyone, and it was really only a matter of time before the news was shared. She was actually a bit surprised it hadn't been already.

But then this postdinner drawing room time with the ladies might yet see it out.

"Kiss the Nun, Kiss if You Can, that sort of thing," Violet said.

Hannah's eyes flickered with understanding—and interest. "I see. Who kissed whom? I can tell from your demeanor that *something* happened."

"Several kisses were exchanged." Violet hoped the heat she felt rising up her cheeks wasn't noticeable, but knew that was a fantasy. "I was paired with Nick—the Duke of Kilve—in Kiss if You Can."

"And he was successful." Hannah's mouth spread into a wide grin. "How wonderful." She sobered, her eyes taking on a darker glint. "It was wonderful, wasn't it?"

Beyond wonderful. "It was on the lips."

Hannah's eyes rounded, and she lifted her hand to her open mouth. "Well, *now* I understand your hesitation. However did you manage it?"

Did she think Violet had initiated it? "I jumped up to evade him, and he pulled me down. We lost our balance, and I…landed on top of him. *He* kissed *me*." She gave Hannah a wry look. "That *is* how the game is played, if you recall."

"How splendid." She lowered her tone to just above a whisper. "Shall I arrange for you to have an assignation? I don't know that anyone's ever done that at one of my parties."

Violet tried not to laugh and failed. "Of course they have."

Hannah blinked. "I guess they were quite skilled, since I was unaware." She shrugged and smiled briefly before glancing at the drawing room. "I suppose I should go in." She sounded resigned. "But if you *do* need assistance with a liaison, you need only ask."

"I won't, but thank you."

Hannah gave her a saucy look. "You never know."

No, she didn't. But she wasn't sure she could imagine it. She'd spent so many years pining over what could have been. To consider that it might be within her grasp was too much.

Violet went into the drawing room and was instantly drawn to join the young women in their little corner seating area.

"Lady Pendleton, we worried you weren't coming," Lady Lavinia said.

Violet sat down in the open chair between Miss Colton and Lady Lavinia. "I think it's past time you all call me Violet."

"Then you must call us Lavinia, Sarah, and Diana." She glanced toward Miss Colton and Miss Kingman in succession. They both nodded in agreement.

"It would be my privilege," Violet said.

Lavinia glanced behind her toward where the older matrons were holding court. The buzz of conversation coming from that direction was as constant as ever, like a beehive on a hot summer day.

"We had such a grand time today," Lavinia said effusively, her eyes alight.

"Oh yes," Sarah agreed, her cheeks a fetching shade of pale pink. "I must admit I didn't try very hard to get away from Mr. Woodward in Kiss if You Can," she said softly but with a heady excitement.

Lavinia giggled at this. "I knew it! I thought for certain the Duke of Romsey was going to catch me, but he didn't. Perhaps he was still cross with me for tweaking his ear."

"He was cheating," Diana said with a gentle snort.

"It wasn't as bad as Mr. Seaver saying there was a spider in my hair," Sarah said, blinking at them. "I was terrified. I hate spiders."

After a beat of silence, they all laughed, including Sarah.

"Oh damn," Violet murmured. She glanced apologetically at the others. "I beg your pardon. But steel yourselves. Lady Nixon and Mrs. Law are coming."

Sarah's eyes widened slightly with fear while Lavinia boldly lifted her chin. Meanwhile, Diana looked as serene as ever, her features reflecting nothing but an air of calm indifference. She really was formidable when it came to putting on appearances.

"You ladies are certainly enjoying yourselves over here," Lady Nixon said. "Do share what is so amusing." Her smile was wide, but her eyes were dark with malicious intent. Or so Violet thought. The woman was unconscionable.

"Nothing really," Violet said. "Just idle chatter." She bared her teeth in a smile, knowing some found that vulgar but hoping Lady Nixon would understand she would not be cowed.

Mrs. Law forced the sort of laugh that had nothing to do with humor and everything to do with trying to manage a situation. "Oh come, you simply *must* share." She looked directly at Sarah, who shrank in her chair. "Are you discussing this afternoon's activities? It sounds as if it was most agreeable."

Violet wanted to leap up and wave Mrs. Law away from Sarah. Perhaps with a sword since it felt as if the woman was targeting Sarah for strategic purposes as if they were in a battle.

"It was," Sarah said uncertainly.

Lady Nixon sat down on the small settee next to Sarah. "What did you do?"

"We, ah, played games."

Mrs. Law perched on the other side of Sarah, though there was scarcely room. This put her rather close to Violet—if she reached out, she could box the officious woman's ears.

"What sort of games?" Mrs. Law asked.

Sarah glanced between the two women who'd surrounded her as if they were conducting a siege. "Kiss the Nun."

Mrs. Law clapped her hands together. "Delightful! Who kissed whom? Should we alert anyone's parents?" She laughed loudly, and the rest of the women from their grouping on the other side of the room came to stand around their chairs and the settee. Violet's neck prickled under all the attention.

She decided to do something good with it.

"All the gentlemen behaved nobly and with enviable charm. I thought the Duke of Romsey, was particularly game. Wouldn't you agree, ladies?" She glanced around at the others and silently prodded them to join in her campaign to rehabilitate Simon.

"Without reservation," Lavinia said. "I tugged his ear a bit too hard in Kiss the Nun, and he was quite magnanimous."

"Did you?" Lady Nixon said with a laugh. "Well, it's hardly anything a gentleman doesn't deserve." She exchanged a look with Mrs. Law, who also laughed, as did several others.

Violet met Hannah's distressed gaze. "Shall we go back and sit?" Hannah suggested nervously. "The gentlemen will likely arrive shortly."

"Oh, and we wouldn't want them to know we're

discussing them," Mrs. Law said, chortling.

"But that's all we do," Mrs. Stinnet said from behind Diana's chair. "Mostly."

This was met with more laughter. Even Lavinia cracked a smile.

Lady Nixon fixed Violet with a penetrating stare. "You seem quite fixated on the Duke. Is it possible you have a tendre for the Duke of Ruin—sorry, *Romsey*?"

Violet gritted her teeth. "I do not. However, he's demonstrated himself to be a kind and admirable gentleman."

"Besides, it was Ice who kissed her." Lavinia cringed the moment the words left her mouth. She shot a pained, apologetic look toward Violet.

"Is that so?" Mrs. Law asked in a deceptively melodic voice.

Every head swiveled toward Violet, expectation painted on their faces.

"It was Kiss if You Can, and we drew cards for partners." Violet's tone was dispassionate, and she didn't care. "Oh look, the gentlemen have arrived." She smirked at Mrs. Law.

"Excellent!" Hannah declared, perhaps a trifle too loudly. "Let us repair to the ballroom for dancing!"

Lavinia jumped up. "Yes, let's!"

Sarah joined her, looking as if she wanted to flee as quickly as possible from the women flanking her.

The gentlemen joined the women, and Violet heard one ask why the women were all clustered together. She walked away before she could hear the answer. She needed air.

Intending to cut through the adjoining sitting room to reach a doorway to the rear garden, she stalked away from the rest of the guests. Well, most of the rest of the guests. As she neared the doorway, she saw Nick standing near the mantel, his eyes hooded. Tonight was meant for brooding, apparently.

He turned his head, his gaze catching hers. She inclined her chin toward the sitting room, silently asking him to join her.

After hesitating a moment during which her irritation increased, he moved away from the mantel. Trusting that he was going to follow her, she continued into the sitting room.

She turned near the exterior door. He strode toward her, tall and handsome in his black and gray evening attire. Heat dashed through her, bringing every sensation of that afternoon's kiss to the fore.

"I'm going to take a walk outside."

He stared at her. "It's cold."

"I need some air. And I need to speak with you."

"You want me to accompany you." It wasn't a question.

So she didn't answer it. Instead, she turned and went outside. To his credit, he followed her.

As soon as they were outdoors, they were plunged into near darkness. Light from the house provided meager illumination, but not enough for her to make out his features. Unless they were close.

He came toward her and shrugged out of his coat, then wordlessly draped it around her shoulders. She was instantly engulfed in his spicy clove scent. The tremors racing through her body since he'd walked into the sitting room behind her intensified.

"I'm afraid our kiss is now common knowledge, but that isn't why I wanted to speak with you." She looked at his face, which she could see better now that he was closer. Even so, she couldn't discern his feelings about what she'd just told him. "I have a plan for Simon," she said.

"Do you?" The question was equal parts interested curiosity and skepticism.

"He's already won over the younger set, but Lady Nixon and Mrs. Law are proving rather horrid." She didn't bother keeping the acid from her tone.

"They've nettled you quite thoroughly," he murmured.

"They're the nastiest sort. I plan on telling Hannah that I refuse to attend any further house parties if they're to be here." She shuddered, and it had nothing to do with the cold but her ire. She was actually feeling much warmer ensconced in his coat. Or maybe it was just his nearness that was causing her body temperature to rise.

"Perhaps now you see why I avoid such things," he said softly and with more than a hint of irony.

"Quite." But she knew he wasn't the Duke of Ice simply to avoid the likes of Mrs. Law and Lady Nixon.

"What is your plan to do with Simon?" he asked.

Violet took a deep breath. The cool night air filled her lungs and cleansed her irritation away, leaving the thunderous hum of her attraction to him. She worked hard to ignore it.

"I should like to make a hero of him again tomorrow in Wells."

His brow knitted. "How?"

"He'll need to rescue one of the ladies. I thought during a tour that one of them could trip or encounter some sort of difficulty."

"And he would help them?"

She nodded.

"She'd have to be privy to our plans. Who would do

that?"

"Me."

Now he reacted. His nostrils flared, and his jaw clenched briefly before he schooled his features once more. He was trying to hide his response. Why?

"What's wrong with that?" she asked.

"His wife died falling down the stairs. We must be careful."

"Even more reason for it to be me, then."

Again, the muscles in his jaw tensed.

She burned to know why this agitated him. "Do you have a better suggestion?"

"Not yet, but I'll let you know if I come up with one."

"Why does this plan bother you?"

He fixed his gaze past her shoulder into the darkness of the garden. "It doesn't."

She didn't believe him, but she was also certain he wouldn't tell her the truth. Perhaps it was just that he was worried about Simon. She hadn't thought about any similarity to his wife's death. "What if I pretend to take ill and faint?"

"Do you really think this will help his reputation? As you said, Lady Nixon and Mrs. Law seem immovable."

Indeed they did. Frustration curled through her, and she stared at his cravat, her lips pursed.

"Please don't do that." His voice sounded strained.

Her gaze shot up to his. "What?"

"Never mind." He avoided looking at her.

What if he was having the same problem she was? What if the desire pulsing through her was also careening through him? "I enjoyed this afternoon. The games," she clarified, not quite brave enough to reveal the entire truth: *I enjoyed your kiss.*

"I apologize for what happened."

He regretted it? She didn't pretend to not know what he meant. "You're sorry you kissed me? I'm not. I'm only sorry it was so short." She stared up at him, her eyes drinking in the cleft in his chin and the sharp, seductive angle of his cheekbone and willing him to look at her.

His gaze dipped to hers finally. Ice and fire seemed to war within his stare. "It won't happen again. There is no future between us, Violet."

The hunger inside her coiled and grew into anger. "You really plan to spend the rest of your life alone? Why would you *choose* to be the Duke of Ice?"

He leaned forward, his face scant inches from hers. "I didn't. It chose me." Their gazes locked for a long moment before he retreated. When he spoke again, his tone had cooled. "Whether I'm alone or not isn't your concern."

The pieces of her heart, broken for so long, seemed to sigh in her chest. "You shouldn't be alone. You deserve happiness."

"Yes, well, we don't always get what we deserve, do we? If I marry again, it won't be for love. Fairy-tale dreams of a happy ever after aren't for me, Violet. And I suspect they aren't for you either."

It was like a physical blow. She gasped. Because there was truth in his words. She'd wronged him so badly. "No, I suspect they aren't." She barely heard her muted response.

That should've been the end of it, but she was wearing his coat.

She found the courage to look up at him and was shocked to see stark desire in his eyes before the wall of ice fell back into place. "Is this all an act?" she asked, her distress bubbling to the surface.

"What?"

She resisted the urge to kick him. "Your frigidity. I see hints of the Nick I knew. Just when I think you're not really the cold man everyone thinks, you're coated in frost once more. What the devil is wrong with you?"

His jaw twitched, and everything about him heated. "Everything," he growled. "I was fine until I came to this bloody party and saw *you*." He swayed toward her again. "I don't like the way you make me feel."

He was so close. She ached to touch him. "How is that?" The question came out in a low rasp.

"As if I'm not in control." His mouth was just an inch from hers.

If she leaned forward, she could kiss him...

But he turned and started toward the house. She still had his coat.

Dashing in front of him, she blocked his path. She shrugged out of his garment and held it out to him. He didn't immediately take it, but when he did, he was careful not to touch her hand.

Without another word, he disappeared inside.

Violet exhaled, her breath rattling from her chest. She began to shake, and she knew it wasn't entirely from the cold. Closing her eyes briefly, she heard him say, *as if I'm not in control.*

That was precisely how she felt. For years. What's more, she was certain she'd feel that way forever. For if she could control anything, she would choose not to love him anymore.

Chapter Nine

❦

"HERE WE ARE," Simon called as they rode into Wells the following afternoon.

Nick dragged his mind from where it had been focused all morning and last night: on Violet. Kissing her had been a foolish mistake. If he'd been thinking clearly, he would've realized that. *If* he'd been thinking at all. Instead, his body had taken over.

And it had tried to do the same last night when he'd accompanied her outside. He'd come so close to kissing her again and perhaps even ravishing her right there.

He'd behaved abominably, but he couldn't seem to help himself. He wanted her. He didn't want to want her. It was a bloody disaster.

Stalking back into the house, he'd gone straight for his room and a bottle of whiskey. Except she'd accompanied him. Or it had seemed like it. Donning his coat when he'd stepped inside, he'd been instantly enveloped in her warmth and her scent. The torture had been keen and long-lasting. Even now, he smelled wild roses and longed for a touch he couldn't have.

Only he *could*. He was fairly certain she would've been receptive to him last night. She'd said as much when saying she wished their kiss had lasted longer. That had nearly driven him over the edge of his control. And therein lay his blasted problem. He refused to lose control.

They slowed their horses as the cathedral came into

sight. The other guests were traveling by coach and would arrive soon.

"What happened to you last night?" Simon asked.

Nick snorted. "Took you long enough to ask."

"Does that mean you're eager to tell me? Excellent."

"No, it means I know you," Nick said. "That you didn't besiege me immediately is perplexing."

Simon guided his horse to a walk. "It's difficult to have a conversation while riding as fast as we did. And since you kept to yourself all morning, I had no choice but to bide my time. Stop avoiding the question. What happened last night? I can tell you're in a foul mood. Or is this all due to yesterday afternoon's mischief in the ballroom?"

"Can we just not discuss it?" Nick massaged the bridge of his nose.

"We could, but that would be dull as hell. I must admit I was shocked when you kissed her. Did you shock yourself?"

"Yes." And he'd just done it again by answering honestly.

"How wonderful," Simon said. "And now you're back to brooding. Angrily, I think. I take it she rebuked you?"

"No." On the contrary, she'd all but invited him to do it again. Which he should have.

No.

Simon grinned. "Even better."

Nick scowled at him. "No, it's not. I told you I didn't want to talk about this."

"Actually, you asked if we could avoid the topic, which was rather polite of you."

"You're being the opposite of polite."

"Not at all. I think you'll feel better if you talk about

it. Although I'm confused as to what happened. She didn't rebuke you, and yet you're clearly in knots. Explain yourself."

Nick drew his horse to a stop in front of the cathedral and dismounted. Frustration, building inside him since yesterday afternoon, exploded from him in waves. "What the hell do you want me to do?"

Simon slid to the ground, his eyes widening for a moment. "Bloody hell, man, you're really in a fit. I should think what you ought to do would be obvious. She wants you. You want her. I think you know what happens next."

Yes, he did, and damn it, his cock was fairly twitching at the thought of it. In front of a bloody cathedral.

He took a deep breath of the cool autumn air. The day was overcast but dry, and the breeze had strewn leaves around them as they'd ridden to town. The journey had been bucolic and would have been pleasant if not for his wretched mood.

Nick tied his horse to the post. "We had our time eight years ago, and it's finished."

Simon followed suit. "That's the most ridiculous thing I've ever heard. You have a second chance. What I wouldn't give—" He finished his task with a hard set to his jaw.

Contrite, Nick exhaled. "This is different," he said quietly. "Violet chose another path." One that had led to loneliness and discontent. He could imagine that was his fault, that her time with him had caused her misfortune. He was fucking cursed.

Simon came around his horse and turned to look up at the cathedral rising before them. "You'll regret it, I think. Life is too short. You know that."

Yes, he did. And yes, what he wouldn't give for a second chance to have Elias in his arms again. And Jacinda. Yet he had to admit his feeling for her had never been as strong as what he'd felt for Violet. He attributed that to being young and stupid. He was neither of those things anymore, which was why he would steadfastly guard his heart.

"The only thing I regret is allowing people too close." He shot Simon a disgruntled glance. "You included."

"Nonsense. Without me, you'd be a complete animal instead of just a beastly man." He angled himself toward Nick, his eyes sad. "I don't think you regret that at all, actually. You resent losing them, and I finally understand that you blame yourself for their loss. It's all a risk, Nick. We love, we lose, we *feel*. Even when the pain is enough to make us weep."

Nick hadn't cried since Elias had died. He'd sworn then that he wouldn't shed another tear. And that meant eliminating any vulnerability.

"You can't control everything," Simon said. "As much as we want to, it's all chaos in the end."

Nick couldn't argue with him. Long-suppressed emotion clogged his throat, but he forced it down. "I hate that." He hadn't been able to control anything. They'd all died—his brother, his uncle, Jacinda, Elias.

"I understand." Simon came toward him and gripped his bicep. "It's why I don't drink anymore. I wasn't in control…then." He dropped his hand. "If I had been…"

The unspoken words hung in the air—he could've saved Miriam if he hadn't been drunk. Whereas Nick couldn't have saved any of them. With the exception of Jacinda. Since she'd died giving birth to Elias, he blamed himself.

"I can't go back and change things," Simon said, drawing Nick back to the present. "All I can do is make different choices. And I choose to *live*." He speared Nick with an intense stare.

Nick blinked at him slowly. "I choose not to feel."

Simon threw his hands up. "You're hopeless."

"Would it surprise you to know that I am considering marrying again?" Maybe it was the attraction he felt for Violet. Or maybe it was the fact that he had allowed emotion to creep back in since he'd come to this bloody party. Perhaps it was Violet's insistence that he shouldn't be alone. Whatever the reason, he could marry again, provided his bride understood the requirements."

"Hell yes, it would surprise me." Simon cocked his head in skepticism. "In fact, I don't believe you. You just said you choose not to feel."

"I don't need to feel to marry."

Simon coughed. "Tell that to your wife!"

"I will. She'll understand that I won't ever love her. Contrary to what you say, I'm not really a beast."

"No, just an insensitive, selfish ass. Nonetheless, you will likely have no trouble finding someone to accept your terms. You're a duke and an Untouchable to boot. Many women would sell their souls to the devil to be your duchess." His brow furrowed. "On second thought, I might be wrong. Otherwise, I'd be remarried already."

Nick knew that Simon was trying to bring a bit of levity back to the conversation, if that was possible. "I didn't mean for that to take such a maudlin turn," Nick said. "My apologies."

"I didn't either. I'm just trying to be your friend. I

care about you, whether you want me to or not. And I know you feel the same." He gave Nick a wry smirk. "So much for your plan to ignore emotion. Come on, the coaches are arriving. We need to put on our house party faces."

Nick nodded. He did care about Simon. And if Violet could somehow make him the hero of the day, perhaps his wishes would come true. *That* would make Nick happy.

They walked to the coaches just as Violet stepped down with the assistance of the groom. She wore a dark blue day dress with a rich brown spencer. Blond curls brushed her temples beneath the brim of her fetching hat. She was beautiful, and he wanted her as fiercely now as he had last night.

It was a damn good thing this party would be over after tomorrow.

⊰•❦•⊱

As VIOLET STEPPED out of the coach, her gaze instantly landed on Nick. He stood next to Simon—they'd ridden ahead—about twenty yards away. He looked rugged and handsome in his riding costume, and her body reacted with a jump in warmth.

No. She wasn't spending another day pining after Nicholas Bateman. Rather, the Duke of Ice. He'd made his choice quite clear—he wanted to be alone. Well, she'd let him.

Diana emerged from the coach behind her, followed by her mother and then Hannah. The latter two gravitated toward another group of ladies that had disembarked from another coach, leaving Violet and Diana to walk together toward the stunning west entrance.

The younger woman looked to the side, in the direction of Nick and Simon. "The dukes are here."

"Yes." Violet didn't particularly want to talk about them. She looked up at the impressive façade instead. "The cathedral is gorgeous."

"Indeed. I've visited the cathedral in Canterbury. It's larger than this one, I think."

"Where Thomas Becket was killed?" Violet asked. "What a gruesome event. I don't think Wells has anything so disquieting to offer."

"No, but I hear the library is excellent, and the octagonal chapter house is of special note."

"I'm looking forward to seeing that," Violet said. "What are you hoping to do today?"

"Nothing particular." Again, Diana glanced toward the dukes. "Can I ask you something? I'm afraid it may be a bit forward."

Intrigued, Violet looked at her profile. She was as placid as ever, betraying nothing. Perhaps she and Nick would be a good match, she thought a bit sourly. Annoyed with herself for having such uncharitable thoughts, she exhaled. "Yes, you may ask me anything. I will answer to the best of my ability."

Diana turned her head briefly. There was a bit of apprehension in her gaze. "Is there... Is there something between you and the Duke of Kilve?"

A tremor rippled through Violet, and she tried to emulate her companion's serenity. "No." That was the absolute truth. *Now.*

"Oh. I wondered...after Kiss if You Can. When he kissed you on the mouth."

"I think he simply forgot the rules." And she would be eternally grateful. Just having that one kiss—even if it was the last—meant everything to her. "The Duke of Romsey kissed you on the mouth, but there's nothing to that, is there?" Violet didn't mean to be indelicate but wanted to be clear that yesterday's kiss had meant *nothing*.

"Of course not," Diana rushed to say. "I just wondered when you and the Duke of Kilve disappeared for a while last night."

Damn. Violet had hoped no one noticed. She'd arrived at the ballroom after her encounter with Nick outside, but he never had. It would have looked more suspicious if they'd both arrived, and she'd been relieved when he stayed away. Also because she wasn't sure she could be in the same room with him after what he'd said to her. Knowing that she caused him to feel out of control but that he would do nothing about it was maddening. "I stepped outside for a few minutes. I've no idea where the Duke went. It does seem he doesn't care for dancing."

He had once. He'd danced with her several times during their love affair, and he'd been a wonderful dancer. She wondered if he waltzed. Probably not.

"Thank you for your honesty," Diana said, making Violet's insides squirm. "My parents would dearly love for me to make a match with him. I'm to endeavor to spend some time with him today." She cast Violet a wry smile. "I'm afraid I'm not at all certain how to do that. He doesn't seem overly interested in courtship."

Violet had told him she'd make it known he wasn't interested in marriage. "No, he isn't."

"I heard his wife and child died," Diana said. "So tragic. It makes sense that he's so reserved and perhaps afraid to marry again."

"Yes, I suppose it does." Maybe Diana understood

him better than Violet did. But then Violet had the advantage of knowing him before tragedy had affected him. He'd been a different person. This man—this Duke of Ice—wasn't someone she wanted. And that was perhaps the most painful thing of all. The Nick she'd loved and fantasized about was now a permanent dream.

Violet turned to Diana as they neared the entrance to the cathedral. "Would you be happy with someone like him?" Again she wondered if they wouldn't be a perfect match with their aloof demeanors and carefully constructed exteriors.

"As I could be, I think."

What an enigmatic response.

"Good afternoon, ladies," Simon greeted them.

So intent on her conversation with Diana, Violet hadn't noticed their approach. "Good afternoon." She curtsied to him and then to Nick, though she didn't look at Nick's face. She couldn't.

"May I escort you inside?" Simon offered his arm to Diana.

"Actually, Duke," Violet said, seizing the opportunity to help Diana in her endeavor. "Would you mind escorting me to the chapter house? I'm keen to see it."

"I'd be delighted," Simon said smoothly, giving his arm to Violet.

Nick presented his arm to Diana, and they entered the cathedral first, veering to the aisle on the right side of the nave.

"I believe the chapter house is this way," Violet said, inclining her head to the left.

Simon guided her in that direction and sent her a look of confusion. "Why did you do that?" Simon asked.

"Do what?"

"Pair Miss Kingman off with Nick. Are you pretending to be obtuse?"

Violet ignored his question. "Her parents are hoping for a match."

Simon shook his head. "I do not understand you or Nick. You clearly want each other, are probably in love with each other, yet you run in the opposite direction."

Violet darted a look toward Nick and Diana. He seemed...attentive. Jealousy snaked through her. "Nick has made his position clear. What we shared is in the past."

"So he says," Simon said with a snort. "I saw him yesterday when he kissed you in the ballroom. That is not the action of a man who feels nothing. I don't care what he says."

She'd thought so too, but he'd been absolutely forthright about their future—there wasn't one. She stole another look at him and then jerked her attention back toward the stairs that led to the chapter room. "I've loved him for eight years, and I've clung to a fantasy that I never dreamed possible. Encountering him at this house party seemed like Fate dealing me a second chance, but it isn't meant to be. I have to let him go."

"Nick is an idiot," he muttered.

She couldn't disagree with him there. "Just look at this staircase." Violet was happy to change the subject. "Shall we go up to the chapter room?"

"Yes, let's."

As they ascended the stairs, Violet thought of her plan to help Simon. Perhaps she could faint in the chapter room. She glanced behind her to see if anyone had followed but was disappointed to see they had not.

"Stop looking at Nick," Simon said gruffly. "He doesn't deserve your attention."

"I wasn't, actually. It appears that we're alone."

He threw her a wicked smile. "How scandalous."

She laughed softly as they finished their ascent. The octagonal-shaped chapter room lay before them. A central column supported a ribbed, vaulted ceiling. Windows with ornate, geometric tracery marched around the room, and beneath them were niches topped with a variety of carvings. It was magnificent.

"I see why you wanted to come here," Simon said.

She let go of his arm and walked to one of the niches. It bore the head of a smiling king. She didn't dare touch the ancient stone, but studied it intently, marveling at the beauty the masons had created. "This must have taken so long. All these intricate carvings— and this is just one small part of the building."

"Indeed." Simon stood a few niches away. He ran his gloved fingers over the face of a cleric. "It's marvelous."

They lingered awhile longer, passing each other as they circled the octagon at their own pace. The exploration soothed Violet's mood. Being inside a beautiful feat of spectacular engineering was rather humbling and offered welcome perspective. She'd survived without Nick and would continue to do so, just like this five-hundred-year-old room.

"Are you ready to continue on?" Simon asked near the top of the stairs.

"Yes." She joined him, and he offered his arm. As they descended, she hoped they would run into someone in the nave so that she could launch her plan to make him look like a hero.

He *was* a hero, she decided. His care for Nick—and

for her—made him a rare man.

On the last step before the landing that sent a branch of stairs toward the cloisters, her heel slipped. She tripped, her legs giving out as she tumbled forward.

And Simon didn't stop her.

She fell onto the stone, her hands breaking her fall so that she didn't slam her face into the floor.

"Dear God, *Violet*." Simon was at her side in an instant, rolling her to her back.

She blinked up at him and tried to regain her bearings. Her heart beat furiously, and she felt shaky all over. She closed her eyes and tried to breathe deeply.

He scooped his hand beneath her back, elevating her from the cold stone. He cupped his hand against her neck. She opened her eyes to see him staring down at her.

"Tell me you're all right," he demanded. His usually affable expression was stark with terror, his eyes dark and his lips pale.

"I am. I think." Her hands hurt, but the pain was already beginning to lessen. She'd twisted her ankle a bit, but even that was improving as she began to realize she was out of danger. When she'd slipped, the rest of the staircase had stretched out before her. It would've been a nasty tumble to the nave.

With a shiver, she turned her head to look. And instantly froze. Standing at the bottom of the stairs, their eyes fixated on Violet in Simon's arms were Lady Nixon, Mrs. Law, Mrs. Stinnet, and Mrs. Padmore. The four worst people that could witness this event.

"Simon," Violet whispered urgently.

His gaze shifted down the stairs, and she felt him stiffen immediately.

"Good heavens, what's happened?" Lady Nixon

cried.

"Did you *fall?*" Mrs. Law's question was thick with accusation. The implication was clear—Simon was once again alone with a woman who'd tumbled down the stairs.

"I tripped," Violet said loudly. "Help me up," she said far more quietly, so that just Simon could hear her.

He lifted her to stand. "Are you sure you're all right?" he murmured.

"A little shaken, but I'm fine." She kept her voice low, then flashed a brilliant smile at their unwanted audience. She curled her arm around Simon's, and they started down the stairs.

Others had joined the spectators, including Hannah and her husband, Sir Barnard and Lady Kingman, Diana, and Nick. He stared up at them, his expression far more readable than normal. His eyes were wide with apprehension and his jaw set as if he clenched his teeth.

When Violet and Simon were a few steps from the bottom, someone whispered, "Did he *push* her?" Violet recognized that shrill voice as belonging to Lady Nixon.

Simon's entire frame went completely stiff. Violet could feel the discomfort radiating from him. She squeezed his arm and threw a malevolent look toward the viscountess. "He did *not*. And I won't tolerate such nasty rumors."

Lady Nixon gave her an imperious stare. "There is no rumor. I merely asked a question."

"Which I've answered," Violet said coolly. "Indeed, the Duke saved me from a nasty fall. I'm quite fortunate he was there to rescue me." She turned her head to Simon and smiled. He looked at her in confusion and then abruptly turned his head away.

Offering a bright smile, she said, "Shall we continue our tour?"

He nodded, but turned her back toward the west entrance. "I need to go." His voice was small, strangled.

"No, we should continue the tour as if nothing happened." She exhaled in frustration. "*Nothing* did happen."

"You did almost fall down the stairs. And I didn't save you."

She looked at him again, hating the darkness in his tone. "Nor did you push me. I slipped." She paused, her fingers digging into his arm. "You mustn't blame yourself. I won't allow it."

"You lied. You said you tripped and that I saved you."

"I'll say whatever I need to in order to keep those harpies at bay. You don't deserve their condemnation." He kept walking, and she continued at his side. "Nick and I will make this right—don't worry."

"Nick?" He glanced toward her. "You and Nick are going to fix this." His skepticism weighed the air around them. "You can't find your way to be together, but you can join forces on my behalf? I find that difficult to believe."

"We've actually been doing it all week. The ballroom games were my idea. I wanted everyone to see the man I see."

They'd reached the end of the nave, and Simon took her hand from his arm. He gave her a sad smile. "The man you see is a façade. Or a shell. Or something in between. You can't fix this. Nick can't fix this. No one can." He turned and left, his long legs carrying him from the cathedral as if the very devil were chasing him out.

Violet watched him go, her throat tightening with sadness. That had been an unmitigated disaster. Nothing was turning out as she'd planned or hoped. She wished she could run from the cathedral after him.

Instead, she decided to take advantage of her surroundings and pray.

Chapter Ten

THE BUZZ OF conversation as soon as Simon and Violet had walked half the distance of the nave grew to the point that Nick was forced to walk away from it. Or maybe he just wanted to go after Simon.

What the hell had just happened? His first impression at seeing Simon bent over Violet was that they were having some sort of intimate moment. Simon's face had reflected concern, and he'd touched her in a way that Nick hadn't dared—not in eight years anyway.

But then he acknowledged they wouldn't be engaged in anything romantic in plain sight on the bloody landing of a staircase in a cathedral. One of those gossiping old hens had the right of it—Violet had fallen. However, there was no way in hell Simon had pushed her.

Especially given the way she'd leapt to his defense. She'd clutched his arm, holding him with great care. Seeing them together sent tendrils of jealousy curling through him.

He watched Violet and Simon stop at the end of the nave. Simon said something, then left. Nick didn't think before stalking toward where Violet now stood alone.

His intent hadn't been to speak to her, but to follow Simon. Nevertheless, he stopped at her side. "What the hell just happened?"

"You saw. You heard." Her voice was cool,

detached.

"Yes, I saw. Is there something between the two of you?"

She turned to face him, her eyes blazing. "That is none of your business. Your friend is in pain. You heard what those awful women said."

Yes, he had. He needed to go after Simon. He strode from the cathedral and went to his horse, unsurprised to see that Simon's was already gone. He set off in pursuit, racing out of town toward the Linfords' manor. As he crested a hill nearly halfway to his destination, he caught sight of Simon's mount near a slender brook.

Slowing his horse, Nick veered off the road and guided the beast toward the water. Simon sat on a rock, his gaze trained at some indeterminate point beyond the stream.

Nick dismounted, his thoughts jumbled. He didn't really believe there was something between Simon and Violet, and she was right—his friend needed him right now.

Simon didn't turn his head. "Why did you follow me? I'm fine."

"It should be obvious. I'm your friend. I can't imagine you're fine."

"I'm as fine as you are." Simon stood from the rock. He clasped his hat with one hand, and the wind stirred his hair. "You're turning your back on something most people would die for."

Nick knew how much Simon had loved his wife, how badly he missed her, and how devastating her death had been. Or still was, it seemed. The torment in his friend's gaze flayed him. "You mean you," he said quietly, and he was afraid the wind had carried the words away.

Simon's dark eyes glittered in the sunlight filtering through the mottled clouds. "Yes, I would die if it would bring Miriam and my unborn child back. You have a bloody second chance. But you'd rather toss it away. Violet is an incredible woman. You're a fool."

"Perhaps you should pursue her. She's everything you want in a wife—mature, widowed, experienced. She's intelligent, witty, and she clearly cares for you." Nick couldn't keep the jealousy from stealing into his voice. He was supposed to be helping Simon, not being an ass.

With a slight shrug, Simon turned his head toward the brook. "Maybe I should. She deserves to be happy, and I sense she's not."

White-hot anger crested in Nick's chest, but he'd had too much practice in managing his emotions. He tamped it down while reason told him that Simon was merely provoking him. Or deflecting from the real issue.

Nick took a deep breath and willed his pulse to slow. "Let me worry about Violet." Did he really plan to do that? He couldn't think of that just now. "You mustn't let what happened in the cathedral drag you into darkness."

"Why? Then you'd have company."

Nick couldn't hold on to his frustration any longer, not entirely. "Goddammit, this isn't about me."

"No, it isn't." Simon glanced back at Nick. "But forgive me if I can't take advice from someone who does nothing to improve his lot."

"There is nothing to be done." Nick grappled with his control and held on to it with the barest thread. "I am cursed. There is no hope for me."

"And that is where you and I diverge. I still have hope. God help me, even after today's debacle, I still have hope. If I didn't, I may as well give up. I honestly don't know what keeps you going."

Stunned into silence, Nick stared at him. What *did* keep him going? He woke up every day and did what he must—he managed his estate, he conducted his ducal duties, he took pleasure in riding, fishing... *Hell*. He *was* lonely. And it had taken this infernal house party to wake him to that fact.

He looked down at the ground briefly, then nodded. "I get your point. Finally."

Simon snorted. "Well, that's something. I hope this means you'll make things right with Violet."

A wave of apprehension swept over him. He wasn't sure that was the right course. Realizing he was maybe ready to make a change, to try again to allow something into his life, didn't mean that something was Violet. He associated her with the start of his misfortune. He'd often wondered if his behavior wasn't to blame. He'd carried on a liaison with a young woman out of wedlock, never mind that he'd had every intention of marrying her...

"I don't know." That was all he could say right now. "I'd rather focus on you. I'll make sure everyone knows Violet *fell*."

"It doesn't matter. Society's court long ago passed judgment on me, and I was a fool to think I could expect otherwise. So I live on the fringe." He shrugged, appearing as if he didn't care, but Nick knew better. "I've managed it for some time now."

"It won't always be like this," Nick said. "Lady Nixon and her ilk will forget. Or die."

"I don't know about the former, but the latter is a

certainty. For all of us." He put his hat back on. "I'm going back to the house, and then I'm leaving."

"You can't."

Simon arched his brow as he pulled his glove more snugly around his left hand. "Why not?"

"We have a deal."

The wind buoyed Simon's laugh. "The deal was that you would stay one night."

"We were supposed to leave together for your box."

"I'm not going there. You're welcome to, of course."

Nick narrowed his eyes. "Where are you going, then? It doesn't matter. You should stay. Show those shrews that you aren't rattled. If the tables were turned, you wouldn't let me leave."

Simon grunted. "I'm still leaving. You need to stay and explore things with Violet. Or not. But if you don't, I promise that I'll hound you about the mistake for the rest of your days." He went to his horse and mounted.

"This may be the end of our friendship," Nick called.

Simon stared at him a moment, then shook his head before turning and riding northwest.

Nick picked up a rock and skipped it into the stream, swearing. Without Simon, he truly had no one, and now that he'd realized his life was lacking, he couldn't afford to lose the only friend he had. Did that mean he had to try to work things out with Violet?

He swore again. This wasn't Simon's bloody life. He didn't understand the complexities surrounding their relationship—the broken promises, the guilt, the unresolved emotions. Wouldn't it be better for Nick to just start over?

Miss Kingman was beautiful and charming, albeit reserved. And today in the cathedral, she'd demonstrated a sharp intelligence as they'd discussed the reformation and the Civil War. If he wanted to banish the emptiness in his life, he could do no better than someone like her. If she agreed to his terms—no expectation of love—he'd be in no danger of losing his heart. Or his mind with grief if tragedy struck, as he almost certainly expected it to.

And yet he couldn't ignore the unresolved feelings he had for Violet, the burning desire that pulsed through him whenever she was near. Hell, whenever he even *thought* about her as he was doing now. He recalled that night so long ago when she'd feigned illness, then slipped out of her aunt and uncle's house. Nick had been waiting for her outside, and together they'd gone to his uncle's town house, but his uncle hadn't been there. It had just been Nick and a handful of servants, and it had been easy to secret her upstairs to his chamber. By the light of the moon streaming through his window, they'd made love for the first time, and he'd basked in the joy of knowing they would be together for the rest of their lives.

He closed his eyes and saw her as she was then—her body soft and lush and so responsive to his touch. She'd cried out his name over and over and declared her love between soul-stirring kisses. He'd never imagined their plans would crash down around him less than a week later.

The familiar anger wasn't as strong now as it had been, but seeing her had roused it again. What Simon didn't understand was that Nick had to manage all these conflicting emotions where Violet was concerned. And he wasn't sure he could.

He opened his eyes and went to the rock Simon had vacated. Dropping down, he stared out toward the

Mendip Hills, mindless of the wind picking up or the clouds darkening overhead.

When the first raindrop struck his shoulder, he glanced up. Another drop splattered his cheek. He was about to get drenched.

Muttering an oath, he mounted his horse and thundered back to the manor. He was, as anticipated, thoroughly soaked by the time he arrived at the stables. He looked for Simon's vehicle. Not seeing it, he asked if the duke had left and was informed that he had. Damn, Simon had departed with incredible speed.

Likely he'd wanted to avoid seeing anyone, which he'd done because the coaches were just arriving from the village.

Nick went into the house and asked for a bath and whiskey. Hopefully, the combination would give him some insight on what path to take.

⋅ε·3⋅

VIOLET STOOD IN the upstairs sitting room that overlooked the front drive and watched the ladies climb into the coaches for an afternoon jaunt into Wells to shop. After yesterday's disaster at the cathedral, she'd wanted to close herself in her room for the remainder of the party, but Hannah had convinced her to come to dinner. Violet had relented, agreeing that it would be better for Simon if she showed everyone that she was fine and reiterate that he hadn't pushed her.

She just wished he hadn't left. Everything she and Nick had done to rehabilitate his reputation had been swept away.

Hannah had felt horrible. She'd vowed never to

invite Lady Nixon and Mrs. Law to anything ever again. It was good the house party would conclude after tonight's ball. Violet was looking forward to leaving in the morning.

She wanted to put as much distance between herself and this party as possible. And not just because of what had happened with Simon. No, if she were honest, it was largely to do with Nick.

He'd come to dinner last night and been his usual aloof self. Even so, she'd caught him looking at her several times. Not that she'd been able to discern why. His features had been as impassive as ever.

Still, she'd been aware of his presence and her undying attraction to him the entire evening. She couldn't stand it. Perhaps she could beg off tonight's ball and plead illness. Everyone had seen that she was perfectly fine yesterday. They wouldn't blame Simon.

Of course they would. They already did.

Scowling, she turned from the window and instantly froze.

Standing in the doorway, leaning against the frame, his gaze targeted directly on her, was Nick. He was dressed as he'd been at luncheon—a dark green coat with buff breeches and a waistcoat of warm acorn brown. "You aren't dressed for riding," was all she could think to say. The men were going riding while the women ventured to the village.

"No, they just left." He pushed away from the jamb and closed the door. Then he walked slowly into the center of the room before stopping.

Why had he closed the door? She ignored the invisible magnet drawing her to him. "I was just heading back to my room."

"Stay." He took another step toward her. "Please."

"I shouldn't." And yet she didn't move.

"After tomorrow, I doubt we'll see each other. It seemed..." He cleared his throat and took another step. What the devil was he about?

His brow creased, destroying the careful composure he always wore. Was he going to be the Nick she remembered? The Nick she liked? *The Nick she loved?*

No. She didn't love him anymore. Not this Duke of Ice.

He wiped his hand over his mouth, a gesture he'd done often in their youth. It startled her.

"I'm conflicted." He speared her with a tumultuous look, and she could see the battle in his eyes. "I... I want to move forward, but I don't know that I can. Not until I put the past behind me. I didn't realize that until I saw you here."

And now the conflict ignited inside her. She'd been so happy to see him. Suddenly, all the dreams she'd buried had taken flight, and for the first time, they'd seemed *real*. Until she'd seen what he'd become. Now she had to accept that her dreams were dead, that they'd died eight years ago. And yet here he was, standing in front of her—the man who'd stolen her heart, the man she would've given anything to reclaim. Sanity told her to run away, but she was rooted to the floor.

"I need to move on too." She didn't recognize the sound of her voice. It was dark and steely. Cold.

"I was hoping that together, we could do that. Find a way to leave the past where it belongs."

She'd held her love so close to herself for so long that it was simply a part of her. She couldn't begin to imagine how she'd cut it away and be whole again. "How?"

He closed the gap between them. His eyes, so pale and bright in the afternoon light coming from the window behind her, bored into hers. "Like this."

He reached for her, his hand curling around her waist. She sucked in a breath, desire enflaming her as he drew her against his chest.

Staring down at her as if he hadn't truly seen her in eight years, he traced his forefinger along her forehead, then down over her temple and across her cheekbone until he found her jaw. Dragging his flesh along hers, he came to her mouth. The moment his finger touched her lips, she opened and drew the tip inside, never breaking their eye contact.

His eyelids lowered, and his gaze turned instantly seductive. She suckled his finger, but he pulled it away, and she thought he meant to leave then.

Instead, he lowered his head and kissed her. The contact was like a bonfire catching flame, sending heat licking outward until everything was ablaze.

He tasted of that heat and need. He tasted like home.

This was no gentle brush of lips as in the ballroom the other day. This was the passion she remembered, his body pressed to hers, his mouth opening and invading hers, his tongue tempting hers. And she answered every provocation, straining against him, her arms twining around his neck and pulling him to her, lest he decide this was a mistake.

Maybe it was. She didn't care. This wasn't the Duke of Ice. This was Nick, the man she'd given her heart to, her lover.

His fingers dug into her back as he kissed her with fierce need. She met his desperation with her own, clutching his neck and curling her hands into his collar. Tilting her head, she pressed harder against him, need pulsing between her legs. She hadn't been with a man in so long. And she hadn't known ecstasy with one since him.

He brought his hand beneath her arm, along her rib cage, until he found her breast. He massaged her through the layers of her clothing, and she wanted to weep with want.

"Always too many damn clothes," he muttered against her mouth, not fully breaking their kiss.

She tangled her tongue with his, cutting off further speech. A sound vibrated deep in his throat, which she felt more than heard. Joy spread through her. How long she'd imagined this moment. And it far exceeded the fantasy.

His thumb came up over the edge of her bodice and brushed along her flesh. She wanted to peel her clothes away and do the same to his. Sliding her hand down from his neck to the edge of his collarbone, she tugged at his cravat, loosening the knot.

He ended the kiss with a groan, and she opened her eyes, her body quivering.

He backed away, wiping his hand over his mouth again, his eyes wild with desire. "I thought I would kiss you and that would be enough. Then we'd part on friendly terms."

She wanted to laugh with the absurdity of that. One kiss had never been enough after that first time. Keeping their hands from each other had been a distinct problem in their short but torrid relationship. "And is it? Enough, I mean."

"No," he rasped. But he turned and went to the door. She sagged with disappointment even as every instinct she possessed said this was for the best.

Then she heard the click of the lock just before he

pivoted, pressing his back to the door. "Do you want me to go?" he asked.

She shook her head, unable to speak.

"There are two other doors." He strode to one of them, and she heard him throw the lock while she rushed to the other.

"There's no lock on this one." Before she could turn, she felt him approach behind her. "Then we shall have to be quiet. And hope no one tries to come in. If memory serves, we had to do this once before."

The third—and last—time they'd been together. They'd taken advantage of a seldom-used sitting room while attending a party one evening. They'd been young and foolish, overcome with emotion and physical yearning. They ought to know better now, to practice caution and reservation.

And yet, she didn't think she could do so, especially not when she was enveloped in his spicy scent and his breath tickled the back of her neck. As if reading her mind, his attention focused on that spot as his lips caressed her skin.

She closed her eyes and leaned her forehead against the door. Over the next several minutes, he did things to her neck with his lips and tongue that aroused her more than she ever thought possible. She splayed one hand next to her shoulder against the door for support, and with her other hand, she reached back and gripped his thigh. His muscle was taut beneath her palm, and he brought his body against hers, his groin nudging into her backside.

His breath came hard and fast against her skin. She clutched at him, eager for more. The whisking sound of her skirt filled the near quiet as he lifted her dress from behind. Cool air rushed over the backs of her legs.

When the fabric was bunched between them, she felt his touch, the gentle stroke of his fingertips along the back of her thigh.

His tongue traced the outer shell of her ear. "Part your legs," he whispered.

She did as he bade, widening her stance. His hand moved forward and found her core. He lightly teased her flesh, swirling around the most sensitive part of her as his lips and tongue ravaged her ear. She turned her head and laid her cheek against the wood, her breath rasping from her mouth as her pulse climbed.

"You are very wet for me," he murmured, trailing kisses along her jaw. "Do you remember how it was?"

He'd always tormented her until she was not only wet and begging for release; he didn't stop until she came. Only then would he take his own pleasure. There'd been only one occasion when his pleasure had come first—

Her thought was completely interrupted by the press of his finger inside her. He went slowly, his touch seductively methodical. She gasped softly at the welcome intrusion, and she couldn't keep her hips from arching back.

"Do you want more?" he asked, sliding out briefly before edging in again.

She kept her eyes closed, all her attention focused on the ecstasy building within her. "I want everything." She turned her head farther, seeking his kiss.

His mouth ravished hers as his finger thrust deep into her. She would've cried out if not for the preoccupation of his kiss. Their position was a tad awkward, and it wasn't long before he broke his lips from hers, returning his mouth to her neck. Her hips moved with the thrusts of his hand, and she rose onto her toes as need tightened inside her. Her pleasure built, and her body tensed.

"Come for me, Violet." The soft command came against her ear, and it was all the urging she needed.

Her muscles clenched, and she sucked in a breath as her orgasm crashed into her.

"Shhh." He kissed her ear, her neck, her jaw, all while his hand kept up its relentless assault.

Before the sensations had faded, he scooped her into his arms and carried her to a chaise, where he laid her upon the cushions. She opened her eyes and saw the harsh control etched into his features. His eyes were dark, his lips parted as he pulled his cravat away. He tore his coat from his shoulders and dropped it to the floor.

He stopped and stared down at her. "Was that enough?" he asked tentatively.

She kicked her shoes off and reached for him, her fingers pulling at the buttons of his waistcoat. "My God, no."

"Good." He sounded relieved, which made her smile.

"Keep doing that." He leaned down and kissed her hard and fast, his tongue sliding against hers and his teeth catching her lips as he straightened to remove his waistcoat.

"Smiling?" she asked. At his answering nod, she said, "You rarely do. I miss that."

He stared down at her, his gaze familiarly seductive, and his lips curved up very slowly. The smile broadened until it tautened his cheekbones and lit his eyes.

Her insides turned to jelly. "Nick," she breathed. There he was at last. "Come here. *Please.*" She reclined and parted her legs.

He tossed up her skirts and looked at her sex. Once, she would've succumbed to embarrassment and squeezed her legs closed, but Nick had taught her to be proud and confident, to use her body to please herself and him. When she'd awaited her new husband nude in their bedchamber, he'd chastised her horribly. Then when he'd discovered she wasn't a virgin, he'd called her a whore.

She closed her eyes to banish the memories.

"What is it?" Nick's gentle question jolted her as his lips trailed along her cheek.

She opened her eyes. "Nothing. I don't want to think of anything else. Just you. Us. Here. Now."

Curling her hand around his neck, she pulled his mouth to hers and kissed him, her tongue sliding into his mouth on a quest to reclaim him, even if it was just for now. He settled between her legs, and she tugged her skirts up, wishing she could disrobe. But they didn't dare. This would have to suffice. She felt the length of his cock against her sex, his clothing the only barrier between them.

So long as her hand was in the vicinity, she put it to good use, unbuttoning his fall. She slipped her hand inside and found the warmth of his flesh. He groaned into her mouth.

His hips pressed into hers, smashing her hand between them, but bringing him into delicious contact with her hungry flesh. She worked her hand along his length and, after a few more teasing moments, pulled him free.

His fingers stroked her clitoris, spinning her toward ecstasy once more. Then he parted her flesh, and she guided him inside. He went slowly, and her body greeted his entry with a shudder. Then he filled her completely, and she knew a joy she'd never thought to experience again.

He began to move, retreating from her and then pushing forward with increasing speed. She clutched at his backside, drawing him deep inside her. Lifting her legs, she curled them around his hips. He thrust faster and tore his mouth from hers, gasping.

She dug her fingers into him and rose to meet him, their bodies snapping together in a familiar rhythm. They fit together perfectly, just as she remembered.

Thought receded from her mind as her body took over. She was only aware of his heat, his insistent thrusts, and the hard pulse of his breathing. Pressure built inside her, then broke free. Light exploded behind her eyes, and she worked to keep from crying out.

"*Violet*."

She recognized the desperation in his plea as well as the clenching of the muscles in his backside. She kissed him, devouring his moan as he spilled himself inside her.

They continued to move together, their bodies slowing as satisfaction claimed them. Violet relaxed back against the cushions, releasing his mouth to take in air. He did the same, working to lower his pulse. After another moment, he left her to sit at the edge of the chaise.

He looked over at her and reached down for his cravat before offering it to her. "Do you want to use this?"

She shook her head. "Petticoats can serve more than one purpose." She sat up and pulled her skirts down, covertly tidying their mess. "I'm surprised you don't remember."

"I do, in fact." He'd looked away but now speared her with an intense stare. "I remember everything. Just as I'll remember this."

That sounded rather final. He'd wanted to leave their past behind and apparently thought this would do that. "Is that enough, then?" she asked quietly.

"I think it has to be, don't you?" He swiped his hand across his mouth and briefly pulled on his chin. "We're different people now. Surely you recognize that."

Yes, she did. That had been wonderful and indeed reminiscent of what they'd shared. But it had been different too. There'd been an element of need and desperation, of something lost that couldn't be found. "We can't go back."

He shook his head. "No matter how much we may want to."

She understood. And she was grateful for this. Maybe now she wouldn't think of him with searing regret and abject guilt. Maybe now she could think of him and smile.

He picked up her shoes and slipped them onto her feet as if she were Cinderella. Except this was no fairy tale. There would be no happy endings and no ever after.

She stood up and shook out her skirts. She gave him a smile and said, "I will always cherish you, and I wish you well."

Then she walked softly from the room, careful to close the door behind her.

Chapter Eleven

OBERON'S HOOVES POUNDED the wet sand, sending salt and spray flying as Nick ran him across the beach. The last two days had been too stormy to ride. Both man and beast were ecstatic to be out, even if the heavens were spitting rain periodically.

The last week had passed at a particularly glacial pace. Since arriving home from the house party, Nick hadn't been his usual self. The things he typically did to pass his days—working in his office or on the estate, fishing, even riding as he was now—had failed to keep him satisfied. He'd left the Linfords' feeling remarkably good, his sexual encounter with Violet fulfilling him in a way he hadn't been in years. That feeling had lasted about a day.

By the time he'd gotten back to Kilve Hall, he'd begun to question everything. Hell, he'd started questioning everything the moment he'd met Violet at the party. She'd awakened him from a long, dismal sleep, and he was surprised to find he didn't want to reclaim it.

Which left him wondering what the hell to do next.

Simon had disappeared to parts unknown, which had left Nick to query his staff. And damn if they weren't perplexed by his behavior. Nick nearly smiled at their bemusement. Poor Rand. Nick had asked his valet last night if he ought to marry again. Rand had gaped at him, then assumed he was jesting. When Nick had said he wasn't, Rand's eyes had nearly popped from his head. In the end, he'd said he certainly couldn't offer advice.

So today, Nick was seeking better counsel. He rode up the path from the beach to the small graveyard overlooking the ocean. Dismounting, he let Oberon graze in a familiar spot, then went to Jacinda's grave. Next to hers was the smaller headstone belonging to their son.

"I'm sorry I haven't been to visit in a while. I was at a house party." He bent and brushed sand from her name on the stone. "You would have liked it. There was archery—no, you wouldn't have cared for that. You would have liked the silly games and the dancing. And the shopping trip." At the mention of the latter, he couldn't help but think of Violet and how fortunate he was that she hadn't taken the excursion.

He'd gone to the sitting room to watch the women leave, never imagining that she would be there. He certainly hadn't planned to lie with her, but the opportunity was too perfect. And he *had* hoped that perhaps they could put the past to rest for good. Instead, he feared they'd made it harder to forget.

For him, at least. He'd no idea how she felt. It was entirely possible that she had moved on, and part of him hoped she had. It made it much easier to think of her continuing with her life as opposed to her thinking of him in the same manner in which he was thinking of her.

He dreamed of her. He relived that afternoon. He wanted her.

Looking at his wife's grave, he tried to bring Jacinda's image to his mind. She'd been two years his senior, a dark-haired pale beauty with eyes the color of rich, dark earth after a dousing spring rain.

He'd married her after returning from the war and inheriting the dukedom. He'd needed a wife, and she'd been among the first women he'd met when he'd gone to London for the Season. Eager to avoid the social whirl, he'd decided to marry her rather quickly. She was well-mannered, came from an excellent family, and possessed a keen intelligence. He hadn't been interested in falling love, not after losing Maurice and then his uncle.

"In retrospect, it wasn't very fair to you," he said softly. "I know you loved me, and I'm afraid I didn't deserve it." He hadn't loved her, but he'd been fond of her. He supposed he'd been practicing to become the Duke of Ice, a man who didn't feel. But it had taken one more horrific tragedy, the loss of his son, for him to fully become that man. To love was to hurt, and he'd done enough of that to last him a lifetime.

And he'd been ready to keep himself from that messy emotion forever. Until he'd encountered Violet again. Just as she'd done the first time, she'd cocked everything up.

Still, realizing he didn't want to be alone wasn't the same as wanting to fall in love. He could take another duchess under the exact same circumstances he'd married Jacinda. "It wasn't terrible, was it?" he asked. "You were happy, I think. I tried to make you happy." As best as he could. She'd been well cared for, and he'd treated her with respect and affection. He could do the same for another woman, say, Miss Kingman. She'd make a serviceable duchess.

Serviceable?

Even he knew that sounded awful. She'd make an *excellent* duchess.

What about Violet?

His traitorous mind couldn't stop thinking of her, and his equally perfidious body couldn't stop wanting her. Instead of banishing her to the past, he was as consumed by her as he'd ever been.

Could they try again?

Simon's pleas echoed in Nick's brain. He was so tormented by his wife's death. Simon wouldn't have thought twice if presented with the opportunity for a second chance.

It was just so damn difficult to have hope when your entire life had been filled with tragedy and misfortune—from the loss of four younger siblings and finally his mother as she'd delivered the last of those children to his father and then his brother and uncle to his wife and child. And yes, he'd lost Violet too, even if it hadn't been to death. Which meant of all of them, he could try for a second chance with her.

If he had the courage to risk disaster again.

He looked at his son's name and thought of his perfect, tiny face. If he could feel that sense of unconditional love and devotion, it would be worth it.

Nick touched each stone, his fingertips lingering over his son's name. Then he turned and climbed back on Oberon. The rain fell in earnest as they returned to the stables. By the time Nick entered his chamber, he was already peeling away his sodden clothes.

"Let me help you, Your Grace," Rand offered, rushing to assist Nick with his coat.

"I'll need a bath," Nick said.

"It's already being drawn and will be ready by the time you're undressed." Rand set the coat on the floor as Nick perched on the edge of a chair.

He extended his leg so that Rand could remove his boots. "Excellent. Then I want you to pack for an extended trip."

Rand's head snapped up, and he paused in tugging at the second boot. "So soon?"

"I know it's a surprise. It is to me too."

Rand removed Nick's stockings as Nick shrugged out of his waistcoat. "Where are we going?"

"To Bath. Please inform Mr. Lovell that I need to meet with him after my bath to make preparations." Nick's secretary would likely be just as surprised as Rand.

"Right away." Rand looked at him as if he wanted to say something but didn't.

"Out with it." Nick stood to remove the rest of his clothing.

"I hope you won't find me impertinent, Your Grace, but you're changed since you returned from the house party."

Nick pulled his shirt over his head and handed it to the valet. "So it would seem."

"For the better, if I may broaden my impertinence."

"Thank you, Rand." Nick peeled his breeches down his legs.

"Everyone says so."

"Let's not take things too far." Nick smiled at the man, causing Rand's eyes to widen. Nick finished undressing, then turned to head to his bath.

He couldn't help but think of the city where he'd met Violet. And he could hardly wait to get there.

VIOLET WAS SURPRISINGLY content as she looked at Bath from the window of her coach. For eight years, she'd lived under the shadow of "if only…" and while she was still sad about how things had turned out, for the first time, she had the sense that she could put Nick behind her.

Oh, it still hurt—she knew she'd always love him— but she had a final happy memory to make her smile.

They hadn't been alone together again at the house party after their encounter in the sitting room. But before he'd left, he'd taken her hand and bowed, telling her he wished her every happiness in the future. It had felt like a goodbye, and she knew that it was.

Yes, that was what felt different. Eight years ago, she'd simply left with her parents, and since he'd never received her letter, there'd been a raw wound. Hopefully, it was now closed, and they could both move forward without regret or bitterness.

As she traveled along Great Pulteney Street, she wondered what that way forward looked like. Perhaps Hannah would help her puzzle that out. Violet was delighted she'd come to town and anticipated spending a lovely afternoon with her friend.

She departed her coach in front of the Sydney Hotel and swept inside, where she looked about for Hannah. Her neck pricked, as if something was...off. She'd come here a hundred times—more probably—but had never felt this sensation of having done exactly *this* before. She took in the familiar setting, the windows looking out to the gardens, and then she froze.

As he rose from a table beneath a window, his eyes locked with hers. He was dressed a bit differently, but the colors were the same—a dark blue coat, brown breeches, and the stiffest cravat she'd ever seen. He presented a breathtaking picture of masculine elegance and rugged allure. Even before he'd been a duke, he'd looked ducal, as if he could command the world.

Violet couldn't move for a moment. The familiarity of the situation was so keen, she almost believed it was a dream. On that day eight years ago, she'd left the table she'd been sharing with her aunt and her aunt's friend, leaving them to gossip while she took a turn outside. She'd never imagined that such a simple decision would alter her life forever.

Nick had stood, and she'd seen him, their gazes connecting briefly before she'd continued on her path to the door to the gardens, her maid trailing behind her. All the while, her heart had pounded as the handsome stranger stared at her. Following the past, she put one foot in front of the other and walked toward the door.

He rushed to open it for her, just as he had eight years ago. She stepped out into the cool, late October afternoon, her breath trapped in her lungs.

Nick joined her and bowed deeply. "May I escort you through the gardens?"

Unwilling—or perhaps unable—to break the spell that had been cast, she looked back over her shoulder as if she'd see her aunt inside. Back then, she'd been too engrossed with her gossip to pay attention to what Violet was doing, so Violet had seized her chance.

She gave him a curtsey. "Yes, I'd be delighted."

He offered his arm, and the moment she curled her hand around him, it was as if they'd been transported. The day seemed suddenly brighter, more like July than October, the air full of intoxicating scents of midsummer. Her insides swirled as giddiness swept through her. He exuded charm and magnetism, and he wanted to walk with *her*!

Violet couldn't keep from smiling.

Questions crowded her mind—what was he doing

here? Why had he come? What was this about? But only one made it to her lips. "Hannah isn't here, is she?"

He shook his head.

Hannah's note hadn't been in her hand, which Violet knew as well as her own. She'd said her husband's secretary was drafting it because she'd burned her finger. Nick, it seemed, was as cunning as she remembered.

"Would you like to see the canal?" he asked. "There's a charming bridge done in the Chinese style."

He was doing everything exactly as he'd done eight years ago. She wanted to do the same. "That sounds wonderful. I'd love to see it."

He guided her along the path toward the bridge, saying, "We haven't been formally introduced, which I suppose makes this rather scandalous."

Violet stifled a laugh. Yes, this endeavor had set the tone for their entire relationship. They'd scarcely followed the rules. They'd been swept up in excitement and love and hadn't cared about Society's principles.

"I'm Mr. Nicholas Bateman," he said.

"Miss Violet Caulfield."

"Pleased to meet you, Miss Caulfield. You aren't from Bath, are you? I believe I should know you if you were."

"I am not; however, my aunt and uncle reside here, and I visit them every summer."

"I am deeply saddened that we haven't met before now. I live outside of town with my uncle."

"I am just coming out," she said, taking in his profile. She tried to see it as she had then, but it was difficult. Because she knew him, and she couldn't forget all that had transpired. She could, however, pretend, and she wanted to.

"Does this mean you'll be attending the fancy ball on Thursday?" he asked. The bright sound of hope threaded through his question now as it had eight years ago.

She nodded. "I will. And I'm allowed to go to the Pump Room."

"Tell me when you plan to go, and I will be there too."

They reached the bridge, and she said, "Oh, this is beautiful. Thank you for bringing me." She looked down at the canal, then turned to face him, her arm still twined with his. "Are there boats?"

He pivoted with her, his face so familiar, so dear. The Duke of Ice was nowhere to be found today. This Nick looked younger, softer, more relaxed. Maybe this *was* a dream.

"Yes. Would you like to take one out someday?"

"I should ask my aunt and uncle." She recalled what she'd been thinking then, that she didn't want to tell them about Nick, that she was afraid they'd tell her she couldn't see him. She'd been young, just nineteen, and not quite on the Marriage Mart. "They won't mind," she said as she had eight years ago, intending to take a boat on the canal with him whether they approved or not. She'd known then that something magical was happening, that this chance meeting would alter the course of her life.

"I shall look forward to it," he said, looking down at her with such warmth that she wanted to sway into him, as she'd nearly done eight years ago.

Then she'd caught sight of her maid about five yards away and realized she ought to return to the hotel before she was missed.

"I should go back." She looked up at him but didn't move. She didn't want to go back.

She realized she meant that about the past too. After years of wishing she could rewind time, she didn't want to anymore. She wanted him in the present. She wanted to believe that they *were* meant to be, even if it had taken a long time to get there.

"I hope you don't mind me saying so, Miss Caulfield, but you are very beautiful. The most beautiful woman I've ever seen."

"Still?" The word came out as a husky whisper, barely audible as the breeze stirred the leaves from the near-bare trees.

"Always." He leaned forward, and she anticipated his kiss.

But he only turned and started back toward the hotel, prompting her to quiver in frustration. How had she thought they were finished? That she could move on as if the past were finally resolved? It would never be resolved between them. Not for her. She loved him with all her heart—the gentle, charming man of her youth and the dark, tortured Duke of Ice.

"Tell me, Miss Caulfield, what do you like to do?"

"Embroidery, singing, reading."

He stopped and looked at her, then laughed. "Really?"

She joined his laughter, recalling this moment as if it had happened yesterday. "Reading, yes. The others, maybe not as much as my mother would like. I love to ride, and I'm rather good at archery." She remembered blushing and wishing she hadn't been so self-aggrandizing.

But he'd only laughed more loudly, his astonishing eyes sparkling with mirth. "I should like to see that.

Perhaps I'll find a place for us to shoot." He leaned closer as he said that, and in her mind, Violet heard the gentle clearing of her maid's throat.

Oh, Letty. She'd been Violet's governess and had taken the position of her lady's maid that spring in preparation for Violet's come out. She'd loved Violet as a daughter and had seen—and sympathized with—how deeply Violet had fallen for Nick. In hindsight, Violet ought to have entrusted the letter she'd written him to Letty. But Letty had been dismissed when they'd left Bath and installed a new, far sterner maid. Her parents had blamed Letty, in part, for Violet's behavior. Later, after Clifford had died, Violet had sought Letty out and given her a settlement on which she could retire. She'd passed away last year.

Nick's brow creased, likely in response to her woolgathering. Violet shook the maudlin thoughts from her head and smiled up at him. "I was just thinking of my maid. I think she would like me to return to the hotel."

His gaze moved to some indistinct point behind her. He was perhaps thinking of Letty too. "I liked her," he said, breaking from their eight-year-old script.

"She was a dear woman."

"Was?"

Violet gave a gentle nod. "She passed last year."

His eyes shuttered briefly, and for a moment, she saw the Duke of Ice. No, she wouldn't let him ruin this perfect day.

Violet squeezed his arm. "Come, Letty would want us to enjoy our walk back. She found you quite handsome, you know. But then, I recall all of Bath fell at your feet." When she'd walked into the fancy ball, she'd heard talk of the spectacular Mr. Bateman and whether he might dance with them. She'd been afraid he wouldn't distinguish her among all his admirers. And she'd been silly to think such a thing. She was the first person he'd asked to dance.

"I didn't notice anyone but you," he said, sweeping her along the path.

She knew that to be true, and yet it still made her shiver.

"Now, stop speaking as if this is the past tense, Miss Caulfield." His gentle admonishment drew a smile to her lips. He was apparently insistent that they continue this pretense.

She tried to remember what had happened next… Oh! She brought her hand to her mouth and laughed. Collecting her wits, she sobered. "My goodness, will you look at that?" She pointed at nothing, wondering if he would recall what they'd seen.

He sucked in a breath, and she knew he did. "Good heavens, is that Lady Fairhaven, and is she…dancing?" The Countess of Fairhaven had been careening about the lawn, her hands flailing.

"I don't recall a type of dancing that requires shrieking along with it," Violet said, grinning. As it turned out, the countess had seen a spider crawling on her skirt—the story had been recounted for days after that. That reminded Violet of the games they'd played at the house party and Mr. Seaver saying there was a spider in Sarah's hair.

"No, I daresay there isn't one. Can you imagine?" He lifted his arm and flapped it like a bird taking flight. "Add in the squawking and we should have to give it an ornithological name."

"Perhaps the bittern," she suggested.

He cocked his head to the side as if he could actually

see Lady Fairhaven and her wild exercise. "Indeed. She does look a bit like a bittern with her neck extended and her long nose. Perhaps we should have several names and base them on the dancer. You, for example, would be a swan."

She gasped and looked at him sharply, though humor lifted her lips. "Swans can be quite disagreeable."

"I'm sure you'll agree they are, without question, the most beautiful of fowl." He looked at her intently, his gaze soft but seductive. "And I'm confident you wouldn't know how to be disagreeable if you tried."

He'd said that then, but did he believe it now? For a moment, reality invaded their charming little play. So much had transpired since this day had actually happened. She'd been more than disagreeable. She'd broken his heart. Was it too late for them to reclaim what they'd lost? She'd thought so. She'd reconciled herself to that outcome, had prepared to move on. But now he was here...

The questions she'd ignored came roaring back, and she wasn't sure she could keep them at bay. This was a lovely game, but they couldn't play it forever.

He shook his head, his eyes darkening, as if he read her thoughts. Turning toward the hotel, he escorted her back. "May I meet you at the Pump Room tomorrow afternoon? If you plan to be there, that is."

"I will now." Her mind had gone to work planning how she would convince her aunt to allow her to go. It ended up not being difficult as her uncle had insisted she be seen—it had been, after all, the intent that summer for her to gain confidence and poise.

Nick didn't walk her inside but withdrew her arm, just as he'd done eight years ago. "I should take my leave," he said. "Thank you for the promenade. I look

forward to seeing you tomorrow." After executing a
perfect bow, he left.

Violet stared after him, her earlier banished questions
burning her tongue. Ah well, tomorrow she would ask
them. Tomorrow, she would ensure they lived in the
present. For as much as she loved reliving their idyllic
past, she knew how that ended.

And she refused to let history repeat.

Chapter Twelve

THE MUSIC FROM the gallery provided a lively backdrop to the hum of conversation filling the Pump Room. Nick hadn't been here in eight years. His uncle had bought him a commission the fall after he'd met Violet, and away to war he'd gone, joining his brother in the company of Wellington's newly formed 4th Infantry Division. He quickly shoved those nearly three years from his mind.

Instead, he focused on yesterday, on Violet. His plan had been executed as perfectly as he could've expected. A part of him had feared she would turn away from him, but she hadn't. No, she'd engaged in his make-believe, and they'd spent a thoroughly delightful afternoon.

He stood near the windows and watched the women promenade while others sat and drank the waters. His gaze strayed to the door often in anticipation of Violet's arrival.

And there she was.

She wore a fetching walking dress with a light blue spencer and cunning bonnet that perfectly framed her face. As lovely as she looked, he would strip everything away until she was bare. That, he realized, was how he liked her best. And since he hadn't been able to accomplish that feat at the house party, he was impatient to do so. Assuming she was even interested in rekindling their affair.

She scanned the room until she found him, her

features lighting up. He picked his way along the length of the room as she moved inside.

"Good afternoon, Lady Pendleton." He took her hand and bowed.

She dipped a curtsey and murmured, "I'm Lady Pendleton today?"

He didn't answer but gave her a sly grin. "Shall we take the water or promenade? Or both?"

"Both, I think."

He curled her hand around his forearm and led her toward the opposite end of the room.

"Duke," she started, drawing him to glance in her direction. The word sounded so strange coming from her. He'd had difficulty adjusting to his title, and this took him back to that time. "I am surprised to see you in Bath."

"I imagine so. It seemed after our last meeting that there was perhaps…more to say." Or do.

She flashed him a look of surprise. "I should like to know your intentions."

He let out a low chuckle. "You sound like a concerned mother. If it isn't obvious, I thought we might determine if we would suit."

She lurched forward, tripping, but he tightened his grip before she went down.

"Careful there," he said.

Now the look she threw him was tinged with exasperation. "You think it's that simple?" The question was low and urgent.

"No, but we have to begin somewhere." There were eight years and a multitude of unknown feelings and hurts between them. They would need to sort them out, *if* they could sort them out.

Two women who were a few years older than Violet

stopped before them. They looked at Violet in question before offering curtsies to Nick.

"Allow me to present the Duke of Kilve," Violet said. "We were recently acquainted at the house party of a mutual friend." She turned her head to Nick. "Duke, this is Mrs. Dunweavy and Mrs. Frye."

The women stared at him, slack-jawed for a moment. Mrs. Frye was the first to regain her tongue. "A pleasure to meet you, Your Grace." She curtsied again.

"Have you come to town to see the Queen?" Mrs. Dunweavy asked.

He hadn't, but he grasped that excuse since he couldn't very well tell them he'd come to Bath to seduce his former lover. "Yes."

"How splendid," Mrs. Frye said, smiling. "Everyone is so thrilled she is coming to town. I imagine you'll be at her audience."

Nick hadn't really thought of it, but of course he would. It was part of being a duke. When the Queen came to visit, you attended her. Violet would also go, given her status as a viscountess.

"I'm looking forward to it," Nick said.

They exchanged a few more pleasantries before parting. Nick and Violet continued to the other end of the room.

As they passed a table, a portly gentleman well past middle age leaned forward, squinting at Nick. "I say, is that Nicholas Bateman?"

Nick recognized the man, an old friend of his uncle's. "It is indeed. How are you, Mr. Eames?"

"I'm quite fair, quite fair." His gaze strayed to Violet.

"May I present my friend Lady Pendleton?" Nick said.

She curtsied to the older man with the smile that

never failed to make Nick's heart trip.

Mr. Eames looked back to Nick with a deep chuckle. "I'm afraid I forgot you were a duke, Your Grace." He inclined his head to Violet. "A pleasure, my lady. Would you care to sit and amuse an old man? I've one more cup of water to finish. Don't want to short myself, not when it keeps me young. But then that is why our Queen is coming, isn't it? These waters are magic, I say." He took a long draught, apparently finishing his serving. He handed the empty cup to Nick. "Would you mind refilling it for me, Your Grace?"

No one would have dared ask a duke to do that, but Nick didn't mind. On the contrary, he liked feeling useful, particularly to people he knew and liked. Eames had been a dear friend of his uncle's. Nick felt suddenly contrite for not keeping in touch with the man.

"I wouldn't mind at all." He took himself off and went to have Eames's cup refilled at the pump. While there, he obtained two more cups for Violet and himself. He looked over at her where she sat next to Eames, their heads bent together in conversation. She laughed at something the man said, and Nick could only imagine what story he was relating.

Balancing the three cups, he made his way back to the table. "Here we are."

Eames took his mug. "Thank you, thank you. Now sit. I'm regaling the fair Lady Pendleton with stories of your youth, such as the time you and your brother sneaked into the Cross Bath."

Nick groaned. "We got into so much trouble for that." His uncle had banished Nick and Maurice to the stables for a week.

"Aye, but your uncle and I laughed about it."

"That's nice to know now," Nick said wryly.

Eames looked at Violet as he lifted his cup. "Do you live here in Bath, Lady Pendleton?"

"I do, yes. It seemed a nice place to settle after my husband passed. I spent some time here in my youth and have many fond memories. Residing here kept them close in my mind." Her gaze strayed to Nick, and she gave him a shy look.

She'd moved here to feel closer to him, to what they'd shared? He hated her for years, and apparently, she'd felt the opposite. But what could he have done differently? She'd married someone else.

Eames looked to Nick. "Your uncle's estate is doing quite well. Mr. Prendergast has proved an excellent farmer."

Nick had sold the farm after inheriting the dukedom. He hadn't wanted anything that reminded him of all he'd lost. "I'm glad to hear it."

"You should go and pay him a visit if you can," Eames suggested. "I presume you're here because of the Queen. I imagine it's busy being a duke. So many demands and requirements."

As Nick sipped from his cup, he noted Violet's keen interest. She looked between him and Eames with the fascination of a thrilling shuttlecock match.

"It's certainly not anything I anticipated having to learn."

"Nor did your uncle. He was bloody shocked when his cousin and his heirs passed."

Nick recalled the letter he and Maurice had received after that had happened. Uncle Gilbert had summoned Maurice home because he'd suddenly become heir apparent to a dukedom. But he'd never made it. They'd gone to battle at Badajoz a few days later, and Maurice had died.

"Then your poor brother…" Eames's voice trailed off, and Nick was glad the man hadn't completed that thought. This entire line of conversation was pushing him to a place he was trying to get away from.

Eames drank more of his water, then clacked his cup on the table. He turned to Violet. "How did you make His Grace's acquaintance?"

Violet's eyes darted to his, and he saw the question there. "We were recently in attendance at the same house party."

It wasn't an outright lie.

"A house party? I've never been to one. What do you do there?"

"Any number of things," Violet said. "There was dancing, an excursion to St. Andrew's Cathedral in Wells. And fishing."

Eames looked at Nick, his eyes gleaming. "I expect you enjoyed that. Do you remember bringing me fish?"

"I do." He and Maurice often caught so many, they had to share them with the neighbors. Eames had always been their first stop. "Lady Pendleton didn't mention the archery where she won the ladies' contest."

The older gentleman turned an admiring look upon her. "Did you now? Well done."

She blushed prettily. "The Duke won the men's contest."

Eames chortled. "Well, aren't you a match, then?" He finished the last of his water, then climbed to his feet. Nick started to rise, but Eames waved him down. "Sit, my boy. Er, Your Grace. It was a pleasure seeing you. If you get out to Prendergast's, I hope you'll stop in and visit me."

Nick gave him a warm smile. "I'll do that."

Eames bowed to Violet. "A pleasure, my lady."

"The pleasure was mine," she said softly. As they watched him go, her lips curved up. "What a charming gentleman." She turned to Nick. "You knew him well?"

"He was a good friend of my uncle's."

"I remember you speaking of him—your uncle. I'm sorry I didn't meet him." She sipped her water. "What happened? He inherited the dukedom, and it passed briefly to your brother?"

"No. My brother was killed in battle before he could get home. When I became the heir apparent, I was discharged, but I didn't make it back to England before Uncle Gilbert passed away."

She reached for him across the small table but stopped before she touched his hand. "I'm so sorry."

"I'd rather not speak of it," he said. "At least not today. Not here."

She nodded in understanding, and they were quiet a moment before she said, "I confess I'm not certain how to proceed. You said you wanted to see if we would suit."

"I do. But I suppose that doesn't matter if you aren't in agreement."

"I've spent eight years wishing we could start over, that things could be different." She looked away sharply. "I know that isn't really possible."

He hated the sadness and regret in her tone, but couldn't dispute it. "No, it isn't."

"I suppose we should get to know each other—as we are now. As much as I loved yesterday, we can't continue in that vein."

"No, nor was that my intent." He'd thought to take them back to those glorious days, but he knew they'd have to resolve what lay between them. If they could. There were so many things he didn't know about her and longed to. He started with something simple. "How did you become acquainted with Mrs. Linford?"

Her eyes took on a sparkle, and she laughed softly. "It's a terrible story, actually. Well, not *terrible*, but embarrassing. I was at my first ball in London after being married." She cast him a nervous look, and he made a note to tell her that they couldn't keep letting that come between them, not if they truly wanted to look to the future.

She cleared her throat. "Hannah—Mrs. Linford— was there too. It was her *second* ball since marrying Irving. My husband left me immediately, and I didn't see him again for the rest of the evening. Hannah and Irving were kind enough to take me home."

"He just abandoned you there?"

She nodded. "I hadn't yet realized I would enjoy myself far more. But it didn't take me long to learn."

"He sounds like a complete wastrel." If the man weren't already dead, Nick would like to thrash him for treating her like that.

"That is an excellent description," she said. "Luckily, Hannah found me and stayed by my side all evening. We've been friends ever since."

"She seems a lovely woman," he said, thinking that he ought to have behaved better at her house party. He thought of Violet chastising him for nearly ruining her party and winced.

"What is it?" Violet asked.

"I was just thinking that I should have liked to have gotten to know Mrs. Linford better during her party. I was, er, out of practice when it came to socializing."

"You said as much," Violet said wryly. "Not that

anyone would have mistaken you for a gadfly."

He laughed at that, trying to imagine himself running about chatting with people. "I'm not sure I ever would've been taken for that."

"Doubtful, but I remember you being quite amiable. As I said yesterday, women threw themselves at you—and that was before you were a duke. What happened after you inherited? I would've liked to have seen that." Her voice had grown more tentative with the question and subsequent declaration. Again, she was being cautious, not that he blamed her.

He took a drink of his water. "I went to London for the Season—that was 1813. It was difficult. I hadn't acclimated to being a duke, but it seemed I should just get on with it."

Violet hadn't spent any other seasons in London. Clifford had said it wasn't necessary, but she knew it was so that he could carry on his lascivious activities without her around. "Is that when you met your wife?"

"Yes."

"Did you fall in love?" Violet tried to keep her voice nonchalant.

"Violet," he rasped. "Do you really want to talk about this?"

"We need to understand each other. Learn each other. I would like to know everything that happened to you."

And he wanted the same from her. He'd seen the flash of pain in her eyes when she'd mentioned her husband. Speaking of him couldn't be easy, especially to her former lover.

"I met Jacinda very soon after I arrived in London. She was the epitome of grace and kindness, and I knew she'd make an excellent duchess. I didn't fall in love with her."

"Oh."

He let a laugh escape. "You sound relieved."

She cringed. "I didn't mean to. I've no wish to disrespect your wife."

"She understood that I didn't love her. She used to say that she had enough for both of us." His chest constricted as remorse poured through him. She'd deserved more than he could give. If he'd been honest at the start, he might have felt differently. But then he hadn't known he wouldn't love her. He hadn't realized that his heart had still belonged to Violet. And probably always would.

He finished his water. "Did you love your husband?" He suspected he knew the answer already and was every bit as relieved as she'd been.

"Absolutely not." The words came fast and vehement. "My parents arranged the marriage, and it was as horrid as I'd anticipated it to be." She took a deep breath, and the color that had flooded her cheeks receded a bit. "I blamed myself, thinking it was a terrible match because I still loved you. I tried to be fair, to give it—him—a chance, but he was an awful man."

They'd conversed very quietly, and between the music and the discussion around them, he was certain no one could hear what they said. Even so, this seemed too private to share here.

"Do you want more water?" he asked.

She blinked at him, likely due to the abrupt change in topic. "Are we taking the full recommended amount?"

"I don't feel required to do so, do you?" When she shook her head in the negative, he continued, "Then let us depart." He stood and offered his arm.

She took it, and they walked toward the exit. "Did I say something wrong?"

"Not at all. I just think our conversation might be better suited to a different venue." He escorted her outside. "Is your coach about?"

She inclined her head down the street. "Down there."

"I'll walk you to it." As he pondered what she'd told him and what he'd discerned from her behavior, he concluded that her husband had been someone he'd like to meet in a boxing match—and beat to a pulp. "Did he ever hurt you?" He hadn't intended to ask, but the question rose in his mind and spilled from his mouth.

"Once."

Every muscle in Nick's body tensed. But again he reminded himself, what could he have done? "If I'd known that, I would have killed him," he said quietly, his gaze trained straight ahead.

"It wasn't more than what I deserved after what I'd done."

Nick stopped. He turned, uncaring of the spectacle he might cause, and clasped her hand while she still clutched his other arm. "Don't ever say that." Except he'd wished her ill—and he'd thought he'd suffered for his vengeful thoughts. They'd both lived a tangled mess. "You didn't deserve that."

"I'm glad to hear you say so. Maybe now I'll believe it." She smiled up at him, hope shining in her eyes.

God, he wanted to kiss her. Touch her. Hold her. Never let her go.

But he'd already created enough of a scene. He withdrew his arm and took a step back. "Is this your coach?"

She looked over her shoulder and nodded. The coachman jumped down to open the door for her.

"Will you go to the fancy ball tomorrow night?" he asked.

"I thought we were going to live in the present."

He flashed her a grin and saw the subtle change in her eyes—a seductive darkening that made his cock start to stiffen. "As it happens, there is a fancy ball tomorrow night—in the present."

She smiled back at him, and it took everything he had not to follow her into the coach and take her in his arms. "Then yes, I'll go," she said, turning to the door her coachman had just opened.

Before she climbed inside, she looked at Nick over her shoulder. "Did you really come to pay your respects to the Queen?"

He fixed her with an intense stare that carried the full weight of his desire. "No. I came for you."

Chapter Thirteen

WHEN VIOLET ENTERED the Upper Assembly Rooms the following evening, it was exactly like eight years ago—only worse. The women—and men—clamoring for Nick's attention were four or five deep. She anticipated having to wait at least an hour for him to even see her.

She'd underestimated him.

Taller than most, he'd been able to see over the throng and instantly reacted to Violet's arrival. He'd worked to excuse himself, and a scant five minutes later was at her side.

Then he'd promptly asked to dance with her for the next set. It was the most joyous she'd seen him since running into him at Hannah's. He danced as she remembered—his feet light, his smile broad, his laughter easy. And Violet felt as if she floated on air. If there'd been a more perfect night, she didn't remember.

Except she *did* remember.

They'd danced eight years ago at that fancy ball, and it had been just as affecting. The only difference was that he hadn't been accosted by people as soon as they'd left the dance floor. Now, however, he was a duke, and people liked to talk to dukes, particularly just before the Queen was due to visit and they were wrangling for an opportunity to attend her reception on Monday.

Violet made her way to the tearoom for supper. She

sat at a table with a pair of sisters who lived in Sydney Place. Lady Andromeda Spier was a widow like Violet, and her bluestocking younger sister, Cassiopeia Whitfield, was a committed spinster.

The latter woman, who was the same age as Violet, adjusted her gold-rimmed spectacles. "How was the house party, Violet?"

"Very nice, thank you."

"That was hosted by your friend, Mrs. Linford?" Andy asked. She and her sister were rather bookish and didn't always pay attention to social events. In fact, Violet was a bit surprised to see them here tonight. They hadn't danced, however.

"It was, yes."

"Who was the gentleman you were dancing with?" Cassie picked up a cake and took a bite, her gaze politely inquisitive.

Violet stifled a smile. It didn't surprise her that Cassie had no idea who Nick was.

"Oh, that was Mr. Bateman," Andy said. "I remember him from when he lived here before. Don't you?" She turned her head toward her sister. They looked somewhat similar—Andy with blonde locks while Cassie's had a bit of red along with the gold. But their eyes were distinctive, even when one discounted Cassie's spectacles. Andy possessed serene, intelligent gray eyes and Cassie's were a bold hazel with sharp gold flecks.

Cassie tipped her head to the side, considering her older sister's question. "I'm not sure. Mr. Bateman…"

"He's the Duke of Kilve now," Andy said, turning her head to Violet. "Isn't that right?"

Violet nodded.

"And how do you know him?" Cassie asked rather

absently as she picked up another cake.

"They were acquainted before," Andy answered before Violet could.

Violet froze. She hadn't considered that anyone would know that. But acquaintance was nothing, she reasoned. Andy had just admitted to being acquainted to him back when he'd been Mr. Bateman. "Yes, I met him in Bath eight years ago—before I was married. We were reacquainted at Hannah's house party."

Andy gave her a shrewd smile. "Well, he seems to have taken a liking to you. I remember thinking he liked you then too. Or am I misremembering?" She tapped her finger against her lip briefly before dropping it to her lap. "No, I'm quite certain, but then I am most observant."

Cassie rolled her eyes. "Yes, yes. We know."

Violet preferred to change the subject. She didn't want to draw attention to herself or to Nick. Or worse, to both of them. Together.

Why?

Because what if nothing happened? What if they decided they didn't suit?

Yesterday's conversation at the Pump Room had been revelatory, and even though he'd quite aroused her desire with his declaration that he'd come to Bath for *her*—she shivered again just thinking of the look he'd given her—she didn't hold any illusions that things were perfect. There was still a great deal to resolve. But she'd been encouraged by what he'd said, that she hadn't deserved her unhappy marriage. Perhaps they could find their way back to each other. She was almost afraid to hope.

As if conjured by her thoughts, Nick entered the tearoom. He scanned the room, his gaze moving from table to table until he saw Violet. Upon finding her, he wove his way in her direction.

Violet didn't want him to come here. It would only increase the sisters' speculation. On the other hand, it wasn't as if they were gossips. Contrarily, they were rather private and kept to themselves.

In any case, it was too late, because Nick was already at the table.

"Good evening, ladies," he said.

"Good evening, Your Grace," Cassie said before sipping from her glass of ratafia. "We were just talking about you."

"Were you?" His gaze drifted to Violet, and she detected a bit of humor.

"We were trying to place you," Andy said. "I remembered you from when you used to live here. Before you were a duke. Kilve isn't that far—do you come back often?"

"No, actually. But I may rectify that. I'd forgotten how much I enjoy Bath." He slid a look at Violet, a smile teasing his lips. She stared at him, trying to silently communicate that he should refrain from saying such things. Honestly, it wasn't what he was saying but how he was saying them. He was flirting. In front of people. She wasn't ready for that. And frankly, she was surprised he was.

Cassie abruptly stood. "I need to visit the retiring room. Please excuse me."

Andy's mouth twitched in the barest grimace at her sister's indelicate comment—Cassie was not the most socially astute—and hastened to join her. "I'll go with you." She smiled at both Violet and Nick. "Lovely to see you both. You should come round for tea, Violet."

"I'll do that, thank you." While she wasn't close

friends with the sisters, she would count them above acquaintances. They were quite intelligent, if a bit eccentric.

After they left, Violet sagged against the back of her chair.

"Is something the matter?" Nick sat down beside her.

"They remembered that we'd been acquainted eight years ago."

"So?"

"So they also noticed that we danced tonight." She glanced around, wondering if anyone was looking in their direction. "Do we want to draw attention to ourselves?"

He was quiet a moment. "I hadn't considered that. I suppose we must—consider it, I mean."

"It seems prudent not to appear as if we are courting."

"The rules are a bit different once you're widowed, aren't they?" He gave her a rueful smile. "I admit I don't really know."

She laughed softly. "I don't either. I just know that we need to be careful. And with that, I think I'll go home."

"Did you walk? I could escort you."

"I didn't—my house isn't quite close enough, particularly given tonight's abysmal weather." They'd arrived amid a cold, persistent rain.

"I know where your house is. Mine is at the near end of Royal Crescent."

She stared at him. "That's not far from mine at all. You planned that."

His slow smile was thoroughly self-satisfied. "I've planned everything." He lifted a shoulder. "Almost. It all depends on you, of course. If you'd like to leave now, I think I might too. I may have somewhere to be, actually." He looked at her in question. No, in *invitation*.

"I do believe I'm ready to retire." She stood, and he made a show of taking her hand and bowing.

"Until we meet again, Lady Pendleton."

Violet's heart thundered, and her breathing quickened. Anticipation raced through her, and she had to work to modulate her steps as she made her way from the tearoom. She was achingly aware of his gaze burning into her back.

It took forever to get her coach, and when she didn't see Nick leave the Assembly Rooms behind her, she worried that he wasn't coming. However, as her vehicle departed, she caught sight of him exiting.

As soon as she reached her small town house, she informed her butler that she was retiring. He would also retire, which would leave the night footman. Violet's maid, Chalke, who also served as the housekeeper, would go down to her chamber as soon as she finished helping Violet prepare for bed.

She wondered how Nick would get into the house, but since he'd said he'd planned everything, she had to assume he had things well in hand. Did that include knowing the location of her bedchamber?

Chalke, a middle-aged woman with bright red hair, met her at the door to her room. "Good evening, my lady. Did you have a pleasant time?"

Violet smiled at the maid, whom she'd hired when she'd moved to Bath two and a half years ago. She'd liked Chalke immediately. The woman had a motherly air about her but also a sense of mischief and warmth that Violet had sorely needed in her life after Clifford's death. "I did, thank you." She walked into her dressing room, Chalke trailing her.

Violet set down her reticule and removed her earrings while Chalke unfastened the pearls adorning Violet's neck. "Did you dance?" the maid asked.

"I did." Violet set the jewelry on the dressing table.

After setting the necklace beside the earrings, Chalke began unlacing the back of Violet's gown. "But you didn't stay for the whole ball. Are you feeling all right?"

"Yes, thank you."

Chalke made a noise in her throat that sounded a bit like disapproval. "I can feel how tense you are. If you don't tell me what's the matter, I'll make you drink one of my toddies. And not the ones you like either."

Violet looked over her shoulder and met Chalke's eyes. "Are you threatening me?"

Chalke gave her a smile that was really more of a smirk. "I'm fussing. I think you secretly like that."

"I'm fine, truly."

"You've been on edge a few days now. It's as if you're waiting for something to happen." Chalke helped her out of the dress and took it to the armoire. "You can confide in me. If you want to."

Yes, she could talk to her. In fact, Violet had done that many times during Chalke's employment. She knew all about the man from Violet's past—the one she'd fallen love with and had to walk away from. What Chalke didn't know was that Violet had become reacquainted with that man. Violet hadn't wanted to talk about him, not when it seemed she was moving forward alone. Then when he'd appeared at the Sydney Hotel, she'd been afraid to share her excitement. She was so afraid it would evaporate. Yes, she was waiting for something to happen—good or bad.

Violet kicked off her shoes. "You remember the man

from my past?"

"The one you met here in Bath?" Chalke returned to unlace her corset.

"The same. I didn't tell you, but he was at Hannah's house party."

Chalke's eyes widened as she looked up at Violet. "You've been keeping secrets! How lovely." She chuckled softly. "I imagine it was wonderful to see him."

"It was certainly surprising. Well, he's here now."

Chalke removed the corset and set it aside before returning to help take the petticoat over Violet's head. "Here in Bath? That's extraordinary! Was he at the ball tonight?"

"He was."

"It's no wonder you're apprehensive. Is there a hope that you'll reconcile?"

"Yes." But that was all she had right now—a hope. They'd discussed nothing about the future. Which they shouldn't. Not until they determined if they would suit. She wanted to know so many things about him. Maybe she could ask him tonight, provided he actually came.

Do you think there will be talking?

Violet stifled a smile.

"I can sense the joy in you. I do hope it all works out."

"Thank you, Chalke."

When Violet was ready for bed, she went into her chamber and paced. Her window overlooked the tiny back garden, which was so dark, she wouldn't be able to see him—if he even came that way.

If he came at all.

Why was she doubting him? Because she still couldn't quite believe he was here, that they *might* have a chance.

Teeming with nervous energy, she tightened her dressing gown around her and left her chamber. She made her way downstairs to the front sitting room. The street was somewhat illuminated, with lanterns spilling light at intervals.

Suddenly, she heard a commotion from downstairs. There came the distinct sound of a cat howling followed by a woman shrieking and then crockery shattering.

Violet dashed to the back stairs and flew down to the lower level. What she saw in the kitchen made her slap her hand over her mouth and her eyes goggle in shock.

Sprawled on the floor was Nick. The cook, Mrs. Spindle, stood over him, her chest heaving and her face bright red. She jabbed her finger toward him. "Thief!"

Chalke rushed into the kitchen in a state of half-dress, a robe pulled over her chemise but not yet fastened, carrying a candle. "What the devil?"

"A thief!" Mrs. Spindle repeated.

Violet lowered her hand. "He's not a thief."

Chalke met her eyes for a moment, then laughter spilled from her mouth. "Oh my goodness." She knew precisely who their guest was.

"He's, ah, a friend of mine," Violet said lamely.

"Yes, a friend," Chalke said, trying to stop laughing.

The butler ran into the kitchen at that moment, his coat askew and his hair tousled. "What—" His gaze took in the scene, and he looked to Chalke, blinking.

"We've a minor situation." Violet summoned a serene smile that was quite at odds with the thundering of her heart. "Nothing I can't handle if you'd care to go back to bed, Lavery."

The butler straightened his coat. "I heard Mrs.

Spindle shout 'thief.' Do I need to alert the magistrate?"

"No, thank you, Lavery," Violet said hurriedly. "There's no thievery going on. Just a bit of a commotion." She smiled at him, hoping he would take himself off to bed.

"Look at this mess." Mrs. Spindle gestured to the shards of pottery littering the floor. "He tripped over Ginger's dish of milk and then sent some of the crockery flying. Thief or no, he's a menace."

Ginger, the orange tabby cat, came prowling back into the kitchen. She approached Nick, who gave her a stern stare. In response, she nuzzled his arm and began to purr.

"Traitor," Mrs. Spindle muttered.

Nick stroked the cat's head before standing. "I beg your pardon for breaking the pottery. Perhaps the doorway is not the best place for a cat dish."

"Perhaps stealing into people's houses isn't the best way to spend an evening!" Mrs. Spindle retorted.

"So there *is* thievery?" Lavery asked, sounding incredibly perplexed. He looked at Chalke, who couldn't seem to stop laughing. Violet had to acknowledge the entire situation was rather amusing.

"It's an excellent alarm should anyone—like you— decide to invade Lady Pendleton's house." Mrs. Spindle turned to Violet. "Why would your friend sneak in the back door?"

Chalke stopped laughing with a cough. She touched the cook's arm while gesturing for Violet to take Nick upstairs. "Let me help you clean up, Mrs. Spindle."

Violet took Nick's hand and dragged him up the stairs to the ground floor. She continued up, but halfway to the first floor, she turned and broke into laughter, unable to control herself any longer. "What the devil were you doing?"

The light in the stairwell was dim from the wall sconce, but she could make out the arch of his brow. "Isn't it obvious?"

"I suppose so, yes, but couldn't you have been more…discreet?"

"I rather thought sneaking in through the servants' entrance *was* discreet."

She laughed harder, shaking her head.

"Will this be a problem?" he asked. "Of course not. Otherwise, you would have had me leave."

Taking a deep breath, she wiped at her eyes. "My maid will set things right with Mrs. Spindle."

"What about your butler? He seemed perturbed. When he wasn't confused, that is."

Violet started laughing again, and Nick put his hand beneath her elbow. He guided her up the stairs. "Let's get to your chamber."

She paused on the next landing, gasping for breath. "Do you know where that is?"

He hesitated before saying, "No."

"So, let me understand," she said, trying not to laugh again and failing. "Your plan was to sneak into my kitchen and skulk about my house until you happened upon my bedchamber?"

"I don't, as a rule, skulk—"

She waved a hand to cut him off and managed to stop laughing for a moment. "Oh, I think you skulked plenty at Hannah's party."

"Skulking is not the same as brooding." He snaked his arm around her waist and drew her tight against his chest.

The laughter left her in a whoosh, but her elevated

heart rate didn't calm. If anything, her pulse increased. "I suppose it isn't."

"Now, would you like to lead me to your chamber, or should I continue with my *plan* right here?" His fingers curled into her back and his other hand clasped her waist, holding her firm against him. The fabrics of her night rail and robe were much thinner than her regular clothes. She could feel him—his heat, his hardness, *everything*—quite distinctly. Her knees threatened to give way, and she could just imagine toppling him down the stairs. This night only needed that.

No, this night needed him to take her to her chamber. *Now.*

"Up to the next floor, turn left, first door on the left." She sounded breathless and desperate. Which made sense since she was both of those things and so much more.

"I don't know." He lowered his head and lightly brushed his lips along her neck, causing her to shiver. "There's something delectably naughty about our current situation." He licked a path to her ear.

"The servants could come up at any moment."

"Exactly."

Oh dear, the servants. What on earth would they say? She imagined Chalke would congratulate her—she'd said many times that she only wanted to see Violet happy. But Mrs. Spindle? Or worse, Lavery? He would be shocked. Knowing that didn't change her mind.

She tangled her hands in the thick, dark crop of his hair. "I don't care where we are, so long as we're together."

His hand moved up her back and cupped her neck, positioning her so that he could take her mouth. And take it he did. His lips crushed hers in reckless abandon, his tongue sweeping inside to claim what she would freely offer.

After a thorough and quite pleasurable exploration, he swept her into his arms. She clasped her arms around him as he strode up the stairs. He managed to open the door to the first floor with his hand and keep hold of her quite securely. He easily found her chamber, and once they were inside, he carried her to the bed, where he laid her gently on the coverlet.

"Shall I lock the door?" he asked.

"I'm not sure it's necessary," she said wryly. "Everyone knows you're here. I daresay we won't be disturbed."

He stood near the bed and swiped his hand over his mouth. The light from the candle next to her bed flickered across his handsome features. "Should I go? I didn't mean to create a mess."

"It's not a mess I can't tidy. And anyway, I don't care." She'd spent too many years dreaming of him, wanting him. There was no way she would turn him away. Not now. Probably not ever. She knelt up on the bed and drew her robe away from her body, then dropped it to the floor. "Come here."

He moved next to the bed and looked down at her, his eyes a dark, turbulent gray.

"You are overdressed, Duke."

"Perhaps you'd like to remedy that, my lady."

"With pleasure." Violet tore apart the knot of his cravat and pulled the fabric from his neck. She slid her hands down to his chest and pushed his coat from his shoulders. As the garment fell to the floor behind him, she unbuttoned his waistcoat. All the while, she stared into his eyes, not wanting to break the connection moving between them. It had been so long since she'd felt close to someone. And now that he was here, she wanted to savor every moment.

He shrugged out of the waistcoat and backed away, giving her a flash of alarm. "I'm taking off my boots."

She exhaled, watching as he perched on a chair in the corner and removed his boots. His stockings followed, and he padded barefoot to the bed.

Reaching for him, she pressed her palm against his chest. His heart beat strong and sure beneath the linen of his shirt. She pulled the hem from his waistband and pushed the fabric up his chest. He lifted his arms and whisked the shirt over his head.

As the bare expanse of his chest was exposed to her, she splayed her hands across his muscles. He was so different than he'd been before—harder, wider. "You look as if you do manual labor." She ran her fingertips over his flesh, loving the feel of him.

"I work with my tenants on occasion. And I ride. And fish, of course."

She smoothed her hands over his collarbones, shoulders, and down his biceps. "You still row." She remembered the day he'd taken her out on the canal at Sydney Gardens.

"I do. It's a bit trickier in the ocean."

She looked at him sharply. "Is it safe?"

"Is anything?"

She wondered at his question, but not for long as he drew her night rail over her head. Cool air rushed over her, and her nipples stiffened beneath the chill.

"You look cold. We can't have that." He lowered his head and drew her flesh into his mouth, his lips caressing her breast as he tongued her nipple.

Desire gripped her hard and fast as sensation rioted

through her. It had been so long since she'd been touched like this. She couldn't compare him to Clifford. There was no similarity whatsoever aside from the fact that they were in a bed.

He cupped her breasts, lifting them as he feasted on first one and then the other, his lips and tongue wreaking delicious mayhem on her senses. She closed her eyes and cast her head back, giving herself over to his touch.

With one hand, he clasped the back of her neck and eased her back until she was lying flat across the bed. She stretched her legs out, and they dangled over the edge of the mattress. He stood between them, the wool of his pantaloons brushing her bare thighs.

Continuing to lavish attention on her breasts, he moved one hand to her clitoris. He'd taught her that word eight years ago just before he'd given her the first orgasm she'd ever experienced. Then he'd explained how he was going to put his mouth on her there. She'd tried to stop him, horrified that he would suggest such a thing. But then he'd kissed her flesh, and she'd come undone.

He parted her folds with his fingers while his thumb worked to build the pressure inside her to a boiling point. She cried out as her hips began to move of their own accord. She couldn't have stopped her body's responses if she'd wanted to.

His mouth left her breast, his tongue tracing up her sternum to her collarbone, then ascending her neck until he licked along her jaw. "Violet, do you remember when we were together before?"

"Every moment." She'd lived on those memories.

"Open your eyes."

She did as he bade and saw him looking down at her,

his gaze dark and dangerously seductive. Her body quivered with longing.

"We didn't talk beforehand—last time. If there's anything you don't want me to do, or anything you don—"

"Just kiss me, Nick." She clasped his neck and drew his head down so she could show him how badly she wanted him. She arched up with her whole body, spearing her tongue into his mouth.

He slanted his head, and his fingers dug gently into her neck as he held her captive. The kiss was deep and dark, almost bruising. It was everything she'd wanted for as long as she could remember.

His hips snapped into hers, and she could feel the length of his erection through his garments. She thrust back, wrapping her legs around his hips. The hand that was still between them worked her flesh, tormenting her until she pulled away and cried out, unable to contain her passion.

"Kiss me everywhere," she rasped.

He obliged, his mouth moving across her cheek to her ear and making a slow, seductive descent. He paused at her breasts again, using his teeth this time to lightly nip her tightened flesh. She moaned and rotated her hips, seeking release.

Then his lips were on her abdomen, leaving a trail of fire and need along her flesh. He gripped her hips and dragged his tongue downward. "Open your legs." He pushed her thighs apart and then did the same to her folds, using his thumbs to stroke and tease her. Mindless with need, she arched off the bed.

Then he answered her silent pleas and put his mouth on her. His touch was soft at first, gently licking her with his tongue as his thumb moved across her flesh.

She thrust her hands into his hair and tugged at the locks, urging him to give her what she wanted, what she needed.

He sucked her clitoris, stoking her release to the breaking point. When his finger slid inside her, she fell over the edge as an orgasm claimed her body. She shook with the force of it, her legs quivering and her breath coming in rapid pants.

He tended her, his mouth and fingers taking her through her ecstasy until she emerged on the other side, spent and satisfied.

"God, Violet, you are the most passionate of women." He came over her and kissed her almost savagely. "You're a gift," he growled against her mouth.

Satisfied was perhaps a premature assessment. Need built inside her once more—fast and hot. She reached between them and tried to unbutton his fall, but her fingers were made of jelly.

He broke away from her and unfastened his pantaloons, then shucked them from his body as quickly as possible. While he was gone, she turned on the bed. He climbed up beside her.

She caressed his shoulder, his back, trailing her hand down until she came to his backside. "I dreamed of this moment for so long," she whispered.

He moved between her legs, gazing down at her. "I would be lying if I said I'd done the same," he said hoarsely. "I worked very hard to keep you from my mind."

"I understand." She did, but that didn't keep unshed tears from stinging her throat. "I know I hurt you, and if I could take it back, I would."

"Shhh." He leaned down and brushed his lips over hers. "It wasn't your choice. I know that."

"No, but I *had* choices." A tear leaked from her eye and snaked down her temple into her hair.

He kissed her forehead, her eyelid, her tear-stained temple, then smoothed her hair back, his fingers gently brushing the locks. "You didn't. Not really. And I should have realized that."

"You would have if you'd gotten my letter," she said bitterly.

"We can't look back anymore. I don't want to."

She felt him tense and wondered if he was trying to convince himself as much as her. She cupped the side of his face, feeling the faint scruff of his beard at this late hour. "I want to look forward. With you."

He kissed her again, their mouths melding in perfect harmony. His hand moved between them, stroking her eager flesh. She moaned as he slid inside.

She wrapped her legs around him, but he didn't move. He simply stayed there, filling her, while he kissed her tenderly.

Joy burst through her as ecstasy swirled, ready to explode within her once more. She clung to him as he started to pulse within her, withdrawing slightly, then thrusting back, increasing her sensation of completion. It was as if she'd found the part of her that was missing.

She squeezed his backside and tightened her legs around him. He pulled back then, almost leaving her, before plunging back into her. Then he did it again. And again. And again until she was overcome with need. She clutched at him desperately, her harsh cries filling the room. When she didn't think she could survive another moment, she came, her mind and spirit breaking into tiny, rapturous pieces that she knew he could put back together again. Having him here meant she could be whole.

His body tensed, and she held him tight as his orgasm ripped through him. He shouted and, she laughed, unable to keep the happiness inside her.

She stroked his back until his rhythm slowed, though his breathing was still hard and fast. He kissed her, touching her face, before he rolled to the side. She reached over and laid her hand on his chest as it rose and fell, eventually slowing to an almost normal cadence. His skin was warm, and she leaned close to press a kiss beside his nipple.

"I don't think I have words," he said finally.

"I don't think I do either, but we should probably find some." She rolled away from him and got up to tidy herself at the washbasin in the corner. She returned to the bed with a cloth for him.

He took it, and she turned and went to pick up her robe. Before she could put it on, he said, "No. Please. Come back to me."

He pulled the coverlet back and slipped into the bedclothes, then beckoned her to join him.

She did so, feeling suddenly shy, which was silly. He knew her as intimately as anyone ever had. As anyone ever would.

She slid into bed beside him, and he drew her close. He kissed her hairline, his lips lingering against her. "What words do you think we need to find?"

Gathering her courage, she turned to look him in the eye. "The words that will lead us back to each other."

Chapter Fourteen

NICK WAS CONFUSED. "I thought we had."

She traced her finger along his chest. "There are still things we don't know—eight years is a long time."

Her touch was distracting, and he was already thinking of the next things he wanted to do to her. "If you don't stop that, there will be no words. At least none that aren't 'please,' 'don't stop,' or perhaps 'harder.'"

Her hand stilled, but her lips turned up in a sultry smile. "You're trying to avoid conversing."

"Perhaps." It wasn't that he didn't want to. Actually, it was precisely that. "It's difficult for me to talk about the past." That his present held joy was astonishing. He was afraid of ruining his fortune.

"Would you like me to start?" she asked softly, her lips curving into a gentle, sweet smile.

He brought her head down and kissed her. She pulled back after a moment, and he gave her a lopsided smile. "If you must."

She swatted at his chest and lay down beside him, snuggling into the crook of his arm, her head on his shoulder. "I wished we'd run away together. In my mind, we did. I'd imagine us eloping to Scotland and never coming back. We'd live in a tiny cottage in the Highlands where we would have our children and our love, and we didn't need anything else."

It sounded idyllic. "Why the Highlands?"

She shrugged. "I don't know. Because it was far

away, I suppose."

"I imagined us farther than that—America."

"Did you?" She leaned up to look at him again. "I thought you hated me."

"I did, but once in a while, I'd let myself fantasize about what could have been." Particularly when he'd been miserable on campaign with the Fourth. "If you hadn't been—" He stopped himself before he said something crude he would regret. She didn't deserve that. He'd meant what he'd said, that she truly hadn't had any choices. His twenty-two-year-old self hadn't been smart enough to know that. "Forgive me," he said.

Her gaze turned soft. "There's nothing to forgive." She kissed his cheek, then settled back against him.

He found he wanted to know the specifics. After all this time, he could learn the truth. "How long after you left Bath did you marry Pendleton?" He recalled reading about it, but didn't remember—or maybe he'd purposely forgotten.

"Almost immediately. It was about four weeks, I think. Just long enough for my father to arrange the marriage settlement and have the banns read."

"You had no say in the marriage?"

"None. I sometimes wonder if they chose the worst possible person, someone who was bound to make me unhappy."

When he thought of what she'd already told him about Pendleton, he wanted to rouse the man from the dead and kill him all over again. But perhaps his anger was misguided. Perhaps he ought to direct it toward the living—namely, her mother and father. "Surely your parents wouldn't be so cruel?"

"I wouldn't have thought so, but they refused to let

me marry the man I loved."

Loved. She used the word in the past tense. He thought she loved him still, but she hadn't plainly said so. Did he love her? He'd loved her then—as much as he'd grown to hate her, he didn't doubt that he'd loved her first.

"Tell me about Pendleton," he said gruffly, both wanting to stoke his hatred of the man and realizing it would be torture to hear. He suspected she wanted to reveal her secrets. She'd been the one to ask for this conversation.

She hesitated before asking, "What do you want to know?"

"Whatever you want to tell me." And when it became too much, he would say so.

"He was a philanderer. I hated being married to him."

A philanderer...Nick tamped down his ire. What good would it do now? "I'm sorry to hear you had to endure such a marriage. And there were no children?" He, of course, knew she'd been unable to carry any, as Mrs. Linford had told him. He thought of her dream of the Highlands—there'd been children in it.

"I can't carry them." Her response was so faint, he had to strain to hear it. "I became pregnant several times. After the third loss, Clifford decided I wasn't worth lying with. As sad as I was, my relief was greater."

Nick squeezed her tight against his side. There was a unique pain associated with losing a child, and he suspected the desolation was the same even if they hadn't been born. "Fate hasn't been particularly kind to either one of us. How did Pendleton die?"

"A lengthy illness, compounded by excessive drink, I

believe. And perhaps laudanum. He started taking it for coughing fits. By the end, he was ingesting far more than the prescribed amount."

"I can't imagine you were sad when he passed."

"No, which made me feel a bit guilty."

He kissed her head again. "You mustn't."

"Was your marriage happy?"

"Yes." As happy as he'd expected to be after losing Maurice and then his uncle.

She propped herself up on her elbow and looked at him. "Just yes?"

His muscles tensed as discomfort tripped through him. "What more can I say that you would really want to hear, Violet?" He pushed himself up, thinking it was maybe time for him to go.

She sat up too and moved close to him, placing her hand on his shoulder. "Pardon me, please. I didn't mean to press. I am sure she was a lovely woman; otherwise, you wouldn't have chosen her."

He angled his upper body toward her. She was so beautiful in the faint light of the candle behind her. Her eyes were rich and earthy, her hair pale and ethereal. She was a mixture of light and dark, of his happiest moments and his saddest. He didn't want any more of the latter.

He lifted a lock of her hair from her shoulder and fingered the soft tresses. "I prefer not to look backward. That doesn't mean I don't want to share things with you. I just want to forge ahead."

"I understand."

"And right now, I'm focused on the fact that we are both here, and you make me feel lighter than I have in years." A smile tugged at his lips. "Well, once I surrendered to your persistence."

"My persistence?"

"You don't think you were persistent at the house party?"

"I'm not sure what you mean. I wasn't trying to pursue you."

He ran his thumb along her jaw. "Truly?"

She tried to look him in the eye, but a laugh escaped her parted lips. "I tried not to. Your deterrence was rather effective."

"It's difficult not to be won over by a woman who can hold her own after tumbling out of a boat, who can win an archery contest with ease, and who is eager to help my dearest friend."

"You make me sound far more exciting than I really am," she said softly, looking away in embarrassment.

He put his finger beneath her chin and drew her to look at him. He stared into her eyes, willing her to believe him. "You are everything I want right now." He'd stopped thinking about what he wanted, because those things kept disappearing. Even as he said the words, fear gripped him. Maybe he should go…

Before he could take flight, she cupped his face in her hands and kissed him. When she drew back, but only slightly, her brow curved into a provocative arch. "*Right* now?"

"I think so." He pressed her back onto the mattress and came over her. "Unless you think I should go. I will need to leave before morning, in any case."

She wrapped her arms around him and stroked the plane of his back, one hand trailing down to his backside. Her touch was divine and exactly what he needed to banish the darkness from his mind. He hoped forever, but accepted it would likely just be for now.

Darkness had a way of finding him.

THE GENTLEMAN LOOKING back at him from the glass was hardly familiar. Violet had insisted that he wear something akin to court dress, which he despised and had worn on only a very few occasions. Rather than have something made, he'd sent for one of his suits of clothing from London. Now he was trussed up in a costume of dark green with lilies of the valley embroidered on the coat. The Queen liked flowers.

He looked forward to seeing Violet in her court clothing, almost as much as he looked forwarding to divesting her of it.

They'd spent the last three days in a rapturous bliss. He'd taken her for a boat ride in the canal on Friday, and that evening, they'd happened—on purpose—to encounter each other at a party celebrating All Hallows' Eve. It had been a festive affair, despite Nick exerting a great deal of effort to avoid the various games of divination. He didn't need such things telling him his fortune, not when he could be assured it would be bad.

He'd meant what he'd told Violet—he wanted to live in the present and enjoy each moment. And that was precisely what they'd done. He hadn't seen her today since he'd ridden out to meet the Queen's procession. Tomorrow they would likely visit the Pump Room when the Queen was there, and the following day they would celebrate Gunpowder Treason Day with everyone else in Bath. It was, he realized, the happiest he'd been in a very long time. In forever, maybe.

Nick turned from the mirror. "Will I do, Rand?"

The valet sized him up and gave an approving nod.

"Splendidly." He handed Nick the three-cornered cocked hat, which Nick placed upon his head. "And now you are perfect."

"Harrumph."

Nick departed the house and climbed into his waiting coach. The traffic would be abominable as people had been crowding the streets all day. The city was so illuminated with lanterns that it almost seemed like day.

He wished he were fetching Violet along the way, but they'd decided they couldn't arrive together. Still, he looked out at her house as they passed her street and saw her coach sitting before it. She hadn't left yet. Good, he would watch her entrance.

He was one of the first to arrive at 93 Sydney Place, where he was shown into a sitting room to await the time when the Queen would receive visitors. A scant quarter hour later, he was treated to a sight that took his breath away.

Violet appeared in the doorway. She wore a gown of bishop's blue velvet made wide and full with hoops. Snowy lace trimmed in gold fell from her sleeves, and several ostrich feathers stood high atop her head. Her blonde hair curled gently around her face, and sparkling sapphires adorned her ears and neck. She swept forward, and he couldn't take his eyes from her.

She was intercepted by a few people, but her gaze found his, and her lips teased into a soft smile. Impatient, he went to her. It was then that he realized the embroidery on her dress was also lilies of the valley.

They exchanged pleasantries until the others moved on, leaving them alone, if only for a moment.

Moving to her side, he leaned close to her ear. "You look stunning."

"Not as fine as you." She raked his body with a

lingering stare, causing his blood to heat and his body to harden in highly inappropriate places.

"Stop regarding me like that. We're due to see the Queen at any moment."

Violet gave him a saucy smile just before the footman announced the Queen was ready. There were several peers in attendance, but Nick outranked them all, save the Queen's son, the Duke of Clarence, who was already with her. Of the guests in the sitting room, Nick was admitted to her presence first.

Queen Charlotte sat in a wide gilt chair. She looked a bit pale, but then she'd come to Bath to take the waters in an effort to improve her health. Though seventy-three, her large, dark eyes were still sharp.

After he bowed, she gestured for him to come stand beside her. "You do not come to court very often, Kilve."

"I do not, Your Majesty. I beg your pardon." He offered another bow.

"I know you were in mourning for a while. Presumably you aren't any longer?"

"No."

She nodded. "Good."

Others were shown in, and they bowed and curtsied, answering the Queen's questions with poise and grace. Violet came forward and dropped into a deep curtsey.

"Are those lilies of the valley, Lady Pendleton?" the Queen asked before turning her head to look at Nick. "And you are wearing them too," she noted. "Do I need to be aware of a forthcoming match?" she asked him.

"No, Your Majesty. It is simply a coincidence."

Charlotte's full lips curved into a delighted smile. "A charming one."

Once everyone had paid their respects to Queen Charlotte, she motioned for Nick to come closer. "I would be remiss if I didn't thank you for your service. You fought at Badajoz, did you not?"

"I did, Your Majesty."

"Such a terrible battle. Wellington has told me all about it—as much as I can bear." She looked at him intently for a moment, then seemed to recall something, her eyes flickering. "You fought alongside your brother. Wellington told me that too. He was about to be discharged so that he could return home and inherit."

That wasn't quite right—Uncle Gil had still been alive at that time—but Nick didn't correct her.

"So awful to have lived through such an ordeal and to lose your brother at the same time. I'm sorry for your loss, and we are deeply grateful for his sacrifice."

Nick inclined his head. Misery and despair coursed through him while the old tang of terror soured his mouth. Ordeal wasn't an adequate word. It had been hell on earth, and after Maurice fell, Nick hadn't cared if he lived or died. He'd protected his brother's body, fighting everyone off with a rage that some had later described as otherworldly. Nick couldn't say because he didn't remember the specifics after Maurice had taken his last breath.

His eye caught Violet watching him. She stood nearby, probably close enough to hear what the Queen had said. Observing the creases in her brow and the troubled set of her mouth, he'd say she had.

The audience ended a short time later, and Violet found Nick in the sitting room as people were departing for their coaches. His body thrummed with tension—the conversation with the Queen had unsettled him, and the confines of the reception room had made him restless.

"Are you—"

Nick cut her off before she finished. "I need to walk." He abruptly turned and stalked from the house, taking to the sidewalk and devouring it in long strides.

He tried to push the distressing thoughts to the back of his mind, as he typically did, but for some reason Maurice's face kept appearing to him. Teasing when they were boys, laughing before he'd bought his commission, gray and lifeless in the midst of battle.

The pernicious tendrils of despair wound around him. He clenched his fists at his sides as he walked, moving faster as if he could run from the fear that threatened to send him to his knees.

"Nick! Nick!"

He'd no idea how many times she shouted his name, but by the time he paused and turned toward the street, her coach was stopped several yards behind him. Her footman jumped down and opened the door, then helped her out.

She had to go slowly because of the ridiculous volume of her dress. But once she was on the sidewalk, she rushed to meet him. "Nick?"

He didn't respond, just stared at her. He couldn't think of a thing to say. His mind, overcome with emotion and memory, was shutting down. Good, perhaps then he could forget.

She took his hand. "Come with me."

He didn't object as she dragged him to her coach. He moved much more slowly than before, feeling as though he'd been coated in lead. Everything felt so heavy all of a sudden.

The footman helped her back into the coach, and

Nick climbed in behind her, taking the rear-facing seat because her skirts were completely occupying the other one.

A moment later, they were on their way.

"What happened?" she asked.

"She asked me about Maurice."

"I heard that." Her voice was soft, comforting, and he calmed a little. "Do you want to tell me why you're upset?"

"Not really." He registered the disappointment in her eyes even though she tried to mask it. "I watched him die. I tried to save him, but I couldn't."

She came off the seat and knelt on the floor. Looking up at him, she rested her hands on his thighs. "Nick, I'm so sorry for all you've endured."

All I'd endured. Yes, there'd been so much death, but in many ways, his brother had been the toughest loss. He and Maurice had grown up together. They'd lived while their siblings, their mother, their father had all perished. Through it all, including losing Violet, Nick had known that he would survive, that he would be all right—because he had his brother by his side.

"It's… Sometimes it's too much."

Her hands moved gently over him, massaging his muscles, taking the bitter edge off his tension. "I wish I'd met him. You always spoke of him with such affection."

"I'd give anything to have him back." How many times had he whispered that plea in the dark days following Jacinda's death? And again after Elias passed? If Maurice had been there, Nick could have managed so much better. Maybe the ice wouldn't have taken over.

She knelt at his feet, touching him, stroking him,

infusing him with quiet strength until the coach came to a stop.

"Where are we?" he asked.

"My house. Come inside and have a drink. Then you can walk home—if you want. I'll send my footman back to let your coachman know you've gone home."

A drink sounded good. Hell, several drinks sounded even better.

He climbed down from the coach and helped her to descend. Her skirts crashed into his legs before she moved toward the short flight of steps leading to her stoop.

"I should go." He wasn't fit company.

Her coach pulled away, leaving them alone in front of her house.

She turned to face him. "If you do, I'll follow you. I'm not leaving you alone. Not until I'm satisfied you're all right."

"Violet, I'm fine. I've had years to cope with his death." With all of it.

"Yes, and you became the Duke of Ice." She stepped toward him. "Is that really who you want to be? Or would you rather be the man I've spent the past week with?"

He was content as the Duke of Ice. His life was ordered, simple, and, for the most part, without upset. But over the past week, he'd found joy again—to a point. He realized he was still controlled, still ensuring he managed his emotions.

She took his hand again and pulled him toward the house. He allowed her to move him several steps before he stopped short. She careened backward but quickly regained her balance.

He dropped her hand. "I need to go, Violet."

"I'm not letting you."

His despair hardened to anger. "It isn't for you to decide."

The door to her house opened, and the butler held it wide.

"We can't do this in the street," she said, her eyes narrowing. "*Go. Inside. Please.*"

She clasped his hand once more, her grip like iron, and gritted her teeth as she gave him a tug.

He wanted to dig his heels in, but he couldn't bring himself to make a scene. He'd go inside, tell her to let him the hell alone, and then he'd leave.

Only, he underestimated Violet.

She greeted her butler with a wide smile that utterly belied the tension swirling between them. "We're just going into the sitting room for a drink, Lavery." She sailed into the room, and Nick reluctantly followed her.

As soon as he was inside, she closed the door behind him.

"What will your butler think?" he muttered.

"That we're carrying on an affair, which is what he's been thinking for days. And quite accurately." She went to the sideboard and poured him a glass of something that looked like whiskey.

"You drink whiskey?" he asked, accepting the glass.

"On rare occasion. That's been sitting there for quite a while, I'm afraid."

He didn't care. He tossed the lot down his throat and handed her the empty glass.

She returned to the sideboard and refilled it. This time, she took a sip before giving it to him.

He stopped himself before he drank. He didn't want to be here. He felt his control slipping, and he didn't want that to happen in front of her. "I need to go."

"You keep saying that, but if you'd like to talk to me about Maurice—or anything else, I'm more than happy to listen. What I am not more than happy to do is stand by and watch you freeze over and withdraw."

He glowered at her over the rim of the glass, then took a drink.

She stared at him and crossed her arms. "You can't go back to being the Duke of Ice. It's not good for you. This past week, you've been more like the old Nick, which I think was your intent given the way you recreated things we did before. So, let's do what we can to keep him here."

Yes, he had tried to reclaim what they'd shared, but he wasn't the same person. Too much had happened. "The Nick you met doesn't exist anymore. You keep focusing on the past. I've decided I don't want to do that. I *can't* do that."

Lowering her arms, she came toward him, the feathers atop her head swaying. "Then we'll find the new Nick, someone who doesn't need to shield himself behind a wall of ice."

She stopped in front of him, so close, but didn't touch him. He burned for her just as he ached to leave. She'd push him to places he maybe didn't want to go.

"What if I can't do that? Everything that's happened has made me who I am."

"And I'm a part of that," she said softly. Her gaze turned sad. "We can't go back, but I still hope we can move forward."

He wasn't sure. Even now, those old feelings of bitterness stole over him. In his darkest moments, he'd blamed her for instigating a string of misfortune. Though he knew that none of it was her fault, it was difficult right now to differentiate that in the midst of his anguish.

His body hummed with buried emotions and suppressed need. Before he could force himself to turn and go, she placed her hand against his chest.

It was a simple contact, not even particularly intimate, but he felt it all the way to his core. And it provoked him to move—but not to leave.

He slipped his finger beneath the gold bandeau encircling her head, to which those ridiculous ostrich feathers were attached, and slid it from her hair. He grasped one of the feathers and tossed the headpiece to the floor. Then he pulled the pins from her curls, letting lock after lock of blond silk fall through his fingers.

When her hair was loose, he combed his hands through it, settling it like a veil over her shoulders. She was so beautiful, eyes sensuously narrowed, lips parted. Her tongue darted across her lower lip, and his control collapsed.

Clasping her back, he dragged her against him. He crushed his mouth over hers, seeking immediate entry to the pleasures within. Their tongues met and clashed as his hunger drove him to press her body tightly against his. But the damn hoops beneath her skirt kept him from feeling what he wanted.

He pulled his mouth from hers, nipping her bottom lip. She gasped, but it was an earthy, seductive sound. "Those bloody hoops," was all he could manage to say. His body shook with need.

She stared at him, her eyes keeping his captive while she slowly raised her skirt. "Untie them." She turned, presenting the ties that held the hoops around her waist.

Nick pulled at the ribbons, his fingers trembling. It

took a bit longer than it should have, likely because he was fixated on the curve of her backside, clearly visible beneath the thin linen of her chemise, but he finally tugged them loose. He offered her his hand, helping her to step clear of the article.

She still had so many clothes on. The volume was prohibitive. He didn't want to wait to disrobe her—he needed her now.

"Violet, I need to—"

He cut himself off as she turned and dropped to her knees before him. Wordlessly, she unbuttoned his fall and adjusted his smallclothes so she could find his stiff cock. Withdrawing his flesh, she stroked it from base to tip, using a stroke that was swift and sure, giving him precisely what he craved.

As she did this several more times, he closed his eyes and relaxed his shoulders, letting his head tip back. When the moist tip of her tongue connected with his sensitive skin, he moaned. Blood rushed to his balls, his cock, making him harder. He was desperate for her to take him into her.

Then she did. Her mouth closed over him, moving slowly until she took him as deep as she could. Her retreat was even more enthralling, her lips and tongue sending curls of ecstasy writhing through him. When she moved forward once more, she picked up her pace, and her hands clasped his hips, her fingertips digging into his flesh.

His need built, his pelvis moving with her. He tried not to thrust into her mouth, but it was so hard to hold himself back. He tried to regain the control he'd abandoned a few minutes ago, but it was more than just elusive—it was completely gone.

He opened his eyes an infinitesimal amount and

tipped his head down. Her hair fell around them like a cascade of gold, the silken locks brushing his thighs. Her lips, pink and perfect, surrounded him. It was the most erotic thing he'd ever seen. And he was going to spill himself in her mouth.

Somehow finding a thread of control, he withdrew from her. Reaching down, he gripped her arms and pulled her to her feet.

He stalked to the settee, bringing her with him. When he turned, she was delicately wiping her mouth. Overcome with lust, he kissed her, hot and hard and fast.

"I need you, Violet." He turned her toward the settee. "Lift your skirts and kneel, facing the back."

She hesitated, but only for a second before she lifted her skirts and climbed onto the cushions and settled on her knees. He grasped the bulk of fabric and held it up at her waist. She leaned forward, and with his free hand, he shoved the chemise, which was adamant about clinging to her backside, up to expose her flesh.

She widened her stance, opening herself to him, and it was all the invitation he needed. He stroked his fingers along her folds, eliciting a soft moan from her lips. She was warm and wet, more than ready for him. Good, because he was past ready. He was almost past thinking.

Guiding his cock to her opening, he eased inside, trying to go slow. The thin thread of control he'd found snapped in two as her tight heat engulfed him. Desire raged through him, and he surrendered to the madness, driving deep into her core.

She gasped, thrusting her hips back until her backside was flush with his groin. He gripped her hips, still clutching the mass of bunched-up fabric, and pulled back, trying to go slowly to savor the sensations. But when it came time to push forward, he had no such patience. The momentum of his need took over, and he plunged into her.

She moved with him, rocking back and forth, driving him to delicious torment. Her passionate cries urged him faster. Then she said his name. Over and over. It was part provocation and part plea. And it stole what little remained of his sense.

He dug his fingers into her flesh and claimed her as his orgasm built. Ecstasy coiled inside him and her muscles clenched around his cock, pushing him to the brink. He teetered for a moment before cascading into delirium.

He wasn't sure how long he was mindless, but when awareness returned, their harsh breathing filled the room and their movements had slowed to nearly nothing. His grip on her clothing loosened, and the fabric fell against her leg and tried to drop over her backside. But he was still seated inside her. She felt so good, so right.

And he felt like a beast.

Withdrawing his flesh from hers, he let her dress cover her as he backed away. He tucked his slackening cock into his breeches and buttoned the fall.

She turned and slid onto her backside on the settee, her chest still rising and falling as she worked to regain her breath. She smoothed her wrinkled skirts over her legs and looked up at him.

"I'm sorry."

Her brow creased. "For what?"

"I shouldn't have taken you like that."

"Why? I quite enjoyed it. I look forward to doing that again, preferably without clothing to manage."

"Not the position." He searched to find the right words but didn't think there were any. "Me. I'm... You deserve better." He had too much darkness, too much of the ice she didn't want.

She stood and went to him, her arms coming around his waist. "That's nonsense."

"It isn't," he practically growled, his anger rising again. "You understand who I am now, and you have to accept I'm not the man you once knew, and probably not the man you want."

She frowned at him, her eyes narrowing with a bit of her own ire. "I don't need you to tell me what I should want. I've had quite enough of people deciding things for me, thank you very much."

Yes, he supposed she had. He knew this wouldn't be easy—him trying to regain some semblance of a happy life. And seeing if he could do that with her. He needed air.

"I have to go." He pulled out of her embrace. "And this time, you're bloody letting me."

She held up her hands. "I can't control you," she said softly. "Nor do I want to."

Good, because he could barely control himself.

Chapter Fifteen

❧

THE PAST TWO days had been a blur of social activity. Nick's presence had been sought by the Queen, which Violet understood. Queen Charlotte had also requested Violet's presence, particularly on an outing in Sydney Gardens. Since Violet resided in Bath, the Queen had been keen to hear all about the local sights and activities.

Last night, they'd celebrated Gunpowder Treason Day with an excess of bonfire and illumination, as well as a fireworks display over Sydney Gardens. The Queen had been thoroughly delighted.

They'd also visited Bailbrook House, where war widows and children learned to knit and sew buttons. Violet had watched Nick through the entire visit to see how it affected him. He'd been stoic and aloof. The Duke of Ice had returned.

Except at night.

At night, he came to her house, where they reveled in each other's touch. However, they didn't talk, not about anything substantive, and Violet wondered if there was any hope for them in the long term. She hoped so. She wanted there to be. But Nick had to find a way to let go of the past. He said he didn't want to focus on it. What he didn't realize was that it consumed him.

She stood near the windows in the Pump Room, watching Nick as he spoke with another gentleman. A hush started at the other end of the room, and Violet saw people bending their heads toward each other.

Strolling forward, she went to a table where two of her acquaintances were seated. Someone from the next table leaned over and said, "Princess Charlotte has died."

Violet immediately thought of the Queen, with whom she'd spent so much time in recent days, and her heart twisted. She turned and went to Nick as a member of the Queen's entourage joined him.

"The princess delivered a stillborn son and died shortly afterward," the gentleman said quietly, his features creased with distress.

Violet couldn't help but touch Nick's arm, knowing this had to affect him. He didn't say anything, but some of the color left his face.

"How tragic," Violet murmured.

"The Queen will be leaving posthaste to return to Windsor for the funeral." He looked at Nick. "You must go."

Nick didn't return the man's stare but nodded slowly.

The gentleman moved away to continue sharing the information.

"Nick, are you all right?" Violet kept her voice low but wasn't able to disguise the urgent concern she felt for him.

He looked at her, but she had the sense he wasn't seeing her. "I'll see you later."

She stood, feeling helpless as she watched him stalk from the room. Later... Presumably, he'd come to see her tonight. She would hold him and hopefully break down some of the barriers he'd erected around his heart. If she didn't, she wasn't sure where they could go.

She still loved him, and in the time they'd spent

together, she'd fallen in love with him all over again.
No, he wasn't the same man she'd met, but neither was
she the same woman. He was a man touched by
tragedy who'd inherited a role he'd never expected and,
from what she could discern, had done so masterfully.
He deserved happiness—far more than anyone she'd
ever known—and she wanted to be the one to share it
with him. But she'd begun to think that might not be
possible.

And her heart threatened to break all over again.

◆&3◆

"MUCH BETTER, YOUR Grace." Rand surveyed his
handiwork as Nick wiped his hand over his mouth and
felt the smooth skin of his face for the first time in two
days. He hadn't left his house—hell, he'd scarcely left
his chamber. He'd been too wrapped in grief.

The death of Princess Charlotte and her son had
brought back every emotion he'd worked so hard to
bury. It was as if Jacinda and Elias had died all over
again.

So Nick had crawled into bed and hidden from the
world, just as he'd done after they'd died. He wished he
could say he felt better after succumbing to his
emotions, but he didn't. Instead, he felt drained and a
bit…empty.

"It's good to see you up and about," Rand said,
cleaning up his shaving implements. "Shall we finish
your toilet?"

Nick grunted in response and allowed his valet to
finish dressing him. Once he was finished, Nick
thanked Rand and departed his chamber.

As soon as he reached the hall downstairs, the butler

approached him. "You've received another missive, Your Grace."

It was likely from Violet. She'd sent two notes already, asking after him and, to her credit, filling the page with mindless chatter that took his mind off his sadness, at least for a little while.

He took the letter from the butler and frowned at the unfamiliar handwriting. Opening it, he saw that it was a short missive, and judging from the writing and careless ink splatters, hastily drafted. Quickly scanning it, his heart fell into his feet.

While it wasn't from Violet, it was about her. She'd been in an accident.

Nick dashed from the house without a word to the butler. He tore down the street, uncaring what people thought. He was never more glad that he'd leased a house so close to hers.

Her butler admitted him immediately. "Your Grace, the physician is with her upstairs. Perhaps you'd like to wait in the sitting room?"

No, he didn't want to wait anywhere except at her bedside. He started toward the stairs, but stopped with his hand on the newel post. "What happened?" The note hadn't said.

"Lady Pendleton went for a walk—I believe to the Royal Crescent." To see him, Nick thought. "There was some sort of commotion involving a runaway coach. She fell and struck her head. She has not regained consciousness, I'm afraid." The butler's tight, dark tone said more than his words ever could.

Panic rose in Nick's throat along with bile. One would think he would be numb to loss—he *should* be. He wanted to be. The alternative was excruciating. He didn't know if he could go through it again.

THE DUKE OF ICE 229

He slowly ascended the staircase as apprehension rioted through him. He felt cold and shaky, as if he had a fever.

When he reached her room, he saw that the door was half-open. He heard voices from within but couldn't make out what they were saying. Fear rooted him to the carpet.

The door opened farther and her maid, Chalke, filled the gap. The woman's round face was pale, her eyes red as if she'd been crying. Nick thought he might be sick.

"Oh, Your Grace," she said. "Come in, come in." She stepped inward and gestured for him to follow her into Violet's room.

He was terrified of what he'd see and learn. It took him a moment, but he went inside. His gaze immediately fell on Violet lying in her bed—the bed in which they'd brought each other so much joy. She was so pale that she was actually a bit gray. A deathly pallor, someone would say. Icy sweat broke out along Nick's neck, and his palms grew clammy.

"Dr. Paulson, this is His Grace, the Duke of Kilve. He's, ah, a friend of Lady Pendleton."

The physician was perhaps a few years older than Nick, with a sharp blue gaze and long face. He looked well equipped to deliver bad news. He bowed toward Nick. "Your Grace. Lady Pendleton has suffered a severe injury. There's quite a knot on her skull, and she has yet to wake. There is, unfortunately, nothing I can do at present. We must pray that she regains consciousness soon."

Pray? That was what the physician had advised him to do when Elias had failed to take enough nourishment to grow bigger. He'd been small and frail at birth and had only diminished over the weeks of his life. Nick had long since given up on prayer.

"There must be something you can do to help her." It wasn't a question. Nick wanted to grab the man by his lapel and shake him until he made her well again. But it wouldn't help. This was Nick's curse.

"I've instructed Mrs. Chalke to brew some herbs and let them steep beside the bed here."

"Mrs. Spindle is working on that now," the maid said earnestly.

"The aroma may help rouse Lady Pendleton. Beyond that, we'll need to wait and see what happens. Mrs. Chalke will send for me as soon as she wakes."

"You're leaving?" Nick glared at the man.

The physician startled, his frame jerking. "For now. But I'll return the moment you have need of me."

Nick turned toward the bed, dismissing the man before he did something he would regret.

Chalke saw the physician out but returned a moment later, joining Nick beside the bed. "She looks so peaceful, doesn't she?"

Her features were in a state of repose, her lashes dark against the paleness of her cheeks. Her hair was loose, the golden curls splayed across the pillow. The top of her night rail was just visible above the bedclothes.

"You changed her clothing." He didn't say what he was thinking—*how long did you wait to send word to me?* It didn't matter. He was just glad they *had* sent word. But then everyone in the household was aware of their affair. Was anyone else? "I'm glad you sent for me. However, it's best if we don't make our…relationship known. For propriety's sake."

"Of course, Your Grace."

To preserve her reputation, he ought to leave. And yet he couldn't. Not while she lay there unmoving.

Oh God. What if she never woke? The tremors that had shook his frame on the way over returned.

Chalke seemed to notice. "I'll fetch you some whiskey. Sit with her. It will do her good to know you're here."

He looked sharply at the maid. "You think she knows?"

The older woman nodded, her lips pressed together. She seemed certain in her conviction. "I do. She cares for you most fiercely, you know."

Yes, he knew. And he cared for her. Too damned much.

After Chalke departed, he pulled a chair from the corner and set it next to the bed. He sank onto the cushion and touched her face. It was smooth and cool. There was a bit of color, but not much. She didn't look lifeless as Jacinda had.

Chalke brought him the whiskey and stayed for a bit, chattering about how she'd come to work for Violet when she'd moved to Bath.

"You weren't with her when she was married?" he asked, grateful for the diversion of conversation but also curious.

"No. She had a maid her husband hired and apparently her ladyship didn't care for her. She moved here to Bath to start fresh—new staff, new everything."

He could understand why she'd wanted to do that. She'd endured a marriage she'd never wanted, and she hadn't even been able to make the best of it.

"You've known her ladyship a long time," Chalke said softly, her knowing gaze clearly communicating that she was aware of their history.

He didn't respond since it wasn't a question. Instead, he pictured Violet as she'd been then, her eyes bright, her cheeks flushed in the midday sun as they strolled through the park. Suddenly, he thought of her parents. "Have you sent a note to her parents?"

Chalke pursed her lips. "I was waiting to see if she'd wake. She doesn't like to see them very often. I've only met them once."

This didn't surprise him either. But it made him sad. What he wouldn't give to have his parents alive and well. Still, it wasn't as if she could control the Caulfields' behavior. He wondered what they would think of him being here. They'd probably be thrilled. He was, after all, a duke now.

"You should also send a note to Hannah Linford." While Violet might not want her parents here, she'd want her closest friend. Simon rose in Nick's mind. He still hadn't heard from him, and Nick's mail had been diverted to the house in the Royal Crescent.

"Oh yes, I should. I'll go and do that straightaway. Here, give me that." She took his empty glass. "Would you prefer to write to Mrs. Linford?"

He shook his head.

The maid patted his shoulder, startling him with the physical display. "You'll keep a good eye on her."

Alone with Violet, he watched her sleep. Was she sleeping? Was that what happened when you hurt your head? He leaned over the bed and gingerly felt for the lump she'd sustained. Christ, it was the size of a goose's egg. Distraught, he sat back in the chair and sat vigil for who knew how long.

He'd loosened his cravat and unbuttoned his waistcoat long ago. He considered removing his boots when she twitched.

Instantly alert, he leapt to the edge of the chair. "Violet?"

Her eyes fluttered, and her body convulsed. Vomit streamed from her mouth, drenching her front. She gasped, fighting for breath.

He jumped to his feet and put his hands beneath her back, elevating her. "Chalke! Help me!"

He continued to shout until the maid and the butler and another member of her staff came running into the chamber.

"Oh my goodness," Chalke breathed.

Violet trembled in his arms, and then another seizure racked her body. More of her stomach contents came pouring forth.

The butler dashed to the other side of the room and came back with the empty washbasin. He thrust it beneath her mouth as Nick tried to prop her up.

She sucked in air, her breathing loud and harsh. They all waited, tense, to see if she would be sick again, but after a few minutes, she seemed to be past the crisis. Nevertheless, she continued to shake, and they set to work stripping the bed. The butler removed the soiled bedclothes, leaving the two women to peel away Violet's night rail.

All the while, Nick whispered soothing words to Violet and rubbed her back. He didn't know what else to do. He wished he could say he'd never felt so helpless. But he'd felt this way before. Many times. God, he hated this sensation of being absolutely powerless.

Someone fetched water, and they moved Violet to the other side of the bed so Chalke could clean her up. Then the maid braided her hair to the side without the lump. Nick swept Violet up so they could completely change the bedclothes, holding her close against his chest while the maids worked quickly and efficiently.

He was loath to lay her back down but was glad she'd grown calm. Even her shaking had stopped. Once they had her tucked back into the bed, the maids left to work on washing the linens and tidying themselves.

Why hadn't she awakened? It seemed that something like that—her body had reacted quite violently—would force her into consciousness.

But she'd gone back to the way she'd been before. Still. Practically lifeless.

He paced the room, suddenly anxious to be anywhere but here.

When Chalke returned, he went for a turn in the garden. He wasn't sure how long he was gone, but he stopped in the sitting room downstairs for another glass of whiskey before going back up.

He was met with a familiar stench. "She was ill again?" he asked.

"I'm afraid so," Chalke said worriedly. "I've sent for the physician."

They cleaned her up in the same fashion, but this time when Nick held her, she opened her eyes for a brief moment. They looked shiny, like glass, and they couldn't seem to focus on him. One pupil was black and huge while the other was a tiny pinpoint.

"Violet?" When she didn't respond or react, he tried again. "Violet, can you hear me?"

Her eyelids fluttered before closing once more. She went limp in his arms, and his frustration erupted in a loud growl he simply couldn't contain.

He set her back in the now-clean bed and let Chalke cover her up.

"Try not to fret, Your Grace," Chalke said, rather ridiculously.

How could he not fret?

They physician returned but again had nothing of value to say or contribute. Nick wanted to throw him from the window. The vomiting could be a good sign as her body worked to rid itself of whatever poison might be occurring. That theory sounded ridiculous to Nick. How in the hell did one suffer a poisoning by hitting one's head? The physician had calmly—and rather condescendingly—explained that there was perhaps fluid in the lump and that could be poisoning her. Nick had simply stared at the man and imagined him sailing through the air as Nick tossed him to the ground.

After the sun set, Chalke attempted to get Nick to eat, but he refused, as he had all the other times she'd suggested it.

Late in the night, he fell asleep on the other side of Violet's bed, waking at the slightest noise. She roused a few times, thankfully not to be sick anymore, but wasn't able to focus or respond or otherwise demonstrate that she was aware.

By morning, Nick's hope was all but lost.

Then she finally woke.

Except it was for a very short time, and she only asked for water. Chalke supplied the liquid with tears streaming down her face. Violet fell right back to sleep, and Chalke turned to Nick with hope in her eyes. "That has to be a good sign."

"Or it could mean nothing," Nick said coldly.

Chalke's face fell, but she nodded. "You should go home and sleep."

"I can't sleep." He'd tried.

"Change your clothes, then."

He should probably do that.

Chalke seemed to sense his hesitancy. "You won't be far away. We'll send for you if she wakes. But you've seen her—there isn't much happening."

No, there wasn't.

Dejected and exhausted, Nick left. He'd sent a note late yesterday explaining that he wouldn't be home. Since the staff came with the house, he didn't know them and they didn't ask him any questions. Rand, however, was quite distraught over Nick's appearance.

The valet took in Nick's disheveled clothing. "Are you all right, Your Grace?"

"I need a bath. And something to eat." He wasn't particularly hungry, but knew his body needed nourishment.

"Right away." He called for the footmen to fill the bath and helped Nick to undress. "I've packed for London. Do you still wish to leave tomorrow morning?"

Bloody fucking hell.

He'd forgotten about going to the princess's funeral. Could he miss it?

No. The queen expected his attendance. If Violet were his wife, he could beg off...

But she wasn't.

Wife. He hadn't dared to think of her in that capacity. And why was that?

Because of precisely what was happening right now. If he took her as his wife, he'd be open and vulnerable. He couldn't do it.

"Your Grace?" Rand looked at him expectantly.

"Yes, we'll leave tomorrow." He had to. One did not refuse the Queen.

And maybe, if he left Violet, he'd be able to think straight. Because right now, he was tied up in knots, his mind completely twisted with fear and despair. He'd walked that road before, and he knew where it led.

He refused to end up there again.

Chapter Sixteen

FOUR DAYS LATER, Nick rode through Hyde Park, the November wind biting through his clothing. He didn't feel a thing. He hadn't felt anything since he'd left Bath.

He'd visited Violet the evening before his departure. They physician had just left, and Nick was glad to have missed him. Chalke reported that the man still suggested nothing to improve her condition. Beyond frustrated, Nick had found an accomplished physician in London upon his arrival and paid him handsomely to attend Violet in Bath.

He'd received an update in the post that morning: Violet regained consciousness periodically but was too exhausted to do anything but eat and drink before falling back to sleep.

Nick had to admit he'd lost hope that she would recover. That, or he'd convinced himself that he couldn't care. This was too familiar, too painful. He'd rather move on without her of his own accord than risk losing her.

The question was how to move on. In the time they'd recently spent together, she'd become a part of his life. He liked having someone to talk to, someone he looked forward to seeing. He didn't want to go back to being the lonely Duke of Ice. Well, the lonely part anyway. He was destined to live behind his frigid wall. He couldn't see another way.

He considered running off as Simon had done. Maybe they could travel the Isles together.

Consumed with his thoughts, he caught sight of another rider just before he rode directly into his—her—path. He realized at the last moment that the rider was using a sidesaddle.

"Your Grace?"

He vaguely recognized the voice, and once he'd calmed Oberon, he looked over at her. "Miss Kingman."

The petite brunette smiled. "Yes. I'm so pleased you remembered me."

"How could I forget? You were a charming presence at the house party. I enjoyed our tour of the cathedral."

Her eyes flickered with surprise, making him wonder what he'd done.

She seemed to sense his confusion and let out a light laugh. "I didn't realize you'd enjoyed it. That makes me quite happy."

Right, because he'd left the cathedral in a rush, following behind Simon. Plus, he'd behaved like an ass for a majority of the party. Hell, he'd behaved like an ass for years. And suddenly, he'd regained his ability to be pleasant.

Because of Violet. He had to credit her.

His chest tightened, and he pushed her from his mind. "What brings you to London?" he asked.

"This is where we live primarily." Miss Kingman glanced toward his black armband. "Are you going to Windsor for the funeral?"

It was in a few days. "Yes, that's why I've come."

She nodded, and he expected to see sadness in her eyes or that she would comment on the tragedy. Instead, she said, "At least she isn't in pain any longer."

Her manner was so matter-of-fact, so...unemotional that it jarred him. Over the past several days, the miasma of melancholy that pervaded every corner of London had overwhelmed him. The pall had threatened to send him to cower in his bed for the duration of his stay.

Miss Kingman's pragmatism was a welcome respite.

"Yes, that is a blessing," he said.

"It's frightening, though, isn't it?" she said serenely, without a hint of apprehension to accompany her question. "Bearing a child, I mean. I'm not sure I'd want to try." Her frame shuddered delicately.

"I'm sure your husband will want you to."

She pursed her lips briefly and exhaled. "Yes, I'm sure he will."

"I wouldn't." He surprised himself by saying this. "I lost my first wife in childbed. And the child later."

"I'd heard that." Again she refrained from belaboring the tragedy of it. "But what of your title? You need an heir."

He shrugged. "I wasn't meant to inherit—the title came to me after a series of unfortunate events." He opted not to say tragic since she seemed quite fine with leaving emotion out of their conversation. "There are others it will pass to."

"Well, then I can see why you aren't inclined to marry," she said with a smile. "How splendid."

"Splendid?" He was confused by her remarks. "You sound as if you are not in favor of marriage. Forgive me for saying so, but I had the distinct impression at the house party that you were on the Marriage Mart."

"According to my father, yes. He's hoping to match me with a grand title—like yours."

Sir Barnard had made that quite clear every time he'd spoken with Nick at the house party. "He just wants what's best for you, I think."

She let out a rather unladylike snort, showing him a side of her he hadn't seen at the party. "He wants what will elevate his position. If he truly cared what I wanted, he'd let me choose my own husband. Or not."

Yes, he had to conclude she was definitely not in favor of marriage. "You don't wish to marry."

She glanced back toward her groom, who was stationed several yards behind her. "I didn't mean to be so forthcoming. Please forgive me."

"There's nothing to forgive. I admire forthrightness." It was one of the things he'd loved about Violet. When they'd first met, she hadn't played the part of a blushing young lady out to woo a suitor. She'd been honest and plainspoken. He squeezed the thoughts of her from his mind.

"Thank you, Your Grace." She patted her horse's neck. It was a fine animal, and from what he could tell, she had an excellent seat.

"I'm terribly sorry for nearly colliding with you," he said.

"You didn't come very close. Anyway, I'm skilled enough to have avoided you if necessary. I like athletic activity. Aside from swimming. Although I think perhaps I should learn in case I go tumbling out of a boat again. Thankfully I had a knight—rather, a duke— to save me."

"It was my pleasure. I enjoy the water, particularly fishing."

"I love to fish. But of course, the ladies weren't allowed to at the party."

She liked to fish? "Have you ever fished in the ocean?" When she shook her head he said, "I live on the coast. It's quite invigorating. Fishing in the waves is a bit different."

"I'd like to try that someday." Again, she looked over her shoulder. "I should be getting home. It was a pleasure to see you, Your Grace."

"For me as well."

"I hope our paths will cross again while you're in Town." She inclined her head then kicked her horse into a canter.

As he watched her go, her groom following, he realized he felt lighter than he had in days. Miss Kingman had been a welcome breath of serenity in the chaos of his life. He appreciated her undemonstrative demeanor and her candor. It was a pity she didn't want to marry, for she really would make an excellent wife. She'd be a charming hostess, and she'd be undemanding. Furthermore, without children, one needn't worry about losing them. He realized with a start that she was precisely the kind of woman he'd told Simon he wanted.

But was that still true after he'd rediscovered Violet and what they'd shared?

Hell yes. It was even more true now, since her accident. He wasn't the man he'd been eight years ago, no matter how hard he'd tried to recapture that magical time he'd spent with her.

Damn. She would have gotten her hopes up, despite them taking each day as it came. He was angry with himself for going to Bath and opening her up to heartache. She deserved better. She deserved happiness and light and warmth—things he couldn't give her. Maybe it was time to set her free from the past and free from her tether to a beast like him.

•ᴇ•ꝛ•

"SURELY I CAN take a walk around the garden," Violet insisted.

Her mother, lips pressed into a thin, white line, stared down at her. "The physician said you needed another week of rest."

She'd already been in bed ten days. Or so she'd been told. She didn't remember much before about five days ago. Apparently, she'd fallen on the sidewalk and become quite ill as a result. She'd suffered debilitating headaches, barely able to lift her head from the pillow, and her vision had been blurry. Today was the first time she wasn't seeing two of everything.

She blinked at her mother, glad there weren't two of her anymore because, really, one was more than enough. "Then I should at least be able to walk around the room."

Her mother scoffed. "You're a terrible patient."

Violet wanted to suggest she leave, but held her tongue. Instead, she glanced toward Chalke, who gave her a sympathetic smile. The maid had apologized many times for notifying her parents of Violet's injury.

At least Hannah would be arriving soon. She would have come before, but one of her children had been ill.

If only Nick would return. But he'd needed to attend the princess's funeral. Violet looked back toward her mother. "What day is it?"

"Wednesday, the nineteenth." She walked to the window where she had a chair situated in which she did needlepoint. Constantly.

"Is the funeral today?" Violet asked. They'd discussed it a few times, but she couldn't quite recall.

"Yes," her mother answered. "At Windsor. Now that you're feeling better, I'm looking forward to hearing all about your time with the Queen. How splendid that you met her." Mother had brought this subject up several times. "Maybe next time she's in town, you'll invite me to come."

The implication was clear—why hadn't Violet extended her influence to her mother? Maybe because she found her mother's company grating and her behavior self-serving. She and Father had worked very hard to purchase a titled groom, largely so *they* could enjoy the benefits. They'd been far sorrier than Violet when Clifford had died.

"I do believe it's time for luncheon," Chalke said, bustling to the side of the bed and needlessly adjusting Violet's bedcovers. "Then it's probably best if Lady Pendleton rests."

"I could do with a walk myself," Violet's mother said, looking out at the garden below. She flashed a smile at her daughter. "I'll walk *for* you, how's that?"

"That's perfect, thank you." Violet resisted the urge to roll her eyes.

After her mother departed, Chalke patted Violet's arm. "Hopefully she won't stay much longer. Now that you're on the mend, I think your father plans to leave."

It was just as well. He was anxious to get back to the brood of puppies his favorite hound had just birthed. Violet couldn't really tell if he was glad to see her or not. Her mother had at least demonstrated concern and care, helping to feed and dress Violet, much to Violet's chagrin. She hated taking help from her, as irrational as that was.

"Has there been no word from Nick?" Violet asked Chalke.

The maid shook her head. "Not yet, but don't fret. The physician he sent is drafting a letter right now to inform him of your positive progress. I'm sure you'll hear from him soon."

Violet could only imagine how distraught he must be. He'd already been a wreck following the princess's death, and Chalke had told her of his anguish following Violet's injury. She hated that he was at the funeral alone and wished she could be by his side to offer support. And love.

"Hear from who?" Her mother came sailing back into the room. "I forgot my needlepoint." She didn't go anywhere without it.

"No one, just a friend," Violet said. She didn't want to tell her mother about him, not when she'd ruined their happiness eight years ago. A small voice at the back of her head told her it might well be worth her mother's reaction to learn that the man she'd prevented her daughter from marrying was now a duke.

Mother picked up her embroidery and walked to the side of the bed. "He must be a good friend if you're hoping to hear from him." Her coffee-brown eyes lit up with interest. "Dare I hope you're planning to remarry?"

Not planning, but she had to admit she was hoping. She wasn't sure about Nick, however. She wanted him, loved him, but feared he was trapped in the web of past tragedies.

"Not at present." Violet glanced toward Chalke.

"He must be someone important if he sent a physician to care for you. Perhaps I'll just ask *him*." In other words, she'd find out who "he" was one way or another.

Violet decided to listen to the voice in the back of her aching head. "It's the Duke of Kilve. We've actually been acquainted for some time. We met here in Bath eight years ago."

Her mother looked aghast, her eyes widening and her hand fluttering to her chest. "You met a duke eight years ago? How did we not know about this? My sister would have told me."

Violet's aunt *would* have told her, *if* he'd been a duke. "His name was Nicholas Bateman. He wasn't a duke then."

Mother's eyes widened even more—to the point that Violet feared they would pop right out of her head. "That... Oh. How wonderful that he's a duke now and that you've found your way back to each other." She didn't look apologetic in the slightest. But had Violet really expected that? She was satisfied that she'd at least registered shock.

Still, she couldn't resist needling her a little. "Just imagine if I'd been allowed to marry him. I'd be a duchess."

The wrinkled flesh around her mother's mouth twitched. "Maybe you will be after all."

"You mustn't count on it, Mother," Violet said. "The Duke and I are friends, nothing more." She kept her gaze averted from Chalke's, lest they reveal the truth. She and Nick were more than friends, but how much more? And for how long?

"It's not as if you and Father will be able to persuade him into marriage." As they'd practically bribed Clifford—a viscount in need of funds—to wed her. "He doesn't need anything." Except the ability to put the past behind him and reach for a happy future. The question was if he'd changed too much to do that, if he was too weighed down with the burden of loss.

"I suppose not." Mother's brow furrowed. "Doesn't he have one of those nicknames?" She looked at the ceiling as if she'd find the answer hidden in the carved plaster. She shook her head. "Ah well, I'll remember. Have a good lunch and rest, dear." She left again, and Violet relaxed into the pillows.

"How's your head?" Chalke asked with concern.

"It hurts again."

Chalke stared at the doorway where Violet's mother had just gone. "Yes, I imagine it does. I'll fetch some soup and willow-bark tea for your headache. Then, if you'd like, I could read to you until you fall asleep."

Violet settled into the bed, which was beginning to feel more and more like a prison cell. She wished she could go after Nick, to be the light he surely needed right now. Would he let her?

Chapter Seventeen

THE DAY AFTER the princess's funeral, Nick had contemplated returning to Bath. However, the prevalent aura of grief had worked its way into his heart and mind, thrusting him back to the dark period following the loss of Jacinda and Elias. As a result, he stayed in his room all day, and the day after, he'd ventured only as far as his study downstairs.

He'd received a brief note from Violet's physician notifying him that she was improving, but that the progress was slow. His relief hadn't been enough to drive him back to Bath. He was too numb. And afraid. The threat of losing Violet in his current state of despair had incapacitated him. He'd fought against the shadows of the past and was now battling the darkness of the present. Just as he'd decided to try to live again, really *live*, disaster had struck, reminding him that he was cursed.

He wanted to go back to feeling protected, even if it meant he was alone. Over the past five years, and particularly the last three, he'd found a way to manage his grief and loss. Allowing Violet close had opened him back up to that pain. As much as he cared for her, as much as he loved her—and he did—he didn't want to be vulnerable. His heart couldn't bear it if she were taken from him, so it was best that he retreat behind his wall of ice.

Pulling on his gloves, he strode to the hall, where his butler hovered near the door.

"I'm going for a ride."

Bexham, Nick's London butler, an imperious man of nearly sixty years, reached for the door. "It's good to see you back to your regular self, Your Grace."

Nick didn't know what his regular self looked or felt like anymore. Violet had reminded him that he was Nicholas Bateman, and yet he was as much the Duke of Ice as he'd ever been.

After an invigorating run in Hyde Park, Nick felt marginally better. He picked his way back toward the gate, and, as had happened on the days prior to the funeral, he came across Miss Kingman.

She drew her mount to a halt just off the path, and he moved his horse to stand alongside hers. "Good afternoon, Your Grace. I'd despaired of seeing you here again. I was afraid you'd left London after the funeral."

He should have, but he'd shut himself away instead. "I've been busy."

If she detected any upset in his tone—which he didn't see how she could—she didn't reflect it. He had the sense that even if he had displayed a flash of emotion, she would have ignored it. Their conversations had been devoid of weight or importance. They'd talked of fishing, the ocean, and her parents' appalling desperation for her to wed someone Important.

"I hope you weren't reading the newspaper," she said, for the first time revealing a hint of something…anxiety judging by the tense set of her jaw and the glint of concern in her eye.

"No." He'd read *Hamlet*, which had suited his mood, and then a horrid novel, undoubtedly placed next to his bed by Rand, who'd most certainly gotten it from

Bexham, who, amusingly, possessed a small library of such work.

"Ah, well. There's a bit of…speculation about you and me. Our rendezvous here in the park have been noted."

The first thing he thought of was her parents and their desire to see her upwardly wed. "I'm certain your father is thrilled."

"Quite." Her brief smile was both self-deprecating and tinged with irritation. "I tried to tell him that we are merely acquaintances. I apologize for the unwanted attention."

And yet here they were, meeting in plain sight once again.

"I've never cared what people said or thought about me," Nick said. "I suppose that's what happens when you grow up expecting a life of anonymity only to find yourself at the center of Society."

"I don't care either," she said, lifting her chin. "Much to my parents' frustration. But I felt I should caution you—that's why I've been looking for you the past couple of days—my parents are organizing a dinner party next week and plan to extend you an invitation. I would advise you to leave London before they can trap you." She delivered this advice with a tone of utmost gravity.

He laughed at her dire warning. "Would they attempt to snare me in a parson's trap in some scandalous fashion?"

She exhaled. "I wish I could laugh and assure you that would never happen. However, I fear my parents will sink to any level they feel they must to secure a duke, particularly when they realize there is no truth to the rumor in the paper."

He felt a rush of compassion for her—that was an emotion he didn't mind, particularly when it alleviated his own pain. "How awful for you to have to live in this way. I don't suppose you've considered running away?"

Her brows lifted briefly. "I have, in fact. Alas, my purse is not large enough to support more than a few days' journey. And where would I go?"

He considered her question seriously, but before he could answer, she said, "If I fled alone, I would be ruined, no matter where I went."

"If you were in the company of a gentleman you wouldn't mind marrying, it's not a bad plan."

Now she laughed. "I don't know such a gentleman, save you, I'm afraid." She sobered, and color bloomed in her cheeks. "I didn't mean to suggest we should run away together. I only meant that I like you, and you seem to like me—for *me*, not for my fortune or my beauty." Her lips twisted with disgust, and she looked away.

He edged closer to her, speaking quietly. "I *do* like you." He'd been about to say that she'd find a gentleman with whom she felt comfortable, whom she could maybe even love. But then he remembered that she didn't care about such things, particularly marriage. Just as he didn't care about them—or didn't want to anyway.

She squared her shoulders and looked him in the eye. "Rather than run away, I've been thinking I ought to find someone I can marry, someone who will accept me for who I am and not some pretty prize to be won. I truly didn't mean to...*snare* you; however, it occurs to me that we may be of service to one another."

He suspected he knew her intent, but needed to be

sure. "In what way?"

"You need a wife, I presume, since you've a title, and I'd prefer a husband like you. Your lack of ill-behavior and display of extreme equanimity is most appealing."

Nick swallowed a laugh. "I've never been described in such a manner." He supposed it fit, however.

Her brow arched in elegant inquisition. "Am I inaccurate in my estimation of you?"

Once upon a time, she would have been, but she'd captured the man he was now quite well. Except he had behaved poorly in recent days—he'd allowed a relationship with Violet that he never should have in the interest of soothing his own pain and regret. Self-loathing burned his throat like acid.

"No," he choked the answer out.

Her shoulders dipped in relief. "Would such a union be of interest to you?" she asked softly.

Finally, he glimpsed a way to move forward and make a complete break from his past. He could set Violet free so that she could find a bright and happy love that would bring her joy for all the days of her life.

Nick needed to be completely clear with Miss Kingman, now that he understood his limitations. "I wouldn't be a storybook husband. You cannot expect me to fall in love. In fact, I will insist that we keep such emotion from our union." He *had* to. If he wanted love, if he *wanted* to take that risk, he'd run back to Bath—to Violet—this instant. Only, she wouldn't be happy. She'd made it clear she loved the Nick of old, not the frigid man he'd become.

"You want a Duchess of Ice," she summarized perfectly. "That appeals to me, actually. Indeed, I would prefer not to have children, but I understand you require an heir. I would only ask that we wait."

THE DUKE OF ICE 253

She was precisely the type of wife he needed. "I *should* beget an heir, but as I've said before, I have male relatives in line. I have no quarrel with your terms." His chest tightened, threatening to choke him. He struggled to take a deep breath.

"And I agree to yours." She tipped her head to the side and whispered, "Did we just negotiate a marriage contract?"

His body tensed—his mind warring with his heart. "I think we might have."

"My father won't believe it."

Nick's heart thudded, making him wonder if Miss Kingman could hear it. Of course not. As loud as it seemed to him, the voice in his head was just as deafening, insisting that this was the right course of action, the *logical* course. "He will when I tell him in person," Nick said. "Should we go now?" Then his heart wouldn't be able to change his mind, not without causing a scandal.

"If you wish."

"I'm agreeable to whatever you prefer."

Her lips curved up. "Is this how it's going to be? We'll be insufferably polite and deferential?"

"Would that be bad?" he mused. She shook her head and he said, "I don't think so either. Lead the way, if you will." He gestured for her to precede him, and she kicked her horse into a trot toward the gate.

His heart clenched in a hard, fast spasm as he realized what he'd done. Miss Kingman *was* what he needed—a Duchess of Ice, just as she'd said—even if Violet was who he wanted.

Yes, he wanted her, but he wasn't the man *she* wanted. He was damaged and afraid, and she deserved so much more. For both their sakes, he had to walk away. She ought to have a happy future, and he couldn't give it to her.

For that reason alone, he would let her go.

THE PAST FIVE days had been a frenzy of social events, all designed to stir excitement for what was being touted as the wedding of the decade—if Lady Kingman was to be believed. For Nick, it was all torture since he'd awakened in a cold sweat the night after agreeing to marry Miss Kingman. He feared he'd made a terrible mistake, and he'd spent the intervening days alternately feeling ill and drinking—perhaps too much.

Today he would tell his parents-in-law-to-be that there would be no more balls, routs, dinner parties, or levees. The wedding was to take place three weeks hence, and until then, Nick planned to keep to himself.

"What the fucking hell have you done?" Simon's shouted question preceded his entrance into Nick's study.

Bexham followed on his heels, his face pinched with distress. "I'm sorry, Your Grace, he wouldn't allow me to announce him."

"Who needs an announcement when he's bellowed his presence for all of London to hear?" Nick waved his butler away. "It's all right."

Simon moved to stand in front of Nick's desk and glared down at him. "Explain." His jaw was tight, his teeth clearly clenched behind lips pale with anger.

Nick sat back in his chair and rested his hands on the arms. "I presume you're speaking of my engagement?"

"To Diana bloody Kingman! Have you lost your mind?"

It was as succinct—and accurate—an assessment as Nick could've made. "Yes."

"Explain," Simon repeated before lowering himself into a chair.

How could he do that without exposing his weakness, his utter stupidity? "I went to Bath to reconcile with Violet, but it didn't work. Miss Kingman proposed marriage, and I accepted." Like a complete fool.

Simon got up and stalked to the opposite end of the room. "If I still drank spirits, I'd down an entire bottle of whiskey," he muttered, but Nick still heard him. Simon turned around, the anger gone from his face and replaced with sorrow. "If you tried with Violet and it truly didn't work, well then, I have no hope left. I would've bet my last pound that you were written in the stars."

Nick stood and walked around his desk. He leaned on the edge. "You are a hopeless romantic."

"Guilty." He took a few steps back toward Nick. "What happened in Bath?"

Nick grasped the edge of the desk on either side of his thighs. He didn't want to discuss this. "What happened doesn't really matter."

Simon narrowed his eyes slightly. "I'll ask Violet about it when I visit her."

Bloody hell. "You're going to visit her?"

"I'd planned to, yes, and now, because of your idiocy, I think it's vital. She'll be devastated, I expect."

Devastated. Nick winced, his insides twisting painfully, which was no less than he deserved. He'd written to her as soon as he'd returned home from speaking to Diana's father. She hadn't responded. So yes, she was likely devastated. Or furious. Probably both.

"You assume she wasn't the one to break things off."

Simon glared at him again. "I'd wager my last pound that she would never do that. She's loved you for eight years and lived with the agony of her mistake. There's no way she would've hurt you again." He studied Nick briefly. "If you can even be hurt. You *are* the bloody Duke of Ice."

The familiar nausea from the last few days rose in Nick's gut. "This is not a revelation to anyone."

"It is to me. And to Violet, I expect. We know the real you, who you're capable of being."

"Who I *used* to be. That person died with Maurice. And again with Uncle Gil. Yet again with Jacinda and then with Elias. Finally with—" Anguish tightened his body. "Never mind."

Simon advanced on him, his brow dark, his eyes narrowed. "Whom did it die with?"

He was going to find out when he got to Bath anyway. "Violet." Nick cleared the cobwebs from his throat. "She was in an accident. She was unconscious for quite some time and ill. I had to leave her to attend the princess's fun—"

"You *left* her?"

"She's fine now." The physician had arrived back in London a few days ago and reported to Nick. Violet had been weak but was recovering.

Simon goggled at him and ran a hand through his hair, sending it straight up from the top of his head. "This is unimaginable." He barely waited for Nick's nod before raging on. "How did you determine you wouldn't suit? *If* you'd truly tried, as you say you did, I simply can't believe that's true." He moved close enough to Nick to jab him in the chest, which he did. "What did you fucking *do*?"

The emotion he'd struggled to bury since Violet's accident erupted out of him. He shoved Simon, sending him stumbling backward. "I was a coward! She got hurt—badly—and I feared she would die. I *cannot* go through that again."

"Because you love her."

"Desperately." The pain was so keen that he doubled over, sucking in a deep breath to try to right his equilibrium. "So desperately," he whispered brokenly.

Simon's arm came around his shoulders, and he guided Nick to a high-backed chair near the fireplace.

Nick sank down onto the cushion, his head bent as tears tracked from his eyes and dropped to the carpet. The wetness on his face was so foreign, and yet it felt so damned *good*.

Simon stood at his side, his hand a comfort on Nick's shoulder. After a few minutes, Simon coughed. "I understand your fear—I really do. But why on earth you thought marrying Miss Kingman was an acceptable solution is beyond my comprehension. You've made a goddamned mess of things."

Yes, he had. He'd spent the last five days torturing himself but not seeing a way to fix it.

Nick wiped his hand over his face and leaned his head back against the chair. Staring at the ceiling, he gave in to the anguish, realizing—too late—that the loss he'd tried to avoid had found him anyway. He'd been a fool to think he could control his feelings.

"Violet won't want me. She loved who I was eight years ago, not this shell of a man I am now."

"You are not a shell." Simon tipped his head from side to side, reconsidering. "Perhaps you are a *bit* of a shell, but I think you're filling in the holes again. It may take time, but there is no one better suited to help you with that than Violet."

Nick looked at his friend. "What if she doesn't want to?"

"Then you'll be in a sorry state, and I'll help you pick up the pieces. But she *will* want to. She loves you. And you love her." Simon squared his shoulders. "That just leaves the matter of Miss Kingman. Allow me to handle that."

Nick eyed him warily. "How? She doesn't deserve ruination."

Simon's nostrils flared. "Because I'll ruin her? I suppose that *is* what I'm known for."

Nick flinched, his shoulders twitching. "That was a poor word choice. You are *not* known for that."

"Not for ruining young women, but why not expand my depravity?" Simon shrugged, as if his reputation didn't matter at all.

"This isn't a joking matter, Simon. For me to cry off will cast Miss Kingman in an unfavorable light."

"I imagine her parents will be furious," Simon said.

No doubt. And given what Nick knew of her circumstances, she'd have even less choice than she'd had before he'd rescued her. Nick frowned at Simon. "They may try to force her into something terrible. She'll want to get away, I imagine."

"Leave it to me," Simon said. His eyes glinted with determination, and he squeezed Nick's shoulder before letting go. "Now tell me what you're going to do about Violet. Might I suggest going immediately to Bath and telling her what a daft prick you've been and begging her forgiveness?"

Nick sat forward in the chair, a combination of anticipation and dread thrumming through his veins. "I've botched this rather horribly. She may not want me."

"She may not. Will you take the risk?"

The pain of his losses reared in his mind, but he shoved it aside and found the joy he'd shared with Violet. "Absolutely."

Simon's lips spread into a satisfied smile. "Go. Trust me to handle Miss Kingman."

There was no one Nick trusted more. Other than Violet, and he'd done a terrible job of actually doing that. He should have told her what he was feeling, and he damn well shouldn't have cowered in London. "Thank you. I'm not sure I deserve a friend like you."

"I told you long ago that we deserved each other," Simon said dryly. He walked to the door but looked back at Nick before he left. "Give my love to Violet."

Nick nodded, his gaze fixed on the hearth long after Simon had quit the room. Yes, he'd give Violet Simon's love, but only after he offered her his first. He could only hope she'd want it.

Chapter Eighteen

⬦❦⬦

"HOW ARE YOU feeling?" Chalke asked as Violet came in from the garden. It was quite cold, even for the first week of December, and she wondered if it might snow.

"I'm fine, thank you." She looked forward to the day when no one asked her that, but realized it was probably still a long way off. She'd expected extra hovering today from Chalke and the rest of the staff since it was her first day alone.

Hannah had departed yesterday after staying a fortnight, and thankfully, Violet's mother had left shortly after Hannah's arrival. She had, unfortunately, vowed to return and drag Violet "home" for holiday celebrations until Twelfth Night. Violet was still considering how she might avoid such a horror.

Chalke took Violet's thick woolen cape from her shoulders. "Will you nap? That might be a good idea."

Violet rubbed her hands together and walked to the fireplace to warm herself.

"Oh! I think you need a toddy. Yes, that will be just the thing." Chalke's eyes glowed as she clucked her tongue and quickly departed.

It wouldn't matter if Violet didn't want a toddy; Chalke would bring it nonetheless. As it happened, she *did* want a toddy. Preferably with extra spirits to dull the ache of betrayal.

She closed her eyes as she held her hands—palms out—to the fire. She'd memorized the letter Nick had sent to inform her of his betrothal to Diana.

Dear Violet,

It is with great regret that I inform you that we will not suit. I find I cannot return to the days of my youth. I am far too changed, as you well know.

My engagement to Miss Diana Kingman will be announced tomorrow. I never meant to cause you pain. You deserve to be happy and to also be unencumbered by the past. I hope you will see that this is best for both of us.

It gives me great joy to know that you are well and whole. I prayed for you to be safe and am grateful that my prayers were finally answered.

I will always think of you fondly. Be well.

Nick

She'd dissected the letter in her mind a hundred times. He likely believed she'd recovered because he'd decided to leave her. Or, as Hannah had insisted, he'd seized the opportunity for revenge—to revisit upon her what she'd done to him eight years ago. In her angriest moments, Violet agreed. However, she knew better.

He was afraid. She'd seen how the princess's death had affected him and could only imagine how her own accident and near death had likely sent him over the edge. He'd done the only thing he could—he'd run. She'd foolishly believed he would come back to her. Instead, he'd kept on going.

It was one thing to say they didn't suit, but to wed Diana? He didn't love her—of that Violet was certain. And she suspected that was precisely why he chose her.

She opened her eyes and narrowed them at the flames. None of it mattered now. She could replay the events in her mind, hoping for clearer understanding, but the outcome would always be the same. Nick was gone, and he wasn't somewhere she could follow.

Even if he wasn't to be married, she had to let him go. He was right about one thing—she deserved to be happy and unencumbered, and that meant freeing herself of the guilt that had bound her these past eight years.

It also meant unraveling the love in her heart. That, she knew, was going to take some time.

Raised male voices carried from the hall into the morning room, where she stood before the fire. She frowned and pivoted toward the doorway through which Chalke had recently departed.

"Your Grace, you must let me announce you!" Lavery sounded quite agitated.

Violet froze at the appearance of the unannounced visitor.

Your Grace.

Her brain should have made the leap, but she'd truly never expected to see him again and certainly not in her home.

Nick stood just over the threshold, his hat in his hand and his shoulders wet with snow that was rapidly melting into the dark wool.

Her traitorous heart leapt at the sight of him, but she did her best to emulate him and transform herself into the Viscountess of Ice. "You really ought to have let Lavery announce you. It's polite."

"I think we can both agree that I'm past polite," he said, wincing.

"Well past, yes."

Lavery hovered near the door, his ears red with anger. "Shall I escort him out, my lady?" He looked at her before adding, "Please?"

"Yes, I think that would be best." She gave Nick her frostiest stare. "I believe your letter said everything that needed to be said."

"No, it didn't."

"Come, *Your Grace*." Lavery spat the honorific as if it were poison on his tongue.

Nick held up a hand. "Momentarily."

Violet drew herself up and employed her haughtiest tone. "Do not speak to Lavery in that fashion. You'll leave. *Now.*" She let her ire steal that last word, her tone elevating and her hands clenching at her sides.

Lavery, bless him, grabbed Nick's arm and pulled him backward.

"I'm not getting married," Nick blurted as he stepped back out of the room. "I wanted you to know. If there's any way—"

Violet stalked forward and sneered at him. "I don't know what you're going to say, and I don't want to. I have wasted too much of my life on you, and I refuse to give you another minute. *Get out.*"

Lavery gave him a surprisingly vicious tug, causing Nick to stumble. Violet flinched and nearly asked if he was all right. In the end, she held her tongue and watched as Nick turned and walked away, Lavery hard on his heels. She followed them, slowly, perversely enjoying this spectacle.

As soon as the door closed, Lavery spun toward her and tugged at the bottom of his coat to straighten himself. "I'm a bit disappointed I didn't get to throw him out the door."

Chalke hurried into the hall, her eyes wide. "Did I hear His Grace?"

"Yes. He came to inform me that he isn't getting married."

Lavery sniffed. "As if you would care."

Violet stifled a smile. Her retainers knew far too much about her life, but that was her own fault. In the absence of a family, she'd forged relationships with them that were probably too familiar. But she didn't care. She'd followed the rules and look where it had gotten her. Miserably married.

"Exactly right," Chalke said with a definitive nod. She glanced at Violet. "I'm afraid I ran upstairs to see the commotion and left your toddy in the kitchen. I'll just go and fetch it."

Violet retreated to the morning room, where she enjoyed her toddy more than she'd anticipated. Having the opportunity not only to see Nick again but to react to his letter in person made her feel quite satisfied.

And yet her mind was already mulling the implications of what he'd said. He wasn't getting married. He'd come here to tell her. Did that mean he wanted to reconcile? That seemed the logical conclusion, but she'd given up on logic where Nick was concerned. For a man made of ice, he was a slave to his emotions.

She sipped her drink and told herself again that none of it mattered. This changed nothing. She still needed to move on without him.

After she'd finished her toddy and felt sufficiently warm, she stood to find a book on the shelf. Lavery entered, his mouth curved into a half smirk. "He's taken up a position across the street and is watching the house like a dog awaiting his dinner."

Violet whirled about and looked out the window to the back garden. Snow was swirling in the air. It didn't look to be sticking to the ground, but it was still very cold. She walked past Lavery and went to the front sitting room to see for herself.

There he was, his arms crossed and his hat pulled low over his forehead. Snow dusted his shoulders and the top of his hat. He had to be freezing.

Good.

And yet the longer she stood there, the less satisfied she felt. "He can't stay out there indefinitely."

"You don't want to invite him back inside, do you?" Lavery sounded as if he'd battle her on that point.

"No, but neither do I want to watch him freeze to death." She turned to the butler. "Would you go out and tell him to leave? Tell him he's accomplishing nothing but perhaps ensuring he catches cold."

"It would be my pleasure." Lavery bundled himself up and went out into the darkening afternoon.

Violet watched at the window as the two men conversed. The interaction didn't last long, and soon Lavery was back inside removing his greatcoat and hat.

She went into the hall to meet him. "What happened?"

"He refuses to leave until it's dark. What's more, he says he'll return tomorrow and every day after that until you agree to see him."

For the love of God. She was not going to let him make himself ill. "You told him there was no point to that?"

"I told him he could come every day until the end of time and you would still not admit him." Lavery shook his head. "He actually *smiled* and said he'd take that chance, that he'd at least be able to see you coming and going and if that was all he could have, he'd take it."

A loud sigh drew them both to turn. Chalke had come back to the hall. Her gaze had gone limpid, and her mouth curved into a half smile. "That is so romantic."

Lavery scoffed. "It's cracked is what it is."

Violet had to agree it was romantic. And so like the Nick she'd met. Was he still in there?

Of course he was. He was just buried beneath fear and sadness and the inability to cope.

"Are you going to let him in?" Chalke asked.

For a brief moment, Violet considered it. "No." She wasn't sure she believed he'd come back every day for eternity, but decided it might be fun to find out.

Three days later, she decided he wasn't going anywhere. It had snowed a couple of inches that first night, then the temperature had dipped. Through the cold and the snow swirling around his boots, Nick had spent two full days huddled across from the house. Yesterday, he'd worn a blanket draped around his shoulders, and Lavery had reported that someone had brought him something to drink. Something hot, he'd said, given the way Nick had cupped the mug and held it close to his face.

As she stood in front of the sitting room window, Violet decided that she had to put an end to this farce. She turned to Chalke, who'd come into the room a few moments ago. "Bring me my cape, my hat, and my gloves."

Chalke's brow creased, and she clasped her hands together. "You don't need to go outside. That can't be good for you."

"I wasn't ill; I injured my head."

Lavery came into the sitting room, his face awash with surprise. "You can't mean to speak with him?"

"I think I must, don't you? I won't be responsible for him catching cold. And, honestly, I worry the neighbors may complain soon."

Chalke stared at her in confusion. "About a duke standing in front of their house?"

That did sound rather absurd.

"Mrs. Blevins tried to invite him inside earlier," Lavery said.

Violet winced. Mrs. Blevins lived a few houses down the street with her five little dogs and an indeterminate number of cats. She dearly loved visitors, and once inside, you were captive for hours because she rarely stopped talking. "Oh dear, well then, at the very least, I need to warn him away from her."

Against her judgment, Chalke wrapped Violet up tight. Before letting her outside, she made Violet promise to return within ten minutes.

After swearing she would only be gone *five*, Violet went outside and nearly lost her hat to the biting wind. Clamping her hand on the top of her head to keep the accessory from flying away, she walked down the steps. Before she could get to the sidewalk, Nick was in front of her.

"You shouldn't be out here," he said.

She stared at him from beneath her wrinkled brow. "Wasn't your intent to lure me outside?"

"No, I was hoping you'd invite me in."

"I thought it might be nice to get out." Now that she was standing in the wind, she had to admit that thought was ill-advised. She blinked up at him. "I can't believe you've endured this for two and a half days."

"I would endure it forever if it meant I could see you."

"Just *see* me?"

He looked at her intently. "I'll take what I can get."

"Why aren't you marrying Diana?"

"Because I love you."

The words she'd ached to hear for so long made her knees weak and her chest tighten. She pressed her lips together and glowered at him. "You didn't realize that before you proposed?"

His gaze turned sheepish. "I did—I've always known it, no matter how much I tried to fight it."

Violet crossed her arms over her chest and hugged herself tight against the cold. "Is that what you've been doing all this time—fighting it?"

"Among other things. As Simon aptly said, I've been a daft prick." His mouth tipped into a crooked half smile.

She arched a brow at him, surprised at his sense of humor. "I knew I liked Simon."

"I'm only sorry it took him to finally make me see sense. You were very patient with me, and I was... I was a coward."

He *was* a coward, but she understood why. "I've been a coward too. I preferred to live in the past, in the only time I was truly happy."

His answering smile was soft and bright. "That's not cowardice. That's self-preservation—and a much better solution than erecting a wall of ice around yourself." His face darkened, and she tensed. "I know I'm different now. I don't think I can be the Nick you fell in love with, not anymore. Can you accept me as I am?"

He sounded so unsure, so apprehensive, that the old, familiar cracks in her heart trembled. "No, you aren't the same Nick, but I love you even more now than I did then."

"After what I've put you through?" He sounded as if he wanted to thrash himself, and she supposed in some ways he had.

"Stunningly, yes," she said wryly. She touched him tentatively, her hand grazing his great coat over his heart. "We both dealt with loss in our own way. Not that my loss can ever compare to yours."

He stared into her eyes, every emotion she'd ever wanted to see from him naked in their depths. "We've both lost a great deal, especially time. I'd rather not lose another moment."

"I just need to understand about Diana. Is she all right?"

"I'm assured she is. Though her parents are another story that we can discuss another time. Or never. Whatever you decide." His smile came back. "That you're concerned for her welfare only accentuates what a wonderful woman you are."

"I still need... How do I know you won't panic and run off again?"

"I can promise you I *will* panic again, particularly when you end up with child. But I won't run again. At least not away from you. I point in one direction now, Violet—to you."

Despite the cold, heat blossomed inside her. Until her brain processed what he'd said first—about children. She withdrew her hand from his chest. "Nick, I can't give you any children," she said quietly, her gaze dropping.

He clasped her shoulders, drawing her to look back up at him. "Maybe not. Or maybe you will. I will be happy either way."

"Oh, Nick." She stood on her toes and kissed him, but it was brief. The second his frigid nose brushed up against hers, she gasped. "You *have* to come inside."

He grinned. "I thought you'd never ask."

She turned and started up the steps. When they were

inside, Lavery cast him a disgruntled look while Chalke smiled brightly. They each took Nick's and Violet's outerwear, respectively, and left them alone in the hall.

Nick took Violet's hand. "Thank you for bringing me in out of the cold."

"Does this mean you aren't the Duke of Ice anymore?"

"Do you think we could convince people that I'm the Duke of Fire?"

She laughed. "Do you plan to rage at people?"

He shrugged. "I could. Honestly, I don't care what anyone calls me—only you."

She threaded her fingers through his. "And what do you prefer?"

"Friend, lover, husband?" He looked at her in question.

"If that's supposed to be a marriage proposal, you'll have to do much better than that." She lifted their hands and held them to her chest as she moved to stand closer to him. "Are you sure you want to take this risk? Anything could happen—to either of us. You know there are no guarantees?"

He caressed her face, smiling down into her eyes. "There is one, actually: I will love you until the end of time."

She fell into him, her arms encircling his neck. "Well then, how can I refuse?"

Epilogue
❧ ❦ ❧

August, 1818

"YOU'VE A SON, Your Grace!"

Nick, pacing outside his bedchamber where Violet had been laboring for the past nine hours, slumped against the wall.

"I'll fetch the whiskey," Rand muttered before clapping his hand on Nick's shoulder. "Congratulations." He couldn't help but smile as he practically ran to deliver the good news. The entire household had held its breath. No one had mentioned the last time a child had been born at Kilve Hall, and yet he knew they were all thinking about it. How could they not? How could *he* not?

"Can I go in?" Nick tried to keep the fear from his voice, but was certain he'd failed miserably. The physician was quite aware of Nick's terror—Violet had made the poor man promise to inform Nick of her progress every step of the way. She'd even negotiated for Nick to be present during her ordeal, but after six hours of watching her suffer, he hadn't been able to stand another moment.

He really *was* a coward.

"Yes, do come in," the physician urged. He opened the door and motioned for Nick to precede him.

The midwife was finishing up with cleaning Violet, while Chalke, grinning broadly, held the baby.

"Oh, Your Grace, he's just beautiful."

Nick didn't doubt it. He was, after all, Violet's son. And Nick couldn't wait to hold him. But first he had to make sure she was all right.

With leaden steps, he moved to the side of the bed. She turned her head and smiled weakly at him.

Nick turned his head back sharply toward the physician behind him. "What's wrong? She's pale. She looks like she can barely lift her lips to smile."

The man moved up to the bed beside Nick. "She's exhausted, Your Grace, which is to be expected."

Violet gently shook her head at him. "Really, Nick, I'd like to see what you'd look like after what I've been through."

He'd be passed out, probably. He glanced over at the physician. "She's fine?"

"Excellent. That was one of the easiest births I've ever attended. And I appreciated the fine assistance of Mrs. Gowdy here." He nodded toward the midwife.

Violet had wanted both a physician and a midwife, and Nick had agreed. Why have just one child birthing expert when two were better?

"Where is Maurice?" Violet asked, using the name—his brother's, of course—they'd chosen if they'd had a son.

He had a son.

The lad was astonishingly quiet. Last time… He shouldn't think of that. Last time, Elias had squalled incessantly—until he'd become too weak to do so.

"I'm nearly finished here, Your Grace," the midwife said. "Perhaps His Grace would like to hold his son?"

Before Nick could answer, Chalke transferred the babe into his arms. He was already so different from what Nick had expected. His head was covered in a fine blond down, and his eyes were a dark indigo.

Maurice stared up at him in open curiosity, as if deciding whether Nick would measure up.

"Do I pass muster, then?" Nick asked softly. He touched his finger along Maurice's brow. The boy scrunched his face, and Nick thought he might cry, but he didn't. Nick looked between the physician and the midwife. "Why isn't he crying? Shouldn't he be crying?"

"He did at first," the midwife answered, covering Violet's legs and standing back from the bed. "I've cared for many babies who didn't cry much in the beginning. Don't worry. He'll get hungry here in a bit, and then I suspect he'll bawl loud enough to bring the rafters down around us." She laughed.

The midwife proved an excellent prognosticator, because not ten minutes later, Maurice started wailing and didn't stop until he latched on to Violet's breast. Nick watched in wonder, scarcely believing how his fortunes had changed.

Later, when Maurice was asleep in the cradle next to the bed and Violet dozed, Nick stretched out beside her. He closed his eyes, tired but happy. The touch of his wife's hand against his made him open his eyes and turn.

Fear seized him. "Are you all right?"

Her lips curved up, and she patted his chest. "I'm *quite* all right. Isn't he amazing?"

"As perfect as you." Nick kissed her forehead.

She snorted. "There is no such thing as perfect and nor would I want there to be—can you imagine trying to sustain that? I do, however, believe in miracles." She gazed at Maurice in adoration. "I still can't believe we did this. I told you it wasn't possible."

"You did, when I asked you to marry me. And, as

fate would have it, you were already expecting."

She shot him a knowing look. "I still say we have my accident to thank."

"I know your theory—all that rest somehow made the babe 'stick,' but I am not letting you hit your head next time we want to have a child."

She chuckled softly. "I don't need to hit my head. I just need to stay in bed a lot. I can't imagine you'd mind that." She gave him a seductive look.

"God no, but it's far too soon to think about that."

She exhaled in resignation. "Yes, but know that I'm looking forward to it." She narrowed her eyes pointedly.

He kissed her again, this time on the mouth, his lips lingering over hers. "Thank you for giving me a joy I never imagined to feel. I know it hasn't been easy—*I'm* not easy."

"No, but I love you anyway. Our joy is all the sweeter *because* it wasn't easy."

"Such a wise woman. Thank you for persevering, for believing in what we shared and that we could find it again."

"I'm not sure we found it," she said. "I think we created something new." She glanced toward their sleeping son before curling her hand around Nick's neck. "What we have now is wondrous in all its glorious imperfection."

THE END

Are you anxious to find out what happened to Diana and Simon?
Find out in The Duke of Ruin, coming March 27, 2018!

Thank You!

❦

Thank you so much for reading *The Duke of Ice*. I hope you enjoyed Nick and Violet's reunion story! I loved writing them.

Would you like to know when my next book is available? You can sign up for my newsletter, follow me on Twitter at @darcyburke, or like my Facebook page at http://facebook.com/DarcyBurkeFans.

The Duke of Ice is the seventh book in The Untouchables series. The next book in the series is *The Duke of Ruin*. Watch for more information! In the meantime, catch up with my other historical series: Secrets and Scandals and Legendary Rogues. If you like contemporary romance, I hope you'll check out my Ribbon Ridge series available from Avon Impulse and my latest series, which continues the lives and loves of Ribbon Ridge's denizens – So Hot.

I appreciate my readers so much. Thank you, thank you, *thank you*.

Books by Darcy Burke

⊷ξ•3⊷

Historical Romance

The Untouchables

The Forbidden Duke
The Duke of Daring
The Duke of Deception
The Duke of Desire
The Duke of Defiance
The Duke of Danger
The Duke of Ice
The Duke of Ruin
The Duke of Lies

Secrets and Scandals

Her Wicked Ways
His Wicked Heart
To Seduce a Scoundrel
To Love a Thief (a novella)
Never Love a Scoundrel
Scoundrel Ever After

Legendary Rogues

Lady of Desire
Romancing the Earl
Lord of Fortune
Captivating the Scoundrel

Contemporary Romance

Ribbon Ridge

Where the Heart Is (a prequel novella)
Only in My Dreams
Yours to Hold
When Love Happens
The Idea of You
When We Kiss
You're Still the One

Ribbon Ridge: So Hot

So Good
So Right
So Wrong

Praise for Darcy Burke's
Secrets & Scandals Series

HER WICKED WAYS

"A bad girl heroine steals both the show and a highwayman's heart in Darcy Burke's deliciously wicked debut."

—Courtney Milan, *NYT* Bestselling Author

"…fast paced, very sexy, with engaging characters."

—Smexybooks

HIS WICKED HEART

"Intense and intriguing. Cinderella meets *Fight Club* in a historical romance packed with passion, action and secrets."

—Anna Campbell, *Seven Nights in a Rogue's Bed*

"A romance...to make you smile and sigh…a wonderful read!"

—Rogues Under the Covers

TO SEDUCE A SCOUNDREL

"Darcy Burke pulls no punches with this sexy, romantic page-turner. Sevrin and Philippa's story grabs you from the first scene and doesn't let go. To Seduce a Scoundrel is simply delicious!"

—Tessa Dare, *NYT* Bestselling Author

"I was captivated on the first page and didn't let go until this glorious book was finished!"

—Romancing the Book

TO LOVE A THIEF

"With refreshing circumstances surrounding both the hero and the heroine, a nice little mystery, and a touch of heat, this novella was a perfect way to pass the day."

–The Romanceaholic

"A refreshing read with a dash of danger and a little heat. For fans of honorable heroes and fun heroines who know what they want and take it."

–The Luv NV

NEVER LOVE A SCOUNDREL

"I loved the story of these two misfits thumbing their noses at society and finding love." Five stars.

–A Lust for Reading

"A nice mix of intrigue and passion...wonderfully complex characters, with flaws and quirks that will draw you in and steal your heart."

–BookTrib

SCOUNDREL EVER AFTER

"There is something so delicious about a bad boy, no matter what era he is from, and Ethan was definitely delicious."

–A Lust for Reading

"I loved the chemistry between the two main characters...Jagger/Ethan is not what he seems at all and neither is sweet society Miss Audrey. They are believably compatible."

–Confessions of a College Angel

Legendary Rogues Series
LADY of DESIRE

"A fast-paced mixture of adventure and romance, very much in the mould of *Romancing the Stone* or *Indiana Jones*."

-All About Romance

"...gave me such a book hangover! ...addictive...one of the most entertaining stories I've read this year!"

-Adria's Romance Reviews

ROMANCING the EARL

"Once again Darcy Burke takes an interesting story and...turns it into magic. An exceptionally well-written book."

-Bodice Rippers, Femme Fatale, and Fantasy

"...A fast paced story that was exciting and interesting. This is a definite must add to your book lists!"

-Kilts and Swords

The Untouchables Series
THE FORBIDDEN DUKE

"I LOVED this story!!" 5 Stars

-Historical Romance Lover

"This is a wonderful read and I can't wait to see what comes next in this amazing series..." 5 Stars

-Teatime and Books

THE DUKE of DARING

"You will not be able to put it down once you start. Such a good read."

-Books Need TLC

"An unconventional beauty set on life as a spinster meets the one man who might change her mind, only to find his painful past makes it impossible to love. A wonderfully emotional journey from attraction, to friendship, to a love that conquers all."

-Bronwen Evans, USA Today Bestselling Author

THE DUKE of DECEPTION

"...an enjoyable, well-paced story ... Ned and Aquilla are an engaging, well-matched couple – strong, caring and compassionate; and ...it's easy to believe that they will continue to be happy together long after the book is ended."

-All About Romance

"This is my favorite so far in the series! They had chemistry from the moment they met...their passion leaps off the pages."

-Sassy Book Lover

THE DUKE of DESIRE

"Masterfully written with great characterization...with a flourish toward characters, secrets, and romance... Must read addition to "The Untouchables" series!"

-My Book Addiction and More

"If you are looking for a truly endearing story about two people who take the path least travelled to find the other, with a side of 'YAH THAT'S HOT!' then this book is absolutely for you!"

-The Reading Cafe

THE DUKE of DEFIANCE

"This story was so beautifully written, and it hooked me from page one. I couldn't put the book down and just had to read it in one sitting even though it meant reading into the wee hours of the morning."

-Buried Under Romance

"I loved the Duke of Defiance! This is the kind of book you hate when it is over and I had to make myself stop reading just so I wouldn't have to leave the fun of Knighton's (aka Bran) and Joanna's story!"

-Behind Closed Doors Book Review

THE DUKE of DANGER

The sparks fly between them right from the start... the HEA is certainly very hard-won, and well-deserved."

-All About Romance

"Another book hangover by Darcy! Every time I pick a favorite in this series, she tops it. The ending was perfect and made me want more."

-Sassy Book Lover

Ribbon Ridge Series

A contemporary family saga featuring the Archer family of sextuplets who return to their small Oregon wine country town to confront tragedy and find love...

The "multilayered plot keeps readers invested in the story line, and the explicit sensuality adds to the excitement that will have readers craving the next Ribbon Ridge offering."
    -Library Journal Starred Review on YOURS TO HOLD

"Darcy Burke writes a uniquely touching and heart-warming series about the love, pain, and joys of family as well as the love that feeds your soul when you meet "the one."
                    -The Many Faces of Romance

I can't tell you how much I love this series. Each book gets better and better.
                    -Romancing the Readers

"Darcy Burke's Ribbon Ridge series is one of my all-time favorites. Fall in love with the Archer family, I know I did."
                    -Forever Book Lover

Ribbon Ridge: So Hot
SO GOOD

" ...worth the read with its well-written words, beautiful descriptions, and likeable characters...they are flirty, sexy and a match made in wine heaven."
                    -Harlequin Junkie Top Pick

"I absolutely love the characters in this book and the families. I honestly could not put it down and finished it in a day."
                    -Chin Up Mom

SO RIGHT

"This is another great story by Darcy Burke. Painting pictures with her words that make you want to sit and stare at them for hours. I love the banter between the characters and the general sense of fun and friendliness."

-The Ardent Reader

" ...the romance is emotional; the characters are spirited and passionate... "

-The Reading Café

SO WRONG

"As usual, Ms. Burke brings you fun characters and witty banter in this sweet hometown series. I loved the dance between Crystal and Jamie as they fought their attraction."

-The Many Faces of Romance

"I really love both this series and the Ribbon Ridge series from Darcy Burke. She has this way of taking your heart and ripping it right out of your chest one second and then the next you are laughing at something the characters are doing."

-Romancing the Readers

About the Author

❦

Darcy Burke is the USA Today Bestselling Author of hot, action-packed historical and sexy, emotional contemporary romance. Darcy wrote her first book at age 11, a happily ever after about a swan addicted to magic and the female swan who loved him, with exceedingly poor illustrations.

A native Oregonian, Darcy lives on the edge of wine country with her guitar-strumming husband, their two hilarious kids who seem to have inherited the writing gene, two Bengal cats and a third cat named after a fruit. In her "spare" time Darcy is a serial volunteer enrolled in a 12-step program where one learns to say "no," but she keeps having to start over. Her happy places are Disneyland and Labor Day weekend at the Gorge. Visit Darcy online at http://www.darcyburke.com and sign up for her newsletter, follow her on Twitter at http://twitter.com/darcyburke, or like her Facebook page, http://www.facebook.com/darcyburkefans.

71454902R00172

Made in the USA
Middletown, DE
24 April 2018